UNLACING LADY THEA

Louise Allen

First published in Great Britain 2014
by Mills & Boon, an imprint of Harlequin (UK) Limited,
Large Print edition 2014
Harlequin (UK) Limited, Eton House, 18-24 Paradise Road,
Richmond, Surrey TW9 1SR

© 2014 Melanie Hilton

ISBN: 978-0-263-23979-9

Harlequin (UK) Limited's policy is to use papers that are natural, renewable and recyclable products and made from wood grown in sustainable forests. The logging and manufacturing processes conform to the legal environmental regulations of the country of origin.

Printed and bound in Great Britain
by CPI Antony Rowe, Chippenham, Wiltshire

'Turn around,' Rhys murmured.

It should have been easier when she could not see him, but that slight betraying catch in his breathing gave her an unexpected feeling of power, and the last lingering fear that he was pretending desire in order to save her humiliation fled.

'Ah…' The bliss of loosened stay-laces, the sense of freedom as her corset joined the gown on the floor. Her petticoat followed it, leaving her in chemise, stockings and a blush. 'I find I am shy,' Thea confessed.

'And I find I am somewhat overdressed,' Rhys murmured in her ear.

She had thought he would kiss her, touch her, but only his breath stroked her skin. Thea turned. 'Should I undress you?'

'Don't you want to?' There was amusement in his eyes, but not mockery.

AUTHOR NOTE

Last year I spent a wonderful fortnight travelling along the Italian coast from Venice to Sicily on board a small boat. The whole trip was so interesting, and the scenery so beautiful, that I knew I had to put it into a novel.

UNLACING LADY THEA is the result, and it is set in that short space of peace before Napoleon escaped from Elba and it seemed that the whole of Europe was going to be consumed by war again.

I knew Thea immediately—practical, funny, loving and brave—but I had no idea who she was going to share this adventure with until Rhys Denham, rather the worse for wear after an evening out, appeared on the page and began discussing life with the kitchen cat.

It was enormous fun to revisit some of my favourite places in France and Italy in the course of this novel, and I hope you enjoy the journey as much as Thea and Rhys—although hopefully with fewer accidents along the way!

Louise Allen has been immersing herself in history, real and fictional, for as long as she can remember. She finds landscapes and places evoke powerful images of the past—Venice, Burgundy and the Greek islands are favourite atmospheric destinations. Louise lives on the North Norfolk coast, where she shares the cottage they have renovated with her husband. She spends her spare time gardening, researching family history or travelling in the UK and abroad in search of inspiration. Please visit Louise's website—www.louiseallenregency.co.uk—for the latest news, or find her on Twitter @LouiseRegency and on Facebook.

Previous novels by the same author:

THE DANGEROUS MR RYDER*
THE OUTRAGEOUS LADY FELSHAM*
THE SHOCKING LORD STANDON*
THE DISGRACEFUL MR RAVENHURST*
THE NOTORIOUS MR HURST*
THE PIRATICAL MISS RAVENHURST*
PRACTICAL WIDOW TO PASSIONATE MISTRESS**
VICAR'S DAUGHTER TO VISCOUNT'S LADY**
INNOCENT COURTESAN TO ADVENTURER'S BRIDE**
RAVISHED BY THE RAKE†
SEDUCED BY THE SCOUNDREL†
MARRIED TO A STRANGER†
FORBIDDEN JEWEL OF INDIA††
TARNISHED AMONGST THE TON††
FROM RUIN TO RICHES

Those Scandalous Ravenhursts
**The Transformation of the Shelley Sisters*
†*Danger & Desire*
††*Linked by character*

and as a Mills & Boon® special release:
REGENCY RUMOURS

and in the *Silk & Scandal* mini-series:
THE LORD AND THE WAYWARD LADY
THE OFFICER AND THE PROPER LADY

and in Mills & Boon® Historical *Undone!* eBooks:
DISROBED AND DISHONOURED
AUCTIONED VIRGIN TO SEDUCED BRIDE**

Did you know that some of these novels are also available as eBooks? Visit www.millsandboon.co.uk

DEDICATION

The Hussies,
with thanks for all the support, advice
and laughter.

Chapter One

London—June 3, 1814

The skeleton clock on the overmantel struck four. No point in going to bed. Besides, he was thoroughly foxed, although not drunk enough to keep him from lying awake, wondering what had possessed him to make this insane plan. And worse, to follow through with organisation so ruthlessly efficient that to cancel now would throw his entire staff, financial team, estate management and social life into disorder—and make it seem he did not know his own mind.

'Which I do not,' Rhys Denham informed the ragged-eared ginger tom that sat on the hearthrug eyeing him with the disdain that only a feline or a dowager duchess could muster. 'Know my own mind, that is. Always do, just not this time.'

The appearance of the kitchen mouser on the

principal floor, let alone in the study of the third Earl of Palgrave, was unheard of. The household must be stirring already, too distracted by their master's imminent departure for the Continent to notice an open door at the head of the servants' stair.

'It seemed a good plan at the time,' Rhys mused. The brandy at the bottom of the glass glowed in the candlelight, and he splashed in more and tossed the lot back. 'I'm drunk. Haven't been this drunk in years.' Not since he had woken up one afternoon and realised that drink was never going to blot out the disaster of his wedding day, restore his faith in friendship or his delusions about romantic love.

The cat switched its attention to the plate with the remains of the cold beef, cheese and bread that had been left out with the decanters. 'And you can stop licking your whiskers.' Rhys reached for the food. 'I need this more than you do. I have to be more or less sober in three hours.' That seemed improbable, even to his fogged brain.

'You have to admit, I deserve a holiday. The estate is in order, my finances could hardly be better, I am bored to the back teeth with town and Bonaparte has been out of harm's way on Elba for a month,' he informed the cat around a mouthful of beef. 'You think I am a trifle old for the Grand Tour? I disagree. At twenty-eight I will appreciate things more.' The cat sneered, lifted one hind leg and began to groom itself intimately.

'Stop that. A gentleman does not wash his balls in the study.' He tossed it a scrap of fat and the cat pounced. 'But a year? What was I thinking of?' *Escape.*

Of course, he could come back at any time and his staff would adjust to his demands with their usual smooth efficiency. After all, if there was some kind of crisis, he would return immediately. But to cancel on a whim was not responsible behaviour. It put people out, it let them down, and Rhys Denham despised people who let others down.

'No, I am going to go through with this,' he declared. 'It will do me good to have a complete change of scene, and then I'll be in the mood to find a pretty, modest, well-bred girl with a stay-at-home temperament and good child-bearing hips. I will be married by the time I am thirty.' *And bored out of my skull.* A vision of the succession of prime bits of muslin who had worked their magic in preventing just such boredom flitted across his memory. They had never expected dutiful monogamy. A wife would. Rhys sighed.

The friends who had deposited him on his doorstep an hour ago after a convivial farewell night at the club were all married, or about to be. Some even had children. And, to a man, they seemed cheered by the thought of someone else falling into parson's mousetrap. As Fred Herrick had put it, 'About time a rake like you stops nibbling the cheese, takes a proper bite at it and springs the trap, Denham.'

'And why is that such a damnably depressing thought?'

'I could not say, my lord.' Griffin stood in the doorway, his face set in the expressionless mask that signified deep disapproval.

What the devil had his butler got to be disapproving about? Rhys levered himself upright in his chair. A man was entitled to be in his cups in his own house, damn it. 'I was speaking to the cat, Griffin.'

'If you say so, my lord.'

Rhys glanced down at the rug. The ginger beast had vanished, leaving behind it only a faint grease stain on the silk pile.

'There is a person to see you, my lord.' From his

tone it was clear this was the cause of the stone face, rather than his master's maudlin conversations with an invisible cat.

'What kind of person?'

'A young person, my lord.'

'A boy? I am not up to guessing games just at the moment, Griffin.'

'As you say, my lord. It *appears* to be a youth. Beyond that I am not prepared to commit myself.'

Appears? Does Griffin mean what I think he means? 'Well, where is it…. Him?' *Her?* 'Below stairs?'

'In the small reception room. It came to the front door, refused to go down to the tradesman's entrance and said it was certain your lordship would wish to see it.'

Rhys blinked at the decanter. How much had he drunk since he got back from White's? A lot, yes, but surely not enough to have imagined that faint hint of desperation in Griffin's voice. The man was capable of dealing with anything without turning a hair, whether it was pilfering footmen or furious discarded mistresses throwing the china.

A faint trickle of unease ran down his spine. *Mistresses.* Had Georgina failed to take her *congé* as calmly as she had appeared to do yesterday?

Surely she was satisfied with a very nice diamond necklace and the lease on her little house for a further year? Rhys got to his feet and tugged off his already loosened neckcloth, leaving his coat where it was on the sofa. Ridiculous. He might seek pleasure without emotional entanglement, but he was no Lord Byron with hysterical females dressed as boys dogging his footsteps. He was careful to stick to professionals and fast married women who knew what they were about, not single ladies and certainly not unstable cross-dressing ones.

'Very well, let us see this mysterious youth.' His feet seemed to be obeying him, which was gratifying, considering the way the furniture swayed as Griffin preceded him down the hallway. Tomorrow—no, this morning—promised a hangover of monumental proportions.

Griffin opened the door to the room reserved for visitors who did not meet his exacting standards for admission to the Chinese Drawing Room. The figure seated on a hard chair against the far wall came to its feet. Short, bundled into an ill-fitting dark suit of clothes that said 'junior clerk' to Rhys's unfocused eye, it had a pair of portmanteaux at its feet and a battered beaver hat on the chair by its side.

Rhys blinked. He wasn't *that* drunk. 'Griffin, if that is male, then you and I are eunuchs in the Great Chan's court.'

The girl in the youth's clothes gave an exasperated sigh, set her fists on the curving hips that betrayed her sex and said, 'Rhys Denham, you are drunk—just when I was counting on you to be reliable.'

Thea? Lady Althea Curtiss, daughter of the Earl of Wellingstone by his scandalous first wife, the plain little brat who had dogged his heels throughout his boyhood, the loyal friend he had scarcely seen since the day his world fell apart. Here, in the early hours of the morning in his bachelor household, dressed as a boy. A walking scandal waiting to explode like a smouldering shell. He could almost hear the fuse fizzing.

Rhys was bigger than she had remembered. More solid. More…*male* as he loomed in the doorway in his shirtsleeves, his chin darkened by his morning beard, the black hair that came from his Welsh mother in his eyes, that blue gaze blurred by drink and lack of sleep. A dangerous stranger. And then she blinked and remembered that it was six years since she had seen him close to. Of course he had changed.

'Thea?' He stalked across the room and took her by the shoulders, his focus sharp now, despite the smell of brandy on his breath. 'What the blazes are you doing here? And dressed like that.' He reached round and pulled the plait of mouse-brown hair out of the back of her coat. 'Who were you attempting to fool, you little idiot? Have you run away from home?'

Rhys was thin lipped with anger. Thea stepped back out of his grip, which made it easier to breathe, although it did nothing for her knocking knees. 'I am dressed like this because on a stage-coach in the dark it is enough to deceive lecherous men. I am perfectly aware that I do not pass muster as a youth in good light. And I have *left* home, I am not *running away*.'

Rhys's lips moved. He was silently counting up to ten in Welsh, she could tell. When he had been a boy he would say it out loud and she had learned the numbers. *Un, dau, tri...* 'Griffin. More brandy. Tea and something to eat for Lady Althea. Who is not, of course, here.'

Thea allowed herself to be shepherded into the study. Rhys dumped her bags on the hearthrug and pushed an ugly ginger cat off one of the chairs that flanked the fire. 'Sit. The cat hairs can't make that suit any worse than it is.' The cat swore at both of them, battered ears flat to its skull.

When she clicked her fingers, it curled its tail into a question mark and stalked off. Hopefully this was not an omen for how her reception was going to be. 'Is it your pet?'

Rhys narrowed his eyes at her. 'It is the kitchen cat and appears to think it owns the place.' He dropped into the opposite chair and ran his hands through his hair. 'Tell me this is not about a man. *Please.* I am leaving for Dover at seven o'clock and I would prefer not to postpone it in order to fight a duel with some scoundrel you fancy yourself in love with.'

If he was sober, it would help. As for duelling, she wondered if he was capable of hitting a barn door with a blunderbuss in this state. 'Of course it is not a man.' *Of course it is, but if I tell you the details we'll never get anywhere.* 'Don't be ridiculous. And why would you be fighting duels on my behalf, pray?' It was surprising how difficult it was to keep her voice steady. She must be more tired than she had realised.

'I always used to be,' Rhys said with a sudden

grin and drew his index finger down the line of his nose. Its perfect Grecian profile had been lost in a scrap with some village boys who had called her names when she was six and he was twelve. The smile vanished as quickly as it had appeared. 'So if it isn't a man…'

'It is, in a way.' She had rehearsed all this in the smelly darkness of the stagecoach through the long hours on the road. Not quite lies, not quite the truth. 'You recall I have had three Seasons. No, of course you do not—our paths never crossed in town. You weren't attending all the Marriage Mart ghastliness that I was expected to.'

His jaw set hard and she bit her lower lip. *Stupid, tactless, to mention marriage. He still cares; it must still hurt.* 'Anyway, Papa said I was wasting money and another Season with all the other girls so much younger would be even worse. So he sent me back to Longley Park and set about finding me a husband locally.'

'Do you mean you didn't have *any* offers—?' Rhys broke off as Griffin brought in a tray, then waved a hand for her to help herself as he sloshed dark liquid into his glass. 'I mean, I know that with your mother…'

'Oh, yes, several very eligible younger sons offered. My dowry is respectable and there's my trust fund, of course.' Both were considerable inducements to make up for the other things—her plain speaking, her intellectual enthusiasms, her very average looks. Not to mention a mother who had been an actress and her father's mistress before their impetuous marriage and her tragic death in childbirth. 'I turned them all down.'

'Why?' Rhys squinted at her over his glass, apparently in an effort to bring her into focus.

'I didn't love any of them.' *They didn't love me.... None of them.* 'Papa has settled upon Sir Anthony Meldreth.' Would Rhys understand if she explained why she felt so betrayed now? Why she had to leave? The old Rhys would have done, but this man, in this condition? No, better to fudge. 'We did not suit, but Papa says that either I marry Anthony or I must remain at Longley and be a companion for Stepmama for the rest of my days.'

'Hell.' Rhys obviously recalled her stepmother's capacity for hypochondria, vapours and utterly selfish behaviour all too well. He rubbed long fingers against his forehead as though to push away a headache, or perhaps push coherent thought in. 'I understand your problem.'

Does he understand? Probably not, a man like

Rhys couldn't be expected to comprehend the sheer mind-numbing dullness a spinster daughter was supposed to dwindle into. It would be like being buried alive. Nor could she expect him to comprehend the horrors of finding herself married to a man she did not like or trust or have a thing in common with.

'I can see it would be tiresome,' he continued, confirming her belief in his lack of understanding. 'But running away...' He frowned at her. 'I do not have time to deal with this now. I am about to leave for a Continental tour.'

'I know, Papa told me. He considers it shows a commendable enthusiasm for culture he had hitherto not recognised in you. Please *listen*, Rhys. I am twenty-two and of age. I am not running away, I am taking control of my life.'

'Twenty-two? Rubbish. You don't look it.' It was not a compliment.

Thea gritted her teeth and ploughed on. 'All I need is the approval of two of my three trustees in order to take control of my money and be independent.' It wasn't a fortune, but it would give her freedom, give her choice. 'If I do not get consent, then I will receive nothing unless Papa approves my marriage.'

'One of the trustees is your father, I presume.' Rhys picked up the decanter, studied it for a moment then put it down. 'Tempting as complete oblivion is at this moment—'

'He is,' she interrupted. 'And Grandmother was quite well aware of what he is like.' There was no point in feigning filial piety. Her father had been a distant, shadowy figure throughout her childhood, only taking any notice when she was of an age where she could not be relegated to the nursery. A girl was bad enough. A girl without a glimmer of her mother's legendary beauty and charm was worthless unless she made a useful marriage. Thea felt she hardly knew him, and, regrettably, felt no desire to do so.

If this stratagem failed and Papa realised what she was about and put pressure on the third trustee, Mr Heale, then she was trapped. She shivered at the memory of her cold, loveless childhood home. The Season had been an escape, but now that had been snatched away the walls were closing in.

'Grandmother had to name Papa as a trustee, for it would have seemed very strange if she had not, but she put in the clause about me only needing the permission of two of them for major decisions in order to get around him.'

She poured another cup of tea, ravenous and thirsty now that her immediate worries about finding Rhys at home were laid to rest. 'One of the others is the younger Mr Heale, the son of Grandmother's solicitor. I have spoken to him and he is perfectly agreeable to my taking control. I have his letter to that effect. So long as Papa does not realise exactly what I am about and try to influence him…' She touched the packet over her heart and felt the crisp, reassuring crackle of parchment. Surely her father's bullying could not negate that letter? 'My other trustee is Godmama Agnes.'

'Godmama. Now, *she* would approve of you having control of your fortune.' The brandy seemed to be having no serious effect on Rhys's understanding, or perhaps the fumes were clearing. 'Although what you'll do with it at your age…'

He was paying attention, even if he still seemed to believe she was sixteen, or incapable of making decisions. Thea took a sustaining gulp of tea, then reached for another scone. It had been a long time since breakfast at Longley Park and a snatched bun at the midafternoon change of horses.

'Has it ever occurred to you how fortunate we have been in our godmother?' Rhys asked. The thought of Lady Hughson was enough to curve his lips into a smile.

'Daily,' Thea agreed fervently. 'When we were all children I never gave it a thought, but now I see how lucky we were that she turned her unhappiness into pleasure in caring for her godchildren.' Godmama's home had been the only place she had experienced love and warmth.

'The fifteen little lambs in Agnes's personal flock?'

'Exactly. She must have loved her husband very much, then she lost him so young, before they could have children.'

Rhys gave a grunt of agreement. 'But that is history and if you ran, sorry, *left*, home to go to her, she's not in London. Have you just discovered that? Is that why you came to me?' The sleepy blue eyes studied her over the rim of his glass.

'I knew she was not in town and I dared not write and risk her reply falling into Papa's hands. She's in Venice. That is why I came straight here. As soon as I discovered where she was and what you were planning...' This was the tricky part. Would it help that Rhys was castaway?

He was not drunk enough to miss her meaning or perhaps he just knew her too well. 'Oh, no. No, no, *no.* You are not coming with me to the Continent. It is impossible, impractical, outrageous.'

'Have you become such a conventional prude that you cannot help an old friend?' she demanded. The old Rhys would rise to that lure.

'I am not *conventional.*' Rightly taking her words as an insult, Rhys banged the glass down, slopping brandy onto the highly polished mahogany. The smell was a physical reminder of what she was dealing with. 'Nor am I a prude. Revolting word. Like prunes and...' He shook his head as though to jerk his thoughts back on course. 'You cannot go gallivanting about Europe with a man you are not married to. Think of the scandal.'

'A scandal only if I am recognised, and who is going to do that? I will be veiled and anyone who sees us will assume I am your mistress.' He rolled his eyes, as well he might. She was hardly mistress material, veil or no veil. 'Frankly, I do not care if I am ruined. It can't make things any worse. Rhys, I am not asking to be taken about as though I was on an expedition of pleasure, merely to be transported. I cannot go by myself, not easily, although if you do not help me then I will hire a courier and a maid and attempt it.'

'Using what for money?' he demanded. 'Or do

you expect me to lend you the funds to ruin yourself with?'

'Certainly not. But my life will be wrecked if I have to stay.' He looked decidedly unconvinced. 'I have eighteen months' allowance with me.' The bundles of notes and the coins sewn into her underwear had kept her warm and comforted her with their solid presence throughout the long journey.

'I suppose your father handed it over without question?' There was the faintest hint of a twitch at the corner of his mouth. It gave her some hope that the old Rhys, the carefree, reckless boy who was up for any lark, was still lurking somewhere inside this rather formidable man.

'Of course not. I have not spent more than a few pounds of my allowance for three months. The rest I took from the money box in Papa's study. I left a proper receipt.'

'And who taught you to pick locks, madam?'

'You did.'

'The devil! I can't deny it.' He did grin then. 'You were very good at it, I recall. Remember the day when you opened Godmama's desk drawer and rescued my catapult? And I had a perfect alibi, clearing up under the nose of the head gardener after I broke three windows in the conservatory.'

'You said that you would be for ever in my debt.' She did not make the mistake of smiling triumphantly.

'I think I was thirteen at the time,' Rhys said. 'That is a very long time to remember a debt.'

'Surely a gentleman never forgets one, especially to a lady.' His eyes flickered over her appalling clothes, but he refrained from comment. 'You have three choices, Rhys. Take me with you, leave me to my own devices in London or send me back to Papa.' Thea smiled to reduce the bluntness of her demand. 'Think of it as one last adventure. Or don't you dare?'

He shook his head at her, then winced as his eyes crossed. 'Do not think you are going to provoke me that way. I am twenty-eight, Thea, much too old for that nonsense.'

Rhys was not too old for anything, she thought as she concentrated on keeping her face open and ingenuous. He looked perfect for one last adventure, one last dream. 'Please?'

It had never failed before. She had no idea why, of all the group of godchildren who had spent their long summers with Lady Hughson, she was the one who could always wheedle Rhys into doing anything she asked. Her, ordinary little Althea, not the other boys, not even Serena, the blue-eyed beauty he had fallen in love with.

'I must be mad.' She held her breath as he took a long swallow of brandy, his Adam's apple moving in the muscled column of his throat. 'I'll take you. But you had better behave, brat, or you'll be on the first boat home.'

Chapter Two

Rhys might have been foxed, but he could still organise his affairs with an autocratic authority. Hurrying upstairs to get changed, a sleepy maid at her heels, Thea recognised the development of the charm she remembered from years before. Then he would smile, explain, persuade—and things happened as the young Earl of Palgrave desired them. Everything except his marriage.

As an adult he still smiled, but he had no need for persuasion, it seemed. What his lordship ordered, happened. Now a travelling carriage was waiting behind the chaise in which she sat, clad in the plain, crumpled gown and cloak she had pulled from her portmanteau. A startled housemaid had received an unexpected promotion to lady's attendant and was chattering excitedly with Rhys's valet, Hodge, while the remainder of the luggage was packed into the carriage.

Thea twitched the side blind to make certain it was securely down, although there was no one in the dawn-lit street to see her inside the vehicle, let alone recognise her with the thick veil that covered her face. She yawned and wriggled her toes, relishing the thick carpet and the comfortable squabs after the Spartan stagecoach. Her new maid—Molly, Polly?—would join her in the chaise and Rhys would travel in the carriage with his valet, she assumed.

That was a good thing. She had not realised quite what a shock to the system this fully grown Rhys would be. Other than some distant glimpses when their paths had crossed while she was doing the Season, her last memories were of a youthful, trusting twenty-two-year-old standing white-faced at the altar as his world fell about his ears. After that he had been in London and, even when she was there, too, following her come-out, the paths of a wealthy, sophisticated man about town with no interest in finding a bride did not cross those of a young lady in the midst of the Marriage Mart.

The door opened and a footman leaned in. 'Excuse me, ma'am, but shall I put your seat into the sleeping position?' As he spoke he tugged a section of the padded facing panel away to reveal the darkness of the compartment that jutted out at the front of the vehicle, then he fitted the panel into the gap in front of the seat. She had heard about sleeping chaises, but had never travelled in one before.

'No, thank you.' She felt too tense to lie down. The maid deserved some rest after being dragged from her sleep to attend to her so she could use the facility.

The door opened again, the chaise dipped to the side as someone put their foot on the step. 'Rhys?'

'Not sleeping?' Shaven but heavy-eyed, he climbed past her, shrugged out of his coat and slid down the bed the footman had created, his booted feet disappearing into the void. 'Wake me when we stop for breakfast.' He closed his eyes and curled up on his side. 'Or for highwaymen.'

Without his coat Thea had an unimpeded view of the back of his head, his broad shoulders, the quite admirable lines of long thigh muscles and— she made no effort to avert her eyes—a firm, trim backside.

She stared for a long minute, being only human and female, then fixed her gaze on the postilions as the chaise lurched into motion. Oh, yes, indeed, her childhood friend had grown up. She felt rather as if she had whistled for a friendly hound to come to her side and had found instead she had summoned a wolf. He might be Rhys, but he was also a *male*. An adult male. With, she recalled, a reputation.

She brought to mind the sight of him in a box at Covent Garden Theatre, plying a beautiful woman with champagne, and hearing the whispers of the married ladies in her party. He had snatched that ladybird from the keeping of Lord Hepplethwaite and the displaced lord had blustered about calling him out—and had then recalled Rhys's reputation with a rapier.

After a few minutes Thea lowered the blind. It was easier on her nerves to see where they were and, if she was looking out of the window, then she was not watching the man slumbering by her side. He was snoring a little, which was not surprising after all he had drunk, she supposed. The sound was oddly comforting.

A glint of water showed her they were crossing Westminster Bridge, the new gaslights disappointingly extinguished. But the view downriver was as dramatic as when Wordsworth had written about it. 'The City now doth like a garment wear the beauty of the morning...' she murmured.

Beside her Rhys sighed as if in protest at the sound of her voice and turned over, his eyes tightly closed in sleep. His hair was fashionably cropped, but one dark lock fell over his forehead, a vivid reminder of the youth she had known. Thea reached out to brush it back, then stopped, her ungloved hand a fraction above the slightly waving strands. They rose to meet her fingertips like the pelt of a cat that had been stroked until its fur crackled.

Thea folded her hands in her lap. Some things were better left as dreams and memories. Some things were safer as girlhood follies. After a few minutes she drew the road guide from her reticule, where she had placed it in case she had needed to set out by herself, and unfolded the map.

They were heading into Southwark. As she had since she had begun this journey, she began to count off milestones in her head. Gathering everything she needed, undetected. Escaping from the house to the King's Head—not the closest inn, but one where she would not be recognised, despite the extra hour's walking it added to her flight. Taking the stage. Finding a hackney carriage to Rhys's house and then, the most difficult part of all, persuading him to take her with him.

Would he have agreed if he had not been drinking or if he had recognised that she was a grown woman now? She glanced down at his face, pillowed on his bent arm. Those blue eyes were closed, the veiling lashes a dark fringe. The bend in his nose was more visible from this angle and his lips moved slightly with his soft snores. There was a small scar just below his ear. That was new.

Thea wrenched her attention back to the map and the view from the window. Houses were thinning out; ahead was Deptford, full of history. According to her guidebook, it was where Sir Francis Drake was knighted and where Tsar Peter the Great stayed when he visited England. She watched eagerly for signs of the glamorous past and was sadly disappointed by crowded, dirty streets. They rattled over cobbles, the chaise jerked to a halt several times but Rhys slept on, much to her relief. When he woke, sobered and doubtless with a crashing hangover, would he change his mind about her?

The road began to climb towards Blackheath. *Wake me for highwaymen,* Rhys had instructed. Well, if they were to find any, this was a likely spot. She found she could not become very apprehensive, not on a clear June morning. More worrying was wondering where he had given the order for the first change. If it was too close to London, then there was the risk he would send her back. They rattled past the Sun in the Sands, the Fox under the Hill and the Earl of Moira as the road kept climbing. Shooter's Hill, she supposed, and relaxed a little.

Now they were slowing. Ahead she could see buildings, swinging inn signs. The postilions turned into the Red Lion's courtyard and ostlers ran out to make the change as the landlord strode across the yard towards them, attracted no doubt by the coat of arms emblazoned on the carriage doors.

Thea dropped the window. 'Shh! His lordship is sleeping,' she whispered to the man. Hodge appeared beside him and she murmured, 'Please have something if you need to, but don't wake his lordship.'

Hodge showed no surprise, but then, he must have been aware of the state his master had been in when he boarded the chaise. He nodded and went into the inn, her maid on his heels. Thea closed the window and sat on guard, her veil in place, jealously watching for anyone who might disturb Rhys's sleep. But after the arrival of a stagecoach, an altercation between two stable dogs and the shrill laughter of a kitchen maid flirting with an ostler all failed to do more than make him bury his head more firmly in his arms, she began to think he might sleep all morning, and began to doze herself.

Hodge opening the door woke her with a start. He passed her a mug of coffee and a napkin wrapped around a bread roll stuffed with bacon and glanced at his unconscious master.

'Does he always sleep like this?' Thea whispered.

The valet shook his head. 'No, my lady.' He took the mug when she had gulped the cooling coffee and closed the door softly, leaving her more than a little disturbed. Did Hodge mean he always drank that much and therefore slept heavily?

It had shocked her to find Rhys castaway and to see him toss off brandy as though it were lemonade. The rumours immediately after the fiasco of his wedding day were that he was a man who did not care, who had been glad to lose the responsibility of a wife and that he had plunged into a life of rakish dissipation.

He *had* cared, of course. She had seen his face in that first shock of betrayal; she had felt his fingers shake as she had pressed her pocket handkerchief into them, had felt his body rigid with pain when she had risked a brief hug. But then he had turned from the altar rail, a rueful smile on his lips, confessed that he had suspected the impending elopement all along and that he wished the scandalous couple happy.

For a man not given to falsehood, it was an impressive performance. It confused the gossipmongers, deflected some of the opprobrium from Serena and Paul and, she supposed, it salved Rhys's pride not to appear a victim, someone to be sorry for.

When she had been in London for her first Season the only news she could discover of him was that he had steadied, taken his seat in the House of Lords and was managing his estates with a firm hand—but that he had a shocking reputation with women. Far from seeking a new bride, he flirted as if it was a form of elegant warfare, while keeping a string of mistresses who were, she gathered from the whispers, both beautiful and expensive. He was either not invited to the entertainments thought suitable for innocent young ladies, or he chose not to attend them.

The mothers of hopeful daughters were outraged: a young, wealthy, handsome earl should be setting up his nursery. Preferably with one of their girls, any of whom had been better brought up than that flighty Lady Serena Haslow. If Lord Denham would stop indulging in the pleasures of the flesh and the gaming room long enough, he would soon come to his senses and marry one of them.

The chaise rattled out of the yard and turned east towards Dartford. No one was forcing Rhys to go on this European trip. A few months ago, with the Continent at war, he could not even have contemplated it. So why was he going now, and why had she sensed such equivocal feelings about it the night before?

The bed, unaccountably bumpy, suddenly tipped. Half awake, Rhys grabbed for the edge, missed it and slid down until his booted feet hit some obstacle. *Boots in bed? A gentleman always takes his boots off, at the very least.* 'Where in Hades…?'

'This is the West Hill down into Dartford. The route guide warns it is uncommonly steep.' The matter-of-fact voice jolted him into a wakefulness that the discomforts of his bed had not achieved.

'Thea?' Rhys sat up, shoved the hair out of his eyes and groaned at the sunlight. If this was a dream, it was an uncommonly uncomfortable one. 'What the devil are you doing in my chaise?'

'You said I might come with you to the Continent. Surely you weren't so foxed last night that you cannot recall promising?' Pin neat, drab in mud-brown wool, as ordinary as a London sparrow and three times as real, she regarded him with what appeared to be disapproval.

'I'd hoped it was a nightmare. And what are you looking at me like that for?' He lifted the section of padded board and slotted it back into position so he could sit. 'My mouth feels like the floor of a cockpit.'

'I am not surprised—you were positively cast-away last night. I suggest you tell the postilions to stop here and have some breakfast. The rest of us ate at Shooter's Hill.'

To retort that he was in charge of this journey and would make the decisions where to stop was to plunge back into the bickering of their childhood. Not that Thea had ever bickered. Or whined, come to that. She merely widened those unremarkable hazel eyes until he felt he had somehow disappointed her. And he did want something to eat and a quart of black coffee and then, with any luck, someone would hit him over the head so he could forget this headache in merciful oblivion.

Rhys dropped the window, leaned out and yelled, 'Next decent inn!'

'That will be the Bull.' Thea frowned at her road book.

'Never mind inn names, what the devil am I going to do about you?' He must have been beyond foxed to give in to the girl. Vague memories of an awful suit of male clothing swam into his memory.

'Take me to Godmama.' She regarded him through eyes suddenly narrowed with suspicion. 'As you promised.'

'You took advantage of me,' Rhys retorted.

'Do women often take advantage of you?' she enquired sweetly.

'When my luck's in,' Rhys muttered and Thea laughed. How could he have forgotten that wicked gurgle of laughter? He bit his lip to stop himself smiling back at her. 'This is an improper conversation and an utterly improper situation. If it ever gets out, you'll be ruined.' He squinted at her. 'You aren't a child any longer.' Was she? She looked about seventeen, if he was generous.

'No, I am not. And as for being ruined—' Thea shrugged as the chaise slowed. 'Good. Then Papa will stop trying to marry me off to devious, fortune-hunting… I mean, then I can have the freedom to live my life as I want to and not dwindle into an old maid.'

What is the matter with her? Every other girl wants a husband, full stop. Why must Thea be so contrary? 'Is that before or after your father shoots me?' he enquired as they stopped and an ostler hurried up. Rhys opened the door. 'No, we do not need a change of horses, but I want breakfast.'

'So do I, now I think about it.' Thea hopped down before he could offer his hand. 'A bacon roll and warm coffee were not very sustaining.'

She had her thick veil down, so he could find no reason to object, but when she returned from, he presumed, finding the privy, he wedged a chair under the door handle of the private parlour.

'Very wise,' Thea observed, taking her seat. 'If this was a stage farce, someone would burst through the door just as I removed my veil to eat. And, of course, by hideous coincidence they would know me very well and have a fatal penchant for gossip. Papa would arrive with a horsewhip....'

'Do you see many farces?' Rhys refilled his cup and added sugar. He needed all the strength he could get.

'Not these days,' Thea said, and sliced the top off an egg with undue force. Eggshell fragments splintered, Rhys winced. 'Papa knows perfectly well that being kept away from London and the galleries and the theatres and the libraries is a torture. I am *so* looking forward to Paris.'

Rhys told himself that it was unmanly to whimper. 'Perhaps you have a friend somewhere in Kent or Sussex? Someone you can stay with?'

'You promised.' And he had. Being drunk was no excuse; a gentleman should be able to hold his liquor. A gentleman never broke his word. And he owed her. Not for that lock-picking incident that he vaguely recalled coming up last night, but for years of friendship culminating in that moment in the church when she had slipped him her handkerchief, had looked at him with a world of understanding in her eyes for his pain, had given him a brief hug.

Thea had said nothing and had broken the contact almost immediately, as though she knew that too much sympathy would break him. The sixteen-year-old girl had offered him the only thing she could: her understanding and a calm presence that stopped him falling apart. That clear-eyed look told him that she trusted him to do the right thing and, somehow, he had.

What would have happened if she had not been

there? Would he have given chase, called out his best friend? Put a bullet in him and left three lives in ruin instead of just his own?

'Yes, I did, didn't I? All right, I won't go back on it.'

'Thank you.' Her hand shook a little as she lifted her cup, but otherwise she gave no sign that she had feared his refusal.

She always was a courageous little thing. Rhys poured more coffee so she wouldn't know he'd noticed that tremble and felt a pang of guilt. He should have kept in touch. But gentlemen did not write to young girls.

'Why were you—?' Thea broke off. 'Nothing.'

'Why was I so drunk last night? Damned if I know. Twelve months suddenly seemed a hell of a long time to be away and I started having doubts about whether I really wanted to do it, whether it was just a whim. I'd told myself I deserve a holiday before—' he almost did not finish the sentence, but then this was Thea and he'd always been able to tell her anything '—before I look for a wife next Season.'

And I despise myself for snatching at Bonaparte's defeat as an excuse to put off that search for another year, and that's why I was drinking. Cow-

ard. You should have dealt with those memories. There was little risk history would repeat itself; it was safe enough to seek to marry. His reason knew it, but apparently his emotions did not. It seemed there were some things he could not confess to Thea after all.

'You always have a plan,' she said, so coolly that he was taken aback. But what did he expect? That she would gasp in shock that he could forget Serena?

'And that involves getting back on the road now. I expect to be in Dover at half past four. That will give us an hour to get the carriages loaded and still catch the tide.'

'You are taking the carriages to France? How?' Her voice was oddly muffled behind the veil as she replaced her bonnet. Had he upset her somehow?

'I've hired a ship. I do not intend roughing it.'

'Excellent.' Thea's voice held nothing but approval. He had obviously been mistaken. 'I do so approve of luxury. And that means much more room for the shopping.'

'Shopping?' The Thea he remembered had no interest in shopping. But then, she had only been a girl and a tomboy at that. Looking at that disastrous gown, he shuddered to think what her idea of shopping entailed. Oh, well, her stepmother would soon sort out her wardrobe before her come-out. The vague memory of her saying she had been out for several Seasons floated into his aching head. And offers, and some man she was supposed to marry... No, surely not.

'Of course. Shopping is the entire point of Paris.'

This time he did not care how weak it sounded. Rhys whimpered.

Chapter Three

Dartford, Greenhithe, Northfleet. They travelled the next five miles in virtual silence, both of them, it seemed to Thea, adapting to their new relationship as travelling companions. Rhys had the excuse of his hangover as well, of course. She almost suggested they stop at the next apothecary's shop for a headache remedy, but this was a grown man beside her, not a boy. The very last thing she wanted to do was mother him.

'What has put you to the blush?' he asked without preamble.

She wished she had resumed her veil, but it hardly seemed friendly, not while they were travelling through open country. 'I was thinking about a man.' After all, she had always been able to tell Rhys everything. *Almost everything.*

'Really?' Rhys stopped slouching in his corner

and regarded her quizzically. 'A very romantic man, by the look of those pink cheeks. Fallen in love with the drawing master?'

'No.' He obviously could not stop thinking of her as a sixteen-year-old. 'Not the drawing master and no one romantic. Men do not woo me romantically. They check that I am not a complete ninny-hammer, assure themselves that I have all my own teeth and do not giggle and then they trot off and talk to Papa about the size of my dowry and whether he can assure them my mother's family will never make themselves known.'

'Thea, give it a chance. Just because you haven't taken yet it doesn't mean you won't get a perfectly reasonable proposal or two.'

'Rhys, I have not *taken* in three Seasons. I am not a beauty. I am not pretty. I am not even interestingly eccentric in my looks. I am perfectly ordinary. Average height, average face, ordinary eyes, mouse-brown hair which does *not* cascade into tumultuous waves to my waist when I take it down.

'If any man wrote poetry to my eyebrows I would fall about laughing and suggest he bought eyeglasses. When I do laugh no one compares it to the trill of a lark or the ripple of running water.

I can sing and play the piano adequately and no one is so foolish as to ask for an encore.'

Rhys looked rather daunted. 'But you—'

'If you say I have a wonderful sense of humour, I will lose all respect for you,' she warned. 'Such a cliché.'

'Well, you do have. But what I was going to say is that you have a talent for friendship.'

'Oh.' Now he had surprised her. What a very lovely thing to say. He had always been generous with his friendship—to her, to Paul who had betrayed him. She had not realised he had valued that in her and she was touched he recalled it now. 'You have made me blush in earnest now,' Thea said as lightly as she knew how. 'I hope I am a good friend. But I do have a talent, and you will see what it is in Paris.'

'Shopping?'

'Not quite. Where are we now?'

'Gravesend. We will change horses again at Strood. But you have evaded the subject. Who is this man that the mere thought of him makes you blush? Did he break your heart?'

He was teasing, that was all. Thea found her smile from somewhere. 'Not deliberately. He had no idea of my feelings, you see, and besides, he was in love with someone else.'

'He *was*?'

'Is, I am sure. He was never the fickle sort. But don't look so indignant on my behalf. It was ages ago.'

Simply a youthful *tendre*, the delicious, painful quivering of first love. Puppy love. That was behind her now, thank goodness. That girl and that young man no longer existed. Except in dreams, sometimes, but it would be too cruel to give up on dreams of love.

But they were dangerous things to hold on to. If she had realised that then, she would never have believed Anthony sincere when he began to court her, never have thought that she could find an adult love, prosaic and sensible perhaps, but true and honest nevertheless. It had made the disillusion even greater when she had overheard her father discussing the terms of her dowry, the extra lands he was adding to compensate Anthony for taking his plain, awkward daughter off his hands.

Rhys had the tact to stop questioning her, which was a relief because she was not certain how long she could maintain a mask of indifference in the face of direct interrogation. She should never have said as much as she had. 'Look,' she said as she drew down her veil. 'This must be Strood.'

They arrived in Dover at a quarter to five and Rhys ushered his small party into private rooms at the Queen's Head on the quayside. 'I'll go along to the ship and send for you in about an hour.'

Thea balked at the threshold. 'I will come with you.' The prospect of sitting in a stuffy parlour with a yawning maid and a ramrod-backed valet perched on the edge of his chair had no appeal. 'You go and lie down and get some sleep, Polly.'

One of the things she had always liked about Rhys was the way he would never try to persuade her out of the harmless things that stuffy convention decreed girls were not supposed to do. She tucked her hand under his arm and walked along the quayside. The wind flipped her veil back from her face, but there was no one around who might recognise her.

'The wind is quite strong.' Waves slapped high against the stonework. 'And the sea looks rather rough, even in the shelter of the harbour.'

'Do you get seasick?'

'I don't know. I am fine in a rowing boat on the

lake and as cool as a cucumber in a punt on the river.'

'They do not have waves.'

'No.' Thea took a deep breath of bracing sea air and found it was composed of an equally bracing mix of rotting seaweed and drains. 'I am sure it is all a case of mind over matter.'

'Or stomach. Perhaps I should acquire a basin.' Rhys nodded towards a chandler's shop. 'They probably have some.'

'We should write a book together. A practical guide to elopement. You do it from the male point of view, I will do the hints for the ladies. It should have a list of things to take that can fit in a small valise....'

'*Very* small. No cabin trunks,' Rhys said with feeling. 'A rope ladder.'

'Sensible shoes for climbing down a ladder. Smelling salts.'

'A road book and plenty of money. A good team of horses to start with and close-mouthed postilions.'

'A compass to make certain the gentleman really is heading for the Border.'

'Cynic! And that obviates the need for a basin. No sea crossing.'

'So it does. Oh, dear,' Thea said mournfully. 'I was so enjoying the vision of an amorous young gentleman, tiptoeing around the corner at the dead of night, lantern in his teeth, rope ladder tripping him up, basin under one arm.'

Rhys chuckled. 'Why would he take the basin with him for the ladder-climbing part of the proceedings?'

'Because he is young and romantic and silly. Of course,' she added hopefully, 'his true love may be overcome with nerves and need it. Or he could use it to knock out a pursuing parent.'

Rhys disentangled himself from her grasp and caught her hand in his. 'You,' he said with a grin, 'are a bad girl.'

'I wish I was. I fear I am simply too prosaic.'

'If leaving home disguised as a boy, bullying a half-cut gentleman into escorting you across the Channel and spinning fantasies about elopements is prosaic, then I hope I may never meet an adventurous lady.' He looked down at her, more intently. 'Thea, *how* old did you say you are now?'

Having Rhys smile at her was such a relief it affected her like one glass of champagne too many. It was going to be all right. He really would take her, not change his mind at the last moment. 'Twenty-two. I am six years younger than you, just as I have always been.' She laughed up at him and, distracted, tripped over a mooring rope.

Rhys spun her round and caught her up in his arms before she fell on the rough cobbles. 'Steady! Are you all right?'

'Oh, yes.' Tight in his embrace, close against his body and breathless with laughter, Thea looked up into intent blue eyes and smiled.

And then he went very still and his arms tightened around her as his eyes went dark. It lasted a second. It lasted an hour. Heat, strength, intensity. A hard, very adult, body against hers. A body that was becoming aroused.

Then he let her go, stepped back, stared at her in horror. 'God! I am sorry. Hell, Thea…I never meant for a moment to…manhandle you like that.'

Rhys was more shaken than she had ever seen him. *It was that bad, holding me in your arms, was it?* 'Please, do not regard it. I most certainly do not, you merely steadied me.' *Once I would have paid with everything I owned to be in your arms.*

'Of course you should regard it,' he snapped. *As though it was my fault, as though I had flung myself into his embrace on purpose…* 'I beg your pardon. Let me escort you back to the inn.' He offered his arm and she slid her fingers under his elbow. Through the kid leather of her glove she could feel his warmth and the thud of his heart against his ribs. *So agitated by discovering I am female!*

'There is no need. I would like to see the ship and the carriages being loaded.' Anything to stop her thinking about how the body that had pressed against hers had been so... A man's body, not a youth's.

Rhys ignored her, as though intent only on setting a brisk pace towards the Queen's Head. Then, just as she was on the point of jerking her hand free, he said, 'You are right not to regard it. Men are creatures of instinct, I am afraid. To find one's arms suddenly full of woman... It is no excuse, but you must not take it personally. It does not mean I do not hold you in the highest respect.' He cleared his throat.

As well he might, he has probably just heard how pompous he sounds. The rake lecturing on propriety, indeed! And he has just admitted that he was aroused and that I would have recognised that, so now he is thoroughly embarrassed and it is all my fault.

'I should regard it in the light of a cat who cannot resist catching a trailing ball of wool or a hound chasing a rabbit?' Thea enquired with all the sweetness of a lemon drop. She could not decide who she was more angry with: Rhys for making it so very clear that never again, if he was in a position to give it a moment's thought, would he take her in his arms, or herself for finding that attitude wounding. She should know better than to care. Caresses were betrayals; Anthony had taught her that.

'I am afraid so, hence the rules young ladies are sheltered by. But please, do not fear that it will ever happen again. You will have severe doubts about travelling with me now, of course. I will change places with your maid for the rest of the journey. Or I could escort you to a friend. Are you sure you do not have one in the area?'

There is no need to sound quite so hopeful, you exasperating man. 'There is no one and, besides, I am so desperate to reach Godmama that I would risk travelling with a carriage full of rakehells if need be. I could not bear to be taken back.' She sensed his frowning sideways glance, but kept her own gaze firmly forward, focused on the uneven stone setts. He really had no idea of what an emotional prison she faced. Men had so much freedom, unmarried women, none. 'You may rest easy.

I have no intention of casting myself upon your manly bosom a second time.'

Delivered with punctilious formality to the custody of her maid, Thea waited until the parlour door had closed, then threw bonnet, reticule and finally herself onto the plush-covered sofa.

'Did the sight of the sea upset you, my lady?' Polly scooped up the scattered things and began to roll the bonnet ribbons neatly. 'I'm used to it, but I know many folks get proper queasy just looking at it.' Thea's silence seemed to make no impression as she chatted on. 'Mr Hodge says as how his lordship's taking the carriages over on deck. Now, that'll be the place for you to sleep, my lady. The chaise with the window open. Fresh air's what you need. Me, I like it nice and snug down below and I'm used to the smell of the bilges, what with being brought up on me dad's sailing barge on the Thames.'

'Really?' Thea made herself listen. It was ridiculous to sit there panicking—besides, what Polly said made sense. 'I'll do that, then. The chaise seats convert into a bed.'

'If you'll take my advice, my lady, you have a nice wash now and leave off your stays when you dress again. That way you can lie down and be properly comfy.'

No stays? It sounded rather…loose. A huff of laughter escaped her at the unintended pun. Loose or not, it also sounded exceedingly sensible, and she could always wrap her cloak around her so any lack of support was not noticeable. Not that there was anything wrong with her figure that made stays a necessity. It was a perfectly nice, perfectly ordinary figure that went in and out where it should. Nothing jiggled unnecessarily, there were no scrawny bits. *Perfectly ordinary…*

'That was a big sigh, my lady. You'll be tired, I'll wager. I'll ring for the hot water and you have a little rest.'

Polly bustled out and Thea sat quite still and kept her hands folded in her lap, nowhere near her lips that tingled as though Rhys's mouth had touched them.

Of all the damn-fool things to have done, embracing Thea came top of the list by a country mile. What had possessed him? The only consolation was that he had not kissed her. Rhys strode along the quayside past a group of loitering labourers who stepped back sharply at his approach.

He was scowling. Rhys unclenched his teeth and slowed his pace. Poor girl, she must have been appalled to find herself being clutched like that by her old friend, the man she so obviously trusted. No wonder Thea had snapped at him. It had never occurred to him to think of her in that light and then, suddenly, there she was in his arms, laughing up at him, and all he was conscious of was warm soft curves pressed against him and smiling lips and the faint scent of roses, and his treacherous body had reacted.

And she had felt it and had understood what was happening. Twenty-two! He still could not get his head around the fact that she was an adult—although when she was in his arms he'd had no trouble with the concept.

Thea had been too shocked to move, he thought, heaping hot coals on his conscience. Why, she hadn't even turned her head away. Her mouth had been… *Stop it!* Even now, thinking about it, he was growing hard, to his shame. *Thea.* Hell, he might have kissed her. He might be an arrant flirt, but he never trifled with virgins. Never.

'My lord?'

Rhys found himself at the foot of a crane alongside a sturdy hoy. With the tide full, its deck was on the level of the quayside and a blue-coated man with his hat pushed to the back of his head was standing, hands on hips, studying him. Men were leading away the teams from the carriages and removing the shafts under the watchful eye of Tom Felling, the coachman.

'I am Lord Palgrave. Are you Captain Wilmott?'

'I am, my lord, and this is the *Nancy Rose* all ready to take you to Dieppe in an hour.'

'How long will the crossing take?'

The captain squinted up at the sky. 'Twenty-four hours, give or take.'

'Give or take what?' Rhys demanded. Twenty-four hours cooped up on a boat with an embarrassed, angry woman was probably fitting penance, but he could do without the uncertainty.

'Give or take sudden changes in the weather, accidents to the sails or rigging or getting stopped and searched by the coastguard,' Harris said. 'Acts of God, men overboard, collisions with whales...'

Rhys bit his tongue. The man was master of his own vessel and wouldn't take kindly to imperious orders to get a move on. 'Try to avoid the whales,' he said with a smile to show he knew it was a joke. *I hope it was,* he thought as he strolled over to watch the men fixing ropes to the chaise to attach it to the crane.

There was something very compelling about watching experts working. Within half an hour the carriages were on deck and were being lashed down and the harness and shafts stowed. Rhys, temper restored, walked back to collect his party. The only possible approach was to act as though nothing had happened.

Thea, he found, was at least as good an actor as he was. 'Polly is an experienced sailor,' she remarked as they left the inn, a lad with a barrow trundling their hand luggage behind them. 'She advises that I sleep in the chaise in order to benefit from the fresh air. Will that inconvenience you, my lord?'

He echoed her tone of careful formality in front of the servants. 'Not at all, Lady Althea. She will be joining you, I collect?'

'She says she prefers to be below decks. There are no other passengers on board, are there? Surely I will be quite safe alone.'

'I will sleep in the carriage with Hodge. You have only to call out if you feel alarmed, but you will be quite secure.'

'Begging your pardon, my lord, but if I might spend the night below decks I would appreciate it. I don't rightly fancy being up on the top like that.' The valet was wearing his usual poker face and Rhys wondered whether it was fear of the sea or the company of Polly that motivated him.

'As you will, Hodge. Make certain there are blankets and pillows for Lady Althea.'

He helped Thea to the foot of the gangplank, then let the sailor stationed on deck take her hand to guide her safely onto the deck. *Same old Thea,* he thought with a rush of affection. Sensible, level-headed, brave enough not to flinch at the narrow bridge of wooden planks, rising and falling over the drop to the water.

Ridiculous to worry that she would be affected by that moment on the quayside. In six years he had forgotten what she was like—intelligent, loyal, full of fun and thoroughly rational. Until she was seized by some madcap idea, and then she was unstoppable.

Even during those awkward years when all the little girls he knew suddenly transformed into mystifying, alarming, thrilling creatures who left him hot, bothered and, ultimately, falling in love with one of them, Thea had stayed an honorary boy, even with her hems down and her hair up.

She had never giggled at him or ruthlessly used him to practise the arts of flirtation or reduced him to stammering incoherence with one look from beneath fluttering lashes. *Good old tomboy Thea. No wonder she never received an offer.* Rhys rested his elbows on the rail next to her. 'Off we go on our adventure.'

Her answering smile was not the carefree grin of the young Thea. There were layers he could not read, a tension about her that he supposed was partly anxiety and partly tiredness. But she would be all right when they were safely across the Channel and she'd had a good night's sleep. Plain little brown mouse—what the devil was the matter with him that she could send that shock of arousal through him? Must be the hangover, that was it.

Thea studied Rhys's profile as he watched the crew working the hoy away from the quayside and into the harbour. He was a trifle heavy-eyed still—hung-over, she supposed.

How long ago had it been when she had first realised how her feelings were changing for the boy who had been a part of her childhood for so long?

And how had he, who had always understood her so well, failed to notice that she had tumbled into love with him with all the disastrous suddenness of their fall out of Squire Gravestock's pear tree, the time he broke his arm?

It must have been almost eight years ago. So long! Rhys always told her she was stubborn and she supposed he must be correct. Certainly her adoration was stubborn, for it had lived for months, flourished in the barren soil of his cheerful, friendly ignorance and then the desert of his total absence. Eventually she'd come to her senses and had grown up and out of love.

It had seemed such a good idea to go to Rhys when she'd heard he was going to the Continent, for any Grand Tour worth the name must include the great cities of Italy. It had not occurred to her for a moment that there was any danger in being alone with him. That girlish infatuation was long over and she could never forget that this was a man who loved another woman. If he did not, then surely he would have married by now.

But she had not taken the passing years into account. She had grown up and so, inevitably, had Rhys. And her mind might be cool and sensible, but her body was having a perfectly outrageous conversation with his, clamouring at her to look at him, admire him, let it explore this fascinating, frightening man. Her entire skin felt sensitive, her fingers itched to touch his....

She had never felt in the slightest danger from any of the dull, dutiful men who had asked for her hand when she was undertaking the Season. Even Anthony... *No, do not think about him.*

Now, alone with a man who was not dull and who was probably anything but dutiful, it was not Rhys who presented a threat, it was her own sensual self, startled into awareness when all she had ever expected to feel for a man again was a dull ache, like an old bruise.

And then she remembered his rejection just now when he had found her in his arms. No, she was quite safe. The only danger was of embarrassing herself thoroughly by allowing him to glimpse her new consciousness of him as a man.

Chapter Four

Being at sea was more pleasant than Thea had anticipated. The sun shone, her heavy cloak kept the wind at bay and seeing how the ship worked was entertaining. The captain took them straight out into the Channel where they met the large waves head on, so, once she had got used to the motion, Thea felt quite comfortable.

'Take my arm,' Rhys urged.

It was a foolish indulgence to cling to him, feel his strength expended just to keep her safe, to be looked after, the sole focus of his attentions. This was how beautiful women felt all the time: cared for, fussed over, treated as though they were fragile and valuable.

'We can stagger drunkenly up and down the deck together,' he added as they set off, surprising a gasp of laughter from her. No, Rhys didn't think of her as a delicate flower. *Good old tomboy Thea, that's me.*

It was difficult to speak, the wind whipping the words from their mouths, so they fell silent, occasionally pointing things out to each other—the famous White Cliffs, shining in the afternoon sun, the ship's boy scampering amidst the rigging like a monkey, the gulls following their wake.

It made it all too easy to think and to remember.

She had been fourteen, a woman for only a few months, still awkward with her changing body and her strange shifting moods. Rhys had just turned twenty and for two years he had spent most of the summers with his male friends. Still, when he came back he treated her just the same, as a younger friend, not as a little girl or a nuisance. Looking back, she supposed that was because he simply did not think of her as female, a lowering conclusion.

She could recall thinking with relief that he hadn't changed at all in the five months since she had last seen him. And then Serena Halstow had walked into the room, seventeen, blonde and pretty, and Rhys was looking at her in a way she had never seen him look at anyone before. Thea had not quite understood what was happening, but she did recognise her own feelings. She'd been violently jealous. In fact, she could have slapped Serena simply for lowering that sweep of dark lashes over her big blue eyes and then biting her lower lip as she peeped up at Rhys, who was looking, Thea had thought viciously, like a stunned cod.

They had taken no notice when she'd stamped off to sulk in the summerhouse, but when she'd calmed down a little she'd applied her brain to the situation and realised that Rhys was besotted with Serena and Serena was by no means averse to that. It had also become clear that her perception of Rhys as her best friend had shifted into something else entirely. She loved him. She was not sure what that meant, she simply knew that she had given her heart. When you are fourteen, love is for ever. She knew better now.

The butterfly-fluttering, pulse-quickening wonder of that feeling had lasted until supper when she'd stood next to Serena and saw them both reflected in the long glass. Her emotions might have decided they wanted to grow up, her body had started the uncomfortable, embarrassing process of doing so, but she was still a girl while Serena, there was no doubt, was already a young lady.

Thea had resented the approach of womanhood.

She'd dug her heels in and fought every step, hating her changing shape, the monthly misery of her courses, the restrictions and the rules. But Serena had run towards it, arms wide, thrilled with her transformation into a beautiful young woman.

Looks had never mattered to Thea, who was far more interested in character. Her stepmother was constantly lecturing. 'Stand up straight. Rinse your hair in vinegar, it might make it shine. Put this cream on those freckles.' But most of the time she would just stare at Thea and sigh.

Gazing into the mirror beside Serena, she'd realised why. She was ordinary. Not ugly, not even interestingly plain. Just run-of-the-mill ordinary. Dull. Men were not attracted to ordinary—not that she wanted men in general, just her Rhys. And her Rhys had eyes only for Serena.

In one evening Thea came to terms with the truth: that she was not fit for the handsome, eligible young man she wanted because handsome, eligible men deserved beautiful wives. She was a disappointment to Papa, which was why he did not love her and she was invisible as a female to Rhys—and so he did not want her, either.

She'd stayed very quiet all that summer and even Godmama, usually so perceptive, put it down to her being at an *awkward stage*. By the time she'd met Rhys again she had conquered that foolish puppy love and had learned to live with reality. It was better in the end—daydreams only led to hurt.

'Penny for your thoughts?' Rhys bent to her ear, his breath hot on her wind-chilled skin.

'Only one penny?' Her laugh sounded as shrill as the gulls' cries to her, but he did not appear to notice. 'Ten guineas at the very least, my lord. They are very deep thoughts about ancient history.'

'Are you a bluestocking, Thea?' he teased.

'I fear I am not serious enough.'

'Thank goodness,' Rhys said. 'That's what I always loved about you, Thea. You are so bright and yet such fun to be with.'

Her stomach swooped with a sensation that had nothing to do with the waves beneath the hull. 'Is that what it was? And I had always assumed it was because I would tell the most outrageous fibs to get you out of scrapes.'

Love me? As a friend, there was no doubt. Rhys had always been a loyal friend. What would it be like to hear him say those words and mean them, as he must have said them to Serena?

He had fallen in love with Serena Halstow, had wooed and won her, so everyone thought. And then

Serena had run away on her wedding day with Paul Weston, Rhys's best friend, leaving Rhys to receive a note on the altar steps. In one shocked moment both Thea and Rhys had realised that Serena had been using Rhys's courtship as a disguise for her love affair with the other man, who had little money and smaller prospects.

Paul, Thea had thought as she stood clutching the bride's useless bouquet until the stems bent in her fingers. *Of course*. Paul, who Lord Halstow had been so vocal in dismissing as a rake and a wastrel.

For a second, a shameful second, her heart had leapt. Rhys was free. Then she realised he might be free, but he was also broken-hearted, however well he covered it up. The last thing he needed was his gawky little friend. Thea had bitten her lip and slammed the door firmly on the silly, romantic girl she had been.

She was grown-up now. When she'd come out, the men who did court her confirmed everything her stepmother had said. Men were not interested in ordinary girls unless they had connections and wealth. She had those in abundance, but her suitors were careless enough to let her see that was all the value she had for them. They were not interested in her sense of humour, her mind, her gift for friendship.

She would never have asked Rhys to let her travel with him if she had not believed those foolish feelings for him were safely in the past. And, of course, they were. Only, she never dreamt he would touch her on the first day like that.

Oh, well, as the Duke of Wellington said, I must tie a knot and carry on. Although she rather doubted whether the duke, famous for his *amours*, ever found such things disturbing his plans.

'Tired?' Rhys was leaning against the rail, supported on both elbows. His coat fell back, exposing the length of those well-muscled horseman's legs, the breadth of his chest, the flat stomach under the watch chain curving across the subdued silk of his waistcoat. 'You look very heavy-eyed.'

Her body felt achy, her lids heavy. She knew the cause, but it was hard to fight it. She was tired, that was the problem. Once she'd had a good night's sleep in a proper bed she would be able to control these infuriating animal urges perfectly easily. She was an intelligent woman, after all. Sensible. That was all it needed—common sense.

'It must be this sea air,' Thea murmured. The same sea air that blew Rhys's shirt tight against his body and tugged his hair back from his face. The young man she had known had grown into the breadth of his shoulders and the strong bones of his face as a hound puppy grew into its big feet and suddenly changed from a friendly, ungainly plaything into a sleek, muscled killing machine.

And it was not just physical. There was an assurance about him. He knew who he was, what he was. He existed in his world with complete confidence. No, his *worlds*, she realised. Even castaway he was master of his household and received only respect. His reputation as a landowner was unblemished. He had a full social life in a shark pool where there was no tolerance for anyone who was less than polished, assured, courageous, physically and mentally adept. How did a young man acquire those attributes? she wondered. He surely never had a doubt, never felt the fear and uncertainty that she was constantly having to suppress.

As for the way he unsettled her, well, she was not a girl any longer. She had read a lot of books, watched from the sidelines many a flirtation and courtship, allowed Anthony liberties that had gone too far, even if they had been disappointing and had taught her little.

What she was feeling was physical desire and

telling herself that ladies did not permit such feelings was no help whatsoever. Either she was the single wanton exception to the rule or well-bred young women were fed a pack of lies about sex. Thea strongly suspected the latter.

'Sea air and the fact that you haven't had a decent night's sleep for at least two days,' Rhys diagnosed. Apparently he could read some of her thoughts, but hopefully not all of them. 'Still, this swell doesn't appear to be upsetting you, so you might manage a few hours tonight.'

'I agree, it is a positively pleasant motion, dip and rise. Very smooth.' She ran her tongue over salty lips.

'My lord, Lady Althea. There is dinner below if you would care to come down,' Hodge announced.

Polly had been right, there was a distinct odour of something unpleasant below decks and the motion of the ship, when one couldn't see the horizon, was far more noticeable than when she had been leaning on the rail. Thea took a plate of bread and cheese, a mug of tea, and went back on deck with a sigh of relief both for the fresh air and the interruption.

Rhys joined her as she perched on a barrel and

sipped cautiously at the black brew. 'Definitely better than down there,' he said with a shudder, and bit into a slice of meat pie.

'Rhys, why not find a wife now?' He looked across, the pie still in his hand, and a chunk of pastry fell unheeded to the deck. *Oh, goodness, whatever possessed me to blurt that out?* Too late now to go back on the question. Thea ploughed on. 'It will be the house-party season very soon, or you could go to Brighton. There would be plenty of opportunities to find an eligible young lady and then you could honeymoon on the Continent.'

'It is too soon,' he said. His expression did not invite her to continue.

Too soon? Six years? How long does it take to get over a broken heart? *But if Rhys jilted me on the altar steps, would I feel able to marry another man even six years later? Probably not. He still loves her, then.*

It felt like kicking his favourite hound, Rhys thought. Thea didn't snap back or even show any sign that he had snubbed her, although he had an indefinable sense that she had withdrawn from him.

'Of course, it was insensitive of me to ask,' she

said, each word laid down so carefully it might have been made of spun glass. 'You are not fickle. You still love Serena. Marrying again, out of duty, will be difficult.'

Still love Serena? Of course not. He almost said it out loud before he realised that would shock Thea. She believed him faithful, steadfast, the sort of man who would love loyally until death, and somehow he couldn't face the risk that she would think less of him if he admitted the truth.

It had taken six months, not six years, to come to his senses. Six months of heavy drinking, a succession of utterly unsatisfying amatory encounters and the crushing sense that if he wasn't worthy of being loved, then he wasn't worthy to behave like a gentleman, to care about his estates, to bother with his friends.

And then he had woken up one morning and asked why he was punishing himself. He had not driven Serena into Paul's arms; she had been there all the time. She had deceived him, lied to him, used him. He knew then he was not going to drink himself into an early grave for the sake of a woman who had never loved him.

'I meant that I need a holiday. I've been working hard on the estate with the new model farm, the changes to the tenants' cottages, the improvements we've been making to the cropping and livestock systems. I just want a break, something completely different.' He had also been burning the candle at both ends all Season and he was feeling utterly jaded with women, gaming... Not that he could tell Thea that.

Rhys took a swig of ale and watched Thea out of the corner of his eye as she chewed on her bread, apparently intent on digesting his words as thoroughly as her food.

What would she say if he told her the truth? *I want all my wits about me before I select a woman who will not betray me, who will fulfil her part of the bargain, will prove to be the bland, undemanding countess that I will be able to coexist with for the rest of my life. But the whole damn thing feels so cold, so...*mechanical*, that I'm clutching at excuses to put it off.*

He didn't need to ask Thea's opinion; he knew what it would be. She would frown a little, making a crease between the brows that were a shade darker than her hair. Then she would twiddle a strand of flyaway brown hair while she thought about it and finally she would tell him that he must wait until he found a woman to love and who loved him. Her obsession with love matches was the only irrational thing he had ever discovered about Thea.

If he waited to stray into the path of Cupid's arrows, he would die a bachelor. No, he would decide on a wife on the basis of her suitability as a countess and the mother of his heir. She would have to be intelligent enough to be a pleasant companion and a good parent, of course. And she would be attractive enough to make sharing a bed no penance—he intended to take his marriage vows seriously—but really, beyond that, he was prepared to be flexible and businesslike about the matter.

The women he would be deciding between—or, rather, their fathers—would make *their* decision based on his title, his bloodlines and his estate. It would be rational, calm and safe on both sides. No messy emotions. No pretence of love. He had no intention of laying his own heart out to be trampled on again and he was wary of doing anything that would make an impressionable young woman fancy herself in love with him.

'Yes, I see.' Thea nodded at last, a firm little jerk of her head. 'It is very sensible to take a holiday if you need a change.'

'Are you cold? You shivered just then.' They were both well wrapped up, but the wind was cutting across the deck, sending tendrils of her hair dancing. It was rather pretty, that soft brown. Not obvious, just…nice. He'd never noticed before. Rhys leaned forward and tucked a strand back behind her ear, and she shivered again. He really should not touch her, not until he was feeling more himself, he thought, and frowned.

'I must be tired. I think I'll retire for the night.'

'Hodge has made up the chaise, by the look of it.' The valet was pulling down the blinds as he backed out of the vehicle.

'I'll just have a word with Polly.' Thea stood up and brushed at the skirts of the serviceable walking dress she was wearing. 'Goodnight, Rhys.' She leaned forward and, before he could react, planted a chaste kiss on his cheek. 'Thank you for bringing me. I'll try not to be a nuisance.'

He must be forgiven for that idiotic moment on the quayside, he decided as he watched her making her way across the gently heaving deck, her skirts caught up tight to stop the wind tossing them.

She had developed some very feminine curves since he had last seen her, he realised as she vanished into the companionway. The memory of them pressed against his body was…stimulating.

Ridiculous chit. What on earth had possessed

her to think those boy's clothes would have been any protection at all once it had become light? It was fortunate that he had been home and she had not been out on the streets in the morning.

With a muttered curse Rhys got to his feet and went to see what Hodge was doing to make the carriage habitable for the night. This was Thea, for goodness' sake! What was the matter with him? He was going to have to find some obliging female company when they reached Paris if a few days' celibacy had this effect on him. *Thea, indeed!*

Hodge had created a snug nest for her with pillows and rugs. Thea took off her shoes and stockings, folded her cloak and lay down. How clever of Polly to suggest she take off her stays, she thought as she wriggled into a comfortable position. There was absolutely no reason why she could not get a perfectly good night's sleep with the boat moving in such a soothing rhythm.

No reason at all, except that her foolish brain decided to worry about Rhys and his marriage plans. Not that he was going about finding a bride differently from most eligible gentlemen, she supposed, punching a pillow into shape. But this was Rhys, and he was too passionate, too involved, too…

alive, to settle for a bland marriage of mutual convenience, surely?

If he would only take an interest in the young women themselves and not in their parentage and dowries, then he might find a soulmate, someone who could heal the wounds Serena had inflicted.

She tried to think what sort of young lady would suit him. *Not blonde, of course. But she'd have to be pretty. And...* Warm, rocked by the waves, Thea drifted off to sleep.

'Ow!' Thea let out a startled cry, more of confusion than pain. It was dark, her whole left side hurt from colliding with something hard and she had no idea where on earth she was. The surface she was lying on rose and fell and she thumped down again, her limbs tangled in blankets.

The chaise. I'm in the chaise on the deck of the ship and we must have hit a rock or something. Get out.... She scrabbled at the door catch but it wouldn't open. *I'm going to drown....* 'Rhys!'

Chapter Five

'Thea?' The door swung open and Rhys landed on top of her with more force than grace, a shadowy form in the dark. 'Are you all right? I heard you cry out.'

'Are we sinking?' She grabbed for him and found a handful of linen shirt. He must have shed coat and waistcoat before settling for the night.

'No, nothing like that, we are quite safe.' The words ended on a grunt of pain as they were jolted up again. 'Damn, I bit my tongue.' He wedged himself into a corner and pulled Thea across his lap, his arms safe and sure around her as the panic drained away.

'The captain has altered course and we're running across some very choppy waves, something to do with the set of the wind and the way the tide is running. Do you feel sick?'

'I was asleep, and when I was thrown into the air I had no idea where I was or what was happening, so I was alarmed, but I don't feel ill, which must be a miracle. This is like being in a butter churn pulled across cobbles.' She clutched at his arms. 'How will we ever sleep?'

'Stay there a moment.' Rhys began to rummage around in the dark, heaping up blankets by the sound of it. 'If I lie down diagonally, I can wedge myself pretty well. You lie down in front of me.'

He reached for her hand and tugged and Thea half slid, half tumbled, across his body.

'*Ugh.* Turn your back and try not to elbow me in the stomach again.'

'Sorry.' It was a very firm stomach. Thea gave herself a brisk mental shake. 'Like this?' He was warm and hard and, when his arms came around her to anchor her in place, she stopped sliding about. It did nothing for the up-and-down jolting.

'Just like this.' His voice in her ear trembled on the edge of a laugh.

'What is so funny?' she enquired tartly.

'This is. I was imagining our eloping couple— the ones from the book you think we should write. Here they are, alone at last, and Neptune has de- cided to act as chaperon.'

'Of course! He is on the seabed, poking up irritably with his trident. Here he goes…again. Ouch.'

'Try to relax.' Rhys ignored her snort of derision. 'We'll get used to it. Just let go. You need the sleep.'

'Impossible! How can I sleep like this?'

'Count dolphins jumping over rocks,' Rhys murmured in her ear. 'Sheep would get too wet.'

'Idiot,' she murmured. *One, two, three…here comes a porpoise….*

Rhys sighed and moved his mouth gently against the head of the woman in his arms. This was the way to wake up. Warm, rocking gently, arms full of soft, curvaceous femininity.

She smelled of roses, whoever she was. He must try to recall her name in a minute; it was ungentlemanly to forget in the morning. Not that he could recall the night before either, but he supposed it must have been good. His body was certainly awake and interested.

When he pulled her more tightly against his groin she snuggled back with an erotic little wriggle that inflamed an already insistent erection to aching point.

'Mmm.' Rhys nuzzled the silky fine hair and let

his right hand stray lightly across her body. They were both dressed, after a fashion, although their bare feet had obviously made friends in the night. Perhaps she had pulled on her gown again afterwards for warmth, because under the fine wool he could feel uncorseted curves and the sweet weight of an unfettered breast. As his thumb moved across the nipple it hardened and he smiled.

His companion stirred, stretched, her feet sliding down against his. She yawned and he came completely awake. He was in the chaise, on the ship, heading for France and in his arms, pressed against his insistent erection, her breast cupped in his hand, was Lady Althea Curtiss.

Rhys bit back the word that sprang to his lips and went very still. Was she awake? Had she realised? Probably not or she'd be screaming the place down, or, given that this was Thea, applying that sharp elbow where it would do most harm. He let his hand fall away from her breast, lifted the other from her hip, arched his mid-section as far back as he could. If he tried to slide his arm from under her, she would probably wake.

Damn it. *Thea*, the innocent, respectable friend whom he had already shocked with that embrace. If his wretched wedding tackle would only take the hint and calm down, that would be a help; he was as hard as teak.

Rhys thought about Almack's, tripe and onions, Latin verbs, tailors' accounts. It didn't work. His brain, apparently having lost all its blood in a mad southwards dash, was disobediently musing on just where Thea had acquired those curves from and when she had begun to smell of roses and how that mousey mane of hair could be so silky.

'Rhys?' His name was muffled in a yawn.

'Yes. Roll off my arm, would you? I've got pins and needles.'

'Sorry.'

Merciful relief. In the dim morning light Rhys grabbed for a blanket and hauled it across his lap as he sat up.

Thea sat up, too, stretching her arms in a way that made him moan as her bosom rose and fell. 'Are you all right? Shall I rub it better?'

'No! I mean, no, my arm is fine now.' Rhys gave it a shake to demonstrate and grabbed for the door handle. 'I'll get out and let you get…get ready. Yes.' He landed on the deck and bundled the blanket back into the chaise. Damn it, he sounded like a gauche seventeen-year-old. 'I can see the shore clearly. We'll be landing soon, I expect.'

'Oh, good.' Thea's voice came faintly through the closed door. 'I won't be long.'

Hell's teeth. Rhys tottered to the main mast, took a firm grip on a rope and dragged cold sea air down into his lungs. *What have I agreed to? That isn't little Thea in there, that is Lady Althea, all grown up...and out and... Stop it.* He was, for Heaven's sake, a sophisticated man with considerable sexual experience. He was a notorious flirt. His wits were normally perfectly capable of dealing with any female. So why couldn't he cope with this one? It would be better when she was up and dressed and looking like Thea again in that drab dress with her cheerful, intelligent, blessedly ordinary face smiling at him. *And her corset on, please, God.*

Thea pulled on her stockings, tied her garters and searched for her shoes, all ordinary, every-morning tasks. Only this was not every morning. Today she had woken up plastered against the body of a virile, aroused man. Which was *interesting*, if ruinous for her peace of mind. She suspected that Rhys had no idea how awake she had been, or that she knew why he had bundled out of the carriage in such haste with a blanket clutched to his midriff.

After her first encounter with an overamorous rake at a ball during her first Season, she had resolved to discover exactly what physical love involved, if only to avoid unwanted advances.

Her researches had involved a fair amount of eavesdropping on her married acquaintances and discreet rummaging in the library, to say nothing of a survey of some Greek vases that had been pushed right to the back of a high shelf. And there was the Home Farm, of course. No country-bred girl could be completely ignorant, although one hoped one's husband, if one did ever marry, had more...*finesse* than Hector, the stud bull. Or Anthony, she thought with a shudder.

Thea felt she was reasonably well informed about the mechanics of the thing and had even gleaned the interesting snippet that men tended to wake up in a state of readiness for the act. That was obviously what had happened this morning. All perfectly natural and normal. Nothing to feel hot and bothered about. It had been quite impersonal, just as Rhys's hand on her breast had been the unintentional result of sleeping so close together. And presumably her own physical reaction to that sleepy caress was automatic and natural, too. *Goodness, he was large....* Even yesterday on the quayside she had not quite realised.

She spared a wistful thought for their innocent childhood as there was a tap on the door and Polly looked in.

'I've got your brushes here, my lady, and some water and a towel. Would you like your breakfast in here or on deck? The ship's cook's got some nice fried herring.'

'Just tea and bread and butter please, Polly. I'll take it outside. Were you all right last night?'

The motion of the boat was gentle enough now for the water in the deep bowl to lap safely at the sides when she wedged it in a corner. She washed her face.

'I was fine, my lady, but Mr Hodge isn't at all happy this morning.' Polly flapped blankets vigorously as she tidied the interior of the chaise. 'Green as pea soup, he is, and properly on his dignity when I twitted him about it. There, all that needs is the seats putting back. And did you manage any sleep, my lady?'

Thea glanced at the maid. Was that a snide question or a perfectly genuine one? She was not going to put herself in the position of appearing defensive. 'I was very alarmed when we started to toss so,' she said. 'In fact, I think I cried out, because his lordship came and wedged me in with the blankets.'

'Oh. Wasn't he…?' The maid caught herself up and bit her lip.

'Wasn't he in here the entire time? Do you assume that I am his lordship's mistress, Polly?'

'Oh! My lady, I wouldn't… I mean, it isn't my place.'

Thea raised one eyebrow and waited.

'Well, yes, my lady. At least, I thought you must be eloping, like. Getting married abroad. Only he's never brought women—ladies, that's to say, home before.' She trailed off. 'I'm sorry, my lady. You won't dismiss me for impertinence, will you?'

'No, of course not. I am not his lordship's lover, nor are we eloping. I have left home and he is accompanying me to Venice where I will join my godmother. We are old friends, that is all. It makes it quite unexceptional for him to have spent the night in the chaise under the circumstances. Why, he might be my brother.'

It sounded to her own ears like a rehearsed explanation and Polly's pursed lips indicated that she was less than convinced. 'Of course, my lady.'

She gathered up the pillows. 'I'm very discreet, my lady.'

'I am glad to hear it. If you wish to become a lady's maid on a permanent basis, then that is essential.' Thea would not stoop to giving the girl money for silence, for that would convince her there really was something to hide, but the subtle hint that good behaviour might result in the privileged position of personal attendant being assured was probably just as effective.

She followed the maid out onto the deck, wrapped securely into the concealing folds of the cloak. Rhys was leaning against the main mast, hands clasped round a steaming mug, watching the coastline slip past. *France, the next part of the adventure.*

'I didn't realise there would be cliffs,' Thea observed as she reached his side. Thankfully her voice sounded perfectly normal, although she suspected she was blushing. It was strange to have intimate knowledge of his body like that, even more disconcerting than the fact that he had caressed her breast.

'They are not as high as at Dover. We'll be in Dieppe soon.' Rhys sounded perfectly normal, too. He could not have realised that she had been awake as long as she had, or perhaps men were completely blasé about that kind of thing.

But he had not been indifferent about that hectic moment on the quayside in Dover. A sharp pain made her realise that she was biting her lower lip. The only thing to be done was to seem entirely unconscious of any reaction on either of their parts, and Rhys would soon realise that she had no interest in him as anything but an old friend.

Polly brought her tea and she leaned on the other side of the mast, scanning the coast for anything particularly foreign and exotic. 'It looks just like England,' she complained as they swung into the harbour.

'That doesn't.' Rhys nodded to a life-sized crucifix set up to dominate the quayside. 'And look at the costumes. Do you think they are fishwives?'

'They are exceptionally clean if they are,' Thea observed as the crowd on the quay came into focus. 'Not like Billingsgate at all!' The women had tight-waisted bodices with vast skirts billowing out and finishing well above their white-stockinged ankles. They wore snow-white caps with flaps hanging down to their shoulders and, as the sails came down and the ship lost way, Thea could see the glint of gold in every ear.

'So many soldiers,' she added as they glided closer. The crowd was full of men in greatcoats, military-looking jackets, cocked hats—all studying the ship and its human cargo with sullen faces. Thea was suddenly very grateful that she was not attempting this journey by herself. They had been at war with these people for years and, it seemed, peace had not made much difference. 'I thought the army would have been disbanded,' she added, trying for a note of bright interest and not apprehension. She had fought down her fears about leaving home, but it had never occurred to her to worry about dangers beyond escaping the shores of England.

'It has, by and large. Those aren't soldiers, at least not anymore. These are just conscripts who have returned home. Look around, virtually everyone is wearing some piece of cast-off uniform, even some of the women. They've been at war for years, poor devils, and they probably don't have much else.'

'Is there a hotel we will go to?' Thea saw jostling porters, lads with barrows, and tried to start thinking in French. It had never been her best subject, much to the disapproval of her governess.

'Of course. It is all arranged. We will be met—

in fact, that must be the agent there.' Rhys raised a hand and a tall, thin man in a dark suit of clothes lifted his hat in acknowledgement.

The ship bumped alongside, almost level with the top of the quay. Ropes were thrown and tied, a ladder let down the few feet to the deck and Rhys went up, then reached out to help Thea, who twitched her veil into place.

'Monsieur le comte!' The man was pushing his way to their side.

'No earls in France,' Rhys observed to Thea. 'With or without their heads. It appears I have become a count.'

'François le Brun, at your service, *monsieur le comte.*' He whipped his hat off again as he saw Thea. 'And *madame la comtesse*! I had not expected the honour.'

'Non, monsieur. Je suis...'

'This is Madame Smith,' Rhys said firmly in French that was considerably better than hers. 'A family friend I am escorting to Paris.'

'But of course!' Le Brun's hands fluttered in urgent signals to indicate his total willingness to oblige. He was desperate to please, Thea realised. The returning English must offer employment and hope after difficult times. 'It is as *monsieur le comte* says. Another chamber will be no problem. I have taken the entire *hôtel* for the convenience of *monsieur le comte.*'

He clicked his fingers and half a dozen men lined up beside him. 'These will unload your carriages. I have engaged two post boys and hired horses of the best quality.' He grimaced. 'At least, of the best quality that is available these days.

'If you will follow me.' He turned, apparently unconcerned by the fight that had broken out between porters over who would load their luggage onto whose barrows. Hodge, in French almost as good as his master's, was laying down the law to some effect and Rhys did not appear concerned, so Thea took his arm and allowed herself to be led through the crowd.

'They are staring,' she muttered in English.

'Of course. We are still a novelty and no doubt they are studying us for the latest in English fashions.'

'Then they will be sadly disappointed in me,' she retorted. 'How long are we staying? I must buy one new gown at the very least. I cannot bear this drab old thing for much longer.'

'It is fine, surely?' Rhys glanced down at her

skirts, protruding limply between the openings of her cloak.

Either he was completely indifferent to fashion or he simply expected her to wear something dowdy. Probably the latter. 'No, it is not fine. I chose it because it is so dull and worn. I had no wish to draw attention to myself in England. It is my gardening dress and the last thing Papa would expect me to be seen out in. I took the precaution of hiding some of my newest gowns so the description of what I was wearing would be wrong.'

'You would make an excellent spy,' Rhys observed. 'But can you not endure your limp brown skirts until Rouen? I was intending to spend just the one night here, but two there. The shops should be better, too.'

'Very well, it does seem sensible. But you are going to disappoint Monsieur le Brun when he has taken over an entire hotel just for one night.' The Frenchman paused to wave them on with a flourish. Behind them, she could hear Hodge nagging the porters to take care with his lordship's luggage. She had seen less dramatic circus processions.

'Monsieur le Brun has been promised a generous fee, so he will be advised to put a good face on it whether I stay ten minutes or ten days.' Rhys regarded their French guide's flamboyant gestures through narrowed eyes. 'This hotel had better be a good one.'

'He did not believe I was just a friend,' Thea murmured, tweaking her veil. 'Perhaps the hotelier will not approve....'

'The hotelier will approve even if we choose to hold an orgy for two, import every one of the Regent's mistresses or spend the evening playing whist,' Rhys said with an edge that startled her. 'It is none of his damn business. I am Palgrave, and if he does not know what that means then he will discover a startling shortage of English visitors of rank over the next few years.'

I am Palgrave. He would never have said that six years ago, and certainly not with that cool threat behind it. He had never spoken to her in that way and suddenly she saw him as others did: an earl, a powerful man by inheritance and his own force of will. Unnerved by his irritation, she stammered, 'I-it is just that I had not regarded what people might think, provided no one recognised me. And now I feel a trifle... I would not wish to cause you embarrassment.'

'Cause *me* embarrassment?' Rhys stopped dead and frowned down at her, six foot plus of exasperated masculinity. 'I doubt anything would put me to the blush, but you are my responsibility now.'

'Th-thank you.' Thea had to take a little run to catch up with him as he strode off across the cobbles. 'I had no intention of being a nuisance.'

'We will talk when we are alone,' Rhys said. 'Here, give me your arm, these stones will turn your ankle.'

In other words, I am *a nuisance.* It felt very much like being summoned to Papa's study for a lecture. Behind the sheltering veil, Thea grimaced at the haughty profile, fell obediently silent and wished very hard that she had the young Rhys back again.

Chapter Six

The hotel, when they reached it, was large, but half seemed in ruin with windows boarded up. There was even a small tree sprouting in the gutters.

'This looks a wreck,' Rhys said to le Brun.

'It is too big these days, too expensive to keep it all in repair. Before the Revolution it belonged to…a family. They no longer needed it, so part was taken over by a *citoyen*, a citizen of the Revolution, you understand? The same has happened all over the town.' He shrugged. 'All over France.'

'No longer needed it? You mean they were guillotined?' A citizen. *Citoyen*, one of the people. Had the landlord been part of the mob who bayed for *the death of aristocrats*? Thea shivered.

'*Madame*, such an unpleasant subject.' He pursed his lips as though she had made a remark in bad taste. Perhaps she had.

'The half that is in use seems decent enough,' Thea said to placate him as he ushered them inside.

He exchanged a flurry of rapid French with the short man who came out to greet them and two maids were despatched upstairs, arms full of linens. 'They prepare another bedchamber for *madame*,' le Brun explained. 'I show you now to the salon of the suite.' The landlord was swept aside. 'There is a chef, a proper man cook,' le Brun announced with a gesture towards a door at the rear. 'Not a female cook as so often is the case in England, I understand.'

They followed him upstairs, leaving the porters and Hodge in energetic dispute over how much extra it would cost to have the luggage carried up.

'Voilà!' Le Brun flung open a door with a flourish.

They were on the principal floor of the house, in a chamber that had once been an elegant reception room. It was whitewashed now and worn rugs were scattered over a floor of soft red brick, but the fireplace was magnificent and marble. The walls were hung with huge mirrors, damp spotted, their ornate frames bearing faint traces of their original gilding, and the assortment of furniture had once seen far better days.

'*Monsieur le comte*, your chamber is here.' Le Brun opened a door on the far side. '*Madame*, they prepare yours there.'

On the far side, thank goodness. 'I trust the beds are aired.' Thea had practised the sentence in French in her head all the way up the stairs.

Le Brun shot her a look of deep reproach. 'But of course!'

'We will need hot baths immediately, and then breakfast.' She threw back her veil and produced a smile. 'If you please.'

The effect on the Frenchman was curious. He smiled back at her with more genuine warmth than he had shown before, then he glanced at Rhys with a faint smirk. 'I see to it at once, *madame*.'

Thea snorted as he closed the door behind himself. 'He has realised that I am not, after all, your mistress. He will treat *me* with slightly more respect and he feels rather less for *you* now.'

'How did you work that out?' Rhys turned from the window and his contemplation of the street outside.

'He saw me unveiled. I told you, I am not mistress material. So he decides I am respectable and you are to be pitied for having the chore of escorting me.'

'Oh, for goodness' sake! As if the suitability of a woman for that role has anything to do with looks.' Rhys's brain appeared to catch up with his mouth and he shut it with a snap.

'What *does* it have to do with?' Thea asked, overcome with curiosity.

'Never mind! Will you please stop talking about mistresses?'

'Certainly! Perhaps, while you are lecturing me, you can tell me what it is we have to discuss in private?'

'Lecturing?' Rhys narrowed his eyes at her. 'Please sit down, Thea.' This was not the just-awakened man who had made her smile with his precipitous exit from the chaise. It was certainly not the inebriated old friend, sprawled in a chair and harassed by the kitchen cat. This was every inch the adult half stranger she had caught unsettling glimpses of on their journey.

'Very well.' She swept cloak and skirts around her with a flourish and sat in a chair that had probably once graced the town house of some now-executed aristocrat. The idea made her shiver.

'You are cold.' From his frown, that appeared to be a fault on her part.

'No, I am…unsettled. Please say what it is you wish to say and then I will go and change.'

'You should never have come to me and I should never have brought you with me,' Rhys stated without preamble.

'I was obviously mistaken in thinking I could rely on an old friend to help me.'

'You should have been able to rely on an old friend to do the right thing. If I had been halfway sober, I would never have brought you. But it is done now and there is no going back from it. I will get you to Godmama safely.'

'Thank—'

'I have not finished. Your position is open to misinterpretation from everyone we meet, servants or otherwise. I will not have a lady under my protection insulted or embarrassed, and I would therefore be grateful if you would do nothing to draw attention to yourself, or our journey is likely to be a turbulent one.'

'Indeed?' Thea got to her feet with a swirl of skirts that would have been considerably more effective if they had not been overwashed old wool. 'Other than being female, I do not believe I have done anything that might be said to draw attention to my person. I regret that I am not able to rectify that grievous fault—unless you wish me to dress as a boy? I still have the clothes.'

'You make an appalling boy—you do not have the figure for it.' Rhys appeared to find the carved overmantel fascinating.

'I could bind my—'

'It is not your... Not the parts that need binding that are the problem. No youth has hips like that, and those can't be bound.'

'Hips? Are you saying that I have a fat posterior?'

'No! Thea, this is a highly improper conversation.' Rhys glared at her. 'You have curves, that is all I am saying.'

'So I should hope.'

'You never had them before.' Rhys's lips twitched into a reluctant smile. 'You used to be all skin and bone and angles. You still have the elbows. I have the bruises from last night.'

'I was sixteen the last time we met face-to-face, for goodness' sake! I was a late developer,' she added mutinously.

'Well, you've developed now, and that's a problem.'

'Not according to Stepmama. She considers that I finally have an adequate figure.' Rhys appeared to be grinding his teeth. 'Anyway, I have no intention of flaunting anything, or of flirting with passing rakes, leaning over the balcony *en negligée* or otherwise drawing attention to myself. Does that reassure you?'

'It does. Thank you, Thea.' They watched each other in wary silence for a minute, then Rhys said, 'I am not used to having to look after an unmarried girl.'

'I am not a girl.' His words might have been intended as a small flag of truce, but her precarious hold on her temper was slipping again. 'If I am old enough to be married, and to inherit my own money, I think that makes me a woman, don't you?' Even to her own ears she sounded remarkably tart. What was the matter with her? She never lost her temper—she was known for cheerful common sense, everyone said so.

'No doubt it does. And that is the problem. At least we understand each other now.'

We do? She opened her mouth to ask that very question as Polly bustled in.

'The room's all ready for you, my lady, and the bath's being filled, although I had a bit of a problem with the servants here to start with. Cobwebs like you wouldn't believe and no proper pillows, just nasty, hard bolster things.' She picked up Thea's discarded bonnet. 'Amazing how they understand if you speak nice and loud and slow, isn't it?'

'French servants or Englishmen?' Thea murmured as she followed the maid out. From the corner of her eye she saw Rhys's mouth quirk up at the corner. So he had heard her. Ah well, so long as that half smile meant they were back on their old footing and he stopped that nonsense about drawing attention to herself. And wanting to fight anyone who insulted her.

It was rather charming, she decided as she rolled down her stockings. Gallant. Up to now gentlemen had not seemed to consider that she might need helping down gangplanks or rescuing from embarrassment. Even when Anthony was making his pretence of courting her so ardently he had never tried the 'fragile flower' treatment.

Not that she did *need* assistance, of course. She would hate to be a helpless female, but it was pleasant to be looked after once in a while. The memory of just how safe Rhys's body had made her feel sent a shiver shimmering across her skin. Odd, she must be tired, or perhaps she was coming down with a chill.

And perhaps *safe* was not the right word, not

when she remembered the shocking pressure of his arousal against her buttocks, or the heat of his body. But that was just a male reflex, nothing to be worried about. Everything would be fine, provided Rhys stopped lecturing her. Even discovery and ruin hardly mattered. Nothing did, provided she was not forced back home into a grey nothingness of an existence. She shivered again. That would be so bad she might even agree to marriage and find herself tied to someone like Anthony.

Polly lifted her gown over her head and Thea shed shift and petticoats before stepping into the bath. 'Heaven.' This would stop the shivers. 'A hot soak and a soft bed that doesn't move. It is soft, I hope?'

'The sort that swallows you,' Polly said cheerfully, and passed the soap. 'They've put me in there.' She pointed at a door. 'Great big room. And Mr Hodge is on the other side next to his lordship. Not exactly cosy, though, is it?'

'Not at all. I think it was a quite grand town house once and this was the main reception floor. These are not really bedchambers.'

'And the owner's come down in the world? He doesn't look much like a gentleman.' Polly began to shake out Thea's clothes. The corset had reappeared, she noticed.

'I suspect the real owner and his family went to the guillotine,' Thea said, repressing another shiver.

'Ooh! I was forgetting that.' Polly's eyes were huge. 'Murdering Frenchies. Why, they're probably eyeing up his lordship and sharpening the blade even now....'

'We are at peace with France,' Thea soothed. 'There is a king on the throne again and Bonaparte is safely banished to Elba in the middle of the Mediterranean.'

'And quite right, too,' Polly muttered. 'Now, I suppose it will have to be the blue gown tonight.' She prodded the limp garment with disfavour while Thea made herself focus on the immediate crisis of her inadequate wardrobe and pushed other, more disturbing, thoughts back into the shadows.

Rhys folded his long legs into the bath and bent his head for Hodge to pour over a jug of hot water. *Thea and that tongue of hers, as sharp as ever.* But she never used it to wound. Only to tease, to create laughter, to press home a point.

He'd missed that laughter and teasing from a

woman. There was laughter enough with his male friends, but his mistresses were always more intent on being seductive than on amusing him, which he supposed was fair enough, that was what he wanted from them—beauty, sensual expertise in bed and sophisticated conversation beforehand.

They were an expensive luxury, but Rhys was prepared to pay for quality. But some things could not be bought from a woman: friendship, laughter, loyalty. For a few weeks he would have those with Thea, he supposed, and felt the smile curve his mouth.

'More hot water, my lord?'

'Hmm?' He must have fallen into a trance. 'Yes. More hot water, more soap.' *Thea. Just as long as you remember that she's an innocent. A bright, clever, independent innocent. It is a good thing she's been stubborn enough to turn down those marriage offers—she isn't cut out for matrimony and they'd only make her miserable, forcing her into the mould of a perfect wife.*

Hodge passed him a back brush and Rhys began to scrub, shifting his shoulders under the pleasurable rasp of the bristles.

But she'd have to be careful, he realised as he considered it further. Life as a single woman would be made smoother with wealth, but it would be all too easy to slip into eccentricity, or worse, if she failed to find a manner of living that met with the approval of society. He would have to talk to her about it, make certain she made the right decisions, just as he had.

'So what are you planning to do with all this money when you have control of it?' Rhys asked.

The wind on the cliff top was blowing her veil in all directions and he could not see her face. With an irritated *'Tsk'*, Thea gave up wrestling with her veil and threw it back over her bonnet. 'There is no one up here to see,' she said, as though expecting him to demand that she lower it again. 'What am I planning? Why, to be independent.'

'I know that, but independently doing what, exactly?' Rhys hitched one hip onto a tumbledown stone wall and half turned as though watching the town and harbour below. Out of the corner of his eye he studied Thea as she paced back and forth over the rabbit-cropped turf.

'Living, of course! What a ridiculous question.'

'Where? With whom? Who will be managing your investments? What will you be spending your money on?' He swivelled to face her and she stopped, a furrow between her brows as she frowned at him. 'What will be your purpose in life?'

'To enjoy myself. To be free.'

'Selfish,' Rhys commented, with the intent of provoking her. Down in the harbour, fishing boats were running out on the tide, and he pretended to watch them. 'That's not like you.' Or perhaps it was. Six years was a long time. He had changed, she must have, too.

'I don't mean mindless frivolity,' Thea protested. 'I mean doing things that I consider worthwhile. Something that will tell me I am alive,' she added so softly he thought he must have misheard her. Surely life in her father's house was not so stifling? 'I will set up a charity—that would be satisfying....'

'To be Lady Bountiful to the grateful poor?' He let the corner of his mouth curl into a sneer. As it had in the past, his goading worked. Thea glared at him, but he had loosened her tongue.

'No, certainly not. People do not need to be patronised, to be done good to. I will find something worthwhile and invest in it. Perhaps set some enterprising women up in small businesses, or provide apprenticeships for bright boys. I have a brain with some ideas in it, Rhys. I will suffocate if I don't use it, if I am not free.'

He hid both his approval and his unease at her vehemence. 'It does not sound as though you have planned it out.'

'Of course I have not.' Thea marched round to stand in front of him, cutting off his view of the harbour. 'I need to find out exactly what my income is, learn how to manage it and, I hope, increase it. I have to find a suitable companion and somewhere to live. I need to work out all those things and then I can see where I am.

'Anyway,' she demanded, 'what is so important about planning? You used to do things on the spur of the moment. Improvise.'

'I do not any longer.' He stood up, rather too close for her comfort, it seemed. Thea cast a harried glance over her shoulder, apparently decided that the cliff edge was a safe distance from her heels and took a long step backwards. 'These days I plan—the estate, my investments, my political life, the way I live.'

'Predictable,' Thea retorted. 'Boring. Do you schedule your mistresses according to a timetable?'

'Responsible,' he flung back, ignoring that last

jibe. Rhys planned so that nothing, nobody would have the chance to let him down again, but he saw no reason to justify himself. He caught at the ragged edge of his temper and said coolly, 'Grow up, Thea.'

'I have.' Annoyance was bringing out the colour to her cheeks. 'But I do not understand why being a responsible adult involves losing spontaneity, joy, surprise. Adventure.' The look she shot him held reproach. 'Have you any concept what it would be like to have to dwindle into an old maid or be married off to a man whom you cannot like, let alone respect?'

No, he could not, and it made him damnably uncomfortable that Thea of all people feared those things. His conscience nudged him. She had been his friend and he had all but forgotten her as he had rebuilt his life. But what did he know about respectable women and their emotional needs? Perhaps some practical common sense would help— it was all he had to offer. 'This is not about me. It is about you, Thea. You have two assets that must last you your lifetime, if you are not to marry.'

She tipped her head to one side, instantly curious. She had never been able to hold on to a bad mood for long. The only time he had seen her stay angry was two hours after the fiasco of his wedding ceremony when he had found her wringing the neck of Serena's bouquet. And even then, when she had seen him, she had smiled ruefully. 'Poor flowers, it isn't their fault.'

'I have my inheritance, that is all,' she said now.

'You have that, and you will need to choose your financial and legal advisers with great care, for those funds must last to finance your independence.'

'So what is the other asset?' Intelligent hazel eyes fringed with dark lashes narrowed in thought.

'Your reputation. Respectable single women with wealth and breeding and a certain interesting eccentricity will be accepted anywhere—look at Godmama. But get a shady reputation, just the hint of loose behaviour, and you will find doors close in your face.'

'Loose behaviour? Me?' Thea gave an unladylike snort of derision.

'Like gadding about the Continent unchaperoned with a man to whom you are not related, for example?'

The charming blush faded. 'Nonsense. No one is going to find out. Godmama and I will concoct a suitable story involving a courier and a suitable female companion, you'll see.' There it was again, just that flash of emotion behind the confidence. Surely it could not be fear of what would await her if she had to return home?

'I hope so. It is getting cold—let's go down and see what there is for dinner.' He stood and offered his arm and she slipped her hand under his elbow. He was apparently forgiven. But then, Thea always did forgive. Rhys felt another twinge of guilt, this time for goading her and, at the same time, for entertaining Gothic imaginings about her father. The earl might not be the best parent in the world, but he would not mistreat Thea, surely?

'Scallops, I hope. Dieppe is famous for them, I believe.'

'That sounds good,' Rhys agreed. 'I was thinking of a fat lobster, personally.'

He waited until they had left the slippery cliff-top turf for the worn path before he asked, 'Would it not be better to find a husband after all? Someone to take care of you—and your inheritance?'

'*His* inheritance, you mean. Once I marry, I lose all control of my money.'

'Is that why you are so set against marriage?' A group of soldiers lounged by a checkpoint on the road out of town. They glanced over at them, then went back to their game of dice. There was something she was not telling him, and he was going to winkle it out of her, however hard she resisted.

Chapter Seven

'I am not set against marriage, as such,' Thea protested. 'But it is such a risk. A woman hazards so much. I am resolved not to marry unless I fall in love, which seems to me to be the only reason for taking the plunge. And I can tell you, that is highly unlikely.'

'What about Sir Anthony Meldreth?'

'As I said, we found we did not suit.'

Perhaps she had sounded unconvincing, for Rhys stopped and looked at her sharply. 'What happened?'

Bother and blast, I am blushing. 'Nothing.'

'Thea…' Rhys's tone told her he would not let this go now. 'Sit down here and tell me.' He gestured to a bench by the side of the path.

'Oh, well, if you must pry into every last detail!' Thea sat down with an inelegant thump and stared at her toes. 'He led me to believe he loved me, that he was interested in the things that I enjoyed, that he respected my opinions, that he wanted a wife who would be an equal.'

'And did you love him?'

'In a way, yes. I thought he would be a good companion and I trusted him when he said he wanted only me, for myself.'

'And he did not?' Rhys's voice was softer now.

'I overheard him discussing settlements with my father. They had agreed on his approach together so that Papa could get me off his hands and Anthony would gain my inheritance and a piece of land he had been wanting for a long time that Papa had previously refused to sell.'

'That must have been…difficult to cope with. What did you do? Confront them?'

'No. I told Anthony that I had changed my mind and I did not think we would suit. He told me I was frigid and not worth what my father offered him.'

'*Frigid?* Did he force you?'

'No.' It was apparently possible to blush this hard without bursting into flames. 'I allowed him certain…liberties. When I thought we were in love, you understand.' Thea fixed her gaze on her clasped hands.

'*Certain liberties?* What the blazes does that mean?' Rhys sounded furious. Thea flickered a glance in his direction and saw his face. He *was* furious.

'Rhys, for goodness' sake, I cannot discuss this with you!'

'Why not? You are under my protection. The man's a bastard to trifle with you. I will deal with him when I get back to England.'

'Call him out? For pity's sake, Rhys—on what pretext?'

'I'll find one. I am certain I can take offence at his hat, or his face or the way he laughs.'

'Oh, Rhys.' There was no point in arguing and, besides, Sir Anthony was a long way away. Rhys's temper would have cooled by the time he got home. He fired up when he saw her predicament as a matter of honour, but he did not truly understand her horror of returning to that life where she was either a pawn or a tool, where her true *self* would simply dwindle and vanish. A man simply would not comprehend how a woman's powerlessness could make her feel.

'Love's an illusion,' Rhys said abruptly. 'You realise that now, I presume?'

'No, I don't. I was mistaken in him and my own

sentiments, that is all. You know that love does exist,' Thea said softly. She reached out and curled her fingers around his forearm for a moment. 'If it did not, you would not be so set on making a love-less, *suitable* marriage this time. Love hurts—that is how we know it is real.'

Rhys moved abruptly, but she kept looking straight ahead so all he would be able to see was the top of her plain straw bonnet. 'Put your veil down,' he ordered.

'Oh. Yes, of course.'

She arranged it carefully, then let him take her hand and help her to her feet. Now that she had satisfied his curiosity, perhaps Rhys would drop the subject and allow her to nurse her battered emotions in peace. Her fears she dared not contemplate.

'Tomorrow I shop,' Thea said firmly three days later as dinner was laid out on the table in their private salon in the Plume d'Or inn near the Louvre. 'Rouen was all very well, but one day was not enough.' All she and Polly had achieved was fresh linen, a pair of stockings apiece and some handkerchiefs.

'You are not tired by the journey?' Rhys took

up the carving knife and began to dismember a chicken with forensic skill. He sounded hopeful. Why were men so anxious when women went shopping? It was not *his* money after all.

'Tired? Not at all. I love travelling. There was so much to look at and the roads are very good.'

'All the better for marching troops along,' Rhys said with a wry smile.

'It seems so strange to be at peace. All my life we have been at war with France. Thank goodness it is over now.' Thea accepted the meat he laid on her plate and began to investigate the steaming dishes that filled the table. 'How many people do they think they are feeding! This looks delicious. I am going to put on pounds if I am not careful.' She chewed a delicious morsel and took a sip of wine. 'Rhys…'

'Yes? That sounds like the start of a question I should be wary of.'

'Nothing of the kind. I just wondered if you could ask the innkeeper to recommend a guide for me tomorrow. My French is not equal to finding my way about and I have no idea where to discover the best shops.'

'I should escort you.'

'Thank you, but I am certain you have your time

already planned out.' She studied his expression. 'I should give you credit for managing to look perfectly calm when I know you are filled with dread at the very idea of being dragged around Paris's shops in the wake of a female.'

'Very true. I am quaking, so the offer is one of great heroism on my part.' She opened her mouth to protest, but Rhys grinned. 'No, I will not inflict myself on you—take Hodge. His French is excellent and he was in Paris during the last peace.'

There, Thea told herself as she ate her dinner with good appetite. *I am safely settled in a good hotel without any scandal or fuss, Rhys and I are conversing quite on our old terms. There is nothing at all to worry about.* But she never had been very anxious about scandal or fuss, so it must be Rhys that she was relieved about....

'What are you frowning about now?' he asked, the old teasing note back in his voice. 'Afraid there are frogs in the casserole again?'

'Provided they are not live ones hidden under the lid, like your birthday surprise for me when I was ten, I am not at all worried, you wretch,' she retorted. *You see? Nothing to worry about at all.*

* * *

'Please tell me there is more than a single item left in the shops of Paris.'

Thea followed Hodge, Polly and two hotel footmen into the private sitting room and peered around the piles of parcels at Rhys. He was dressed to go out, immaculate in black evening breeches and a midnight-blue swallowtail coat.

'Of course there is. These are just some essentials to tide me over until I can pick up the gowns that are being altered for me.' He rolled his eyes as Thea placed two hatboxes on the table. 'You look very elegant, I do admire your neckcloth. Where are you off to?'

'Thank you. I have tickets for the *Opéra*. There is a spectacular soprano I have been hearing about whom I would like to see in action. I was about to leave you a note to say order dinner without me.'

'Have a good time,' Thea called after him as he picked up hat and cane and left. 'Now what are we going to do with ourselves all evening?'

'Us, my lady?' Hodge asked as he came back from carrying the last of the parcels into her bedchamber.

'Are you tired, or shall we go out again after dinner, all three of us?'

'Where to, my lady? I'm not at all tired, I must confess. It is very stimulating, being back in Paris, but his lordship might not like...'

'Oh, pish! What harm is there in going to one of the more popular localities—the Palais Royale, for example?'

'It used to be rather, er...racy, my lady.'

'I am not suggesting going into one of the gaming houses, Hodge. But there are all those lovely coffee shops with tables outside—ladies seem to find it quite acceptable to sit there.'

'*Cafés*, my lady?'

'Yes, we will find a nice *café* and watch the world go by.'

'You could wear the new peacock-blue gown and that little black chip-straw headpiece with the veil,' Polly suggested. 'Perfect, my lady.'

Perfect, indeed. This was what being an independent woman was all about.

The opera singer known as *La Belle Seraphina* moved slightly in her chair and set her elbows tight together on the tiny *café* table, presenting Rhys with an even more spectacular view of her cleavage, its creamy shadows enhanced by a hint of lace in their depths.

He shifted in his seat, time enough to admire those very generous assets after he had discussed the possibility of her appearing at the London Opera House next season. His cousin Gregory had an interest in the place and Rhys had promised to keep his eye open for promising singers. After their negotiations, perhaps he would open discussions about a transaction of an altogether different kind. She certainly appeared to be sending out signals that such a suggestion might be welcome.

And a night spent in mutual pleasure would be more than welcome to him, Rhys acknowledged, wondering what was making him so damned randy. Anyone would think he had parted from his mistress a month ago, not just over a week. He moved again, restless, his body's automatic urging at odds with a surprisingly fastidious unwillingness to come to the point and make the proposition that he was certain the woman at his side was expecting.

Across the clipped box hedges and shorn grass of the central strip of garden, a small party arrived at the *café* opposite. A veiled woman seated herself in a flurry of peacock-blue skirts. *Very nice,* he thought absently, noting the trim figure and the grace with which she sat down between her companions, a plainly dressed maid and a man in sombre black.

'*Hodge?*'

'*Monseigneur?*' the woman at his side purred as she laid a hand on his forearm, the lush curve of her breast pressed against him in a blatant attempt to regain his attention.

'I beg your… *Excusez-moi.*' Rhys scrambled after his French. He might, strangely, be finding her uninteresting, but that was no excuse for bad manners. 'I just saw someone I know.' His valet, Thea's maid and…the elegant figure, her face hidden under a veil of figured lace that just reached her top lip in a way that was pure provocation… that must be Thea. *Thea?*

'I thought I saw someone I knew.' Rhys forced himself to think coherently in French again as he settled back in his chair, contriving to turn it slightly as he did so to bring the other table fully into his line of sight.

What the blazes was Hodge thinking of, to bring Thea here of all places? It was innocuous enough during the day, except for the effect on the wallet of the numerous tiny shops selling exquisite trinkets, jewellery and *objets de vertu*, but at night it was a playground. *And not for infants*, Rhys fumed inwardly.

The place was a very grown-up playground indeed, an ant heap of gaming hells, high-class brothels and intimate eating places. For respectable French couples who were sophisticated enough to know what they were doing it was safe enough, likewise for an escorted lady in a small party, but for an innocent like Thea it was fraught with perils.

He kept the discussion about London theatres going while he fought the instinct to march across, toss Thea over his shoulder and deposit her unceremoniously back at the hotel, sacking Hodge while he was at it. Making a scene was not the way to protect Thea's reputation and, to be fair, he had told Hodge to escort her wherever she wanted to go.

He realised the moment she recognised him. Her whole body stiffened, then her head tilted to one side as she studied him, and, doubtless, the woman at his table. It was strange seeing such a typical Thea pose from an elegant lady, dressed in the height of Parisian fashion and with her face hidden.

'Rhys!'

'I beg your pardon, my lady?' Hodge, standing stiffly behind her, leaned down.

'That is Lord Palgrave over there.'

She thought he muttered, 'Oh, my God,' but the music and laughter and Polly's appreciative, 'That's a looker he's with, and no mistake,' made it hard to hear.

Rhys's companion most certainly was stunning. Thea assumed she was a courtesan, although she had never knowingly observed one before. Her gown was in the height of fashion, cut daringly to the limits of decency. Her hair, her teeth, her gems—all had an expensive gleam to them and she exuded a sensual confidence that was drawing male attention for yards around.

Thea chided herself firmly for having judgemental thoughts; she had spent all day shopping, Rhys was entitled to his…diversions. And this, she knew, was what men did—they sought out beautiful, elegant, sophisticated women and enjoyed them. There was nothing to feel upset about, not if one was a mature, sophisticated, intelligent woman oneself. Which she was.

But really, did he have to make such an obvious choice? The woman pressing her very ample curves against Rhys had tumbling blonde curls, big blue eyes and a quite spectacular amount of exposed cleavage. As Thea watched she touched her fingertips to his cheek and turned his head so she could whisper something in his ear.

A startlingly explicit image filled Thea's imagination. The woman was shedding that amber silk gown and falling back onto a wide bed, gesturing to Rhys, who…

'Oh! Order me a glass of champagne, Hodge, if you please.'

'My lady?' The valet sounded faintly scandalised.

Well, *she* felt scandalised, so that was two of them, and it was very annoying that she was letting herself be affected like this. She had never realised what a prude she must be. 'And for you and Polly, too.'

'But, my lady…'

'Stop dithering! *Garçon!*' She snapped her fingers and the man hurried over. *'Champagne, s'il vouz plaît. Pour trois.* Sit down, Hodge. This is a holiday.'

'I don't know what his lordship would say,' the man said, but he sat, perched on the edge of the little metal chair. Rhys had not seen them, or surely he would have made some sign?

'I am sure his lordship is entertaining himself

very well, just at the moment.' *Nibbling that hussy's fingertips, by the look of it.*

The champagne and glasses arrived. 'Please pour, Hodge.' The wine fizzed into the flutes and Thea raised her glass. 'To Paris!'

'To beauty,' said a deep voice in English at her shoulder. The liquid splashed over her hand as she twisted round. A tall, saturnine man was watching her, his lips curved into an appreciative smile. He raised the wine glass in his hand in a toast. An Englishman, but not, thank Heavens, one she recognised. Hodge's chair scraped on the stone as he got to his feet, a slight figure against the stranger's bulk.

'Sir, we are not acquainted,' Thea said, coolly dismissive as she turned her shoulder, her mouth dry with apprehension. In all her chaperoned life she had never been accosted like this.

'But we have all evening to become so, *madame.*'

'Sir, my lady has told you—' Hodge began, but the stranger slid easily into his empty seat, sending the valet stumbling with a neat shove to the shoulder.

'Will you kindly remove yourself, sir!'

And then there was a swirl of black evening cloak, the table was sent rocking and the man gave a grunt of surprise as he was hoisted out of the chair.

Polly gave a little scream, but Thea could only stare as Rhys caught the stranger a sharp blow on the chin that felled him accurately into a gap between the tables. It was appalling, a brawl in one of the most public places in Paris, involving two Englishmen—and all she could think, she realised, shocked at herself, was how magnificent Rhys looked.

He towered, lean, muscled…fearless. Thea clutched the table with one hand and Polly's shaking arm with the other.

'The lady told you she did not wish for your acquaintance. Do you need me to explain that any more clearly?' Rhys's calm tone sounded utterly lethal.

'Just a misunderstanding.' The man got to his feet, rubbed his jaw and backed away.

Rhys turned back to the three of them. 'Time to go home,' he said between gritted teeth.

'Of course, my lord. I'll just call a cab….' Hodge began.

'You take Polly. I will look after her ladyship.' Rhys's expression had the maid recoiling towards the valet. 'Get yourselves back to the hotel or I may well reconsider my first impulse, which was to dismiss you here and now.'

'My lady?' To do him justice, Hodge looked to her for confirmation.

'Do as his lordship says.' Thea stood up. Over his shoulder she could see his table was empty. 'Your...friend has left. I am sorry.'

'Are you?' He swept a hard stare around the nearby tables and their gawking occupants found something else to interest them. Conversation started again, then became general when no more excitement was forthcoming.

'Yes, of course. She looked...expensive.' As soon as she spoke Thea regretted it. Never mind that it exposed the shocking fact that she knew what manner of woman the blonde must be, but it sounded like a jealous barb. And what had she to be jealous about, for goodness' sake? Or shocked. Rhys was a virile man, of course he wanted...needed...

'That lady,' he said with a curl of his lips which might, to the charitable, be construed as a smile, 'is an opera singer. A soprano known as *La Belle Seraphina*, with whom I was discussing, on behalf of my cousin Gregory, the possibility of her appearance next season on the London stage.' He took her cloak from the back of her chair where it had been draped and flipped it around her shoulders.

'I didn't mean— Oh, yes, I did,' Thea admitted as she fastened the bow at her neck with stiff fingers. 'And I am sorry, I should not have mentioned such a thing, or have leapt to that conclusion in the first place.'

'It was a perfectly correct conclusion,' Rhys said with ominous calm as he took her arm and steered her towards one of the narrow archways leading out of the gardens. 'But we had not reached that stage in the negotiations yet.' Even in the gloom of the passage he must have been aware of her instinctive reaction. 'Why so indignant, my dear? You raised the topic in the first place, and you must know what manner of place this is at night.'

Thea dug her heels in and he stopped. 'No, I did not know! Hodge told me it was lively, that there was a degree of licence in behaviour—it sounded like an evening at Vauxhall, not the antechamber to a brothel!' When Rhys did not speak she added, 'I will be more aware in future.'

'There will be no *future*, you little idiot. This will not happen again. Don't you know what danger you put yourself in?'

The awareness that she was in the wrong and the

reaction to the violence, which had ceased now to be anything but frightening, left her close to tears. And she would *not* finish this disastrous evening by weeping all over Rhys, which left the alternative of losing her temper with him. And this was a Rhys she hardly recognised. He had rescued her from scrapes often enough when they were young, but this possessive aggression, this physical confidence, was new. Something in her responded to it and she recoiled from how primitive that reaction was. 'You mean, in danger from gentlemen like you?'

'No, not like me. A gentleman takes no for an answer. A buck like your friend back there is quite capable of taking other things. What might have happened if Hodge had gone to find the waiter, or to relieve himself? Do you think that maid of yours would have been any protection?'

'Against what?' Thea protested. 'There are people all around.'

'Against this,' Rhys said as he jerked her off balance, out of the archway and into the deserted alleyway beyond.

Chapter Eight

Thea found herself trapped in a corner, her back against the brickwork, her body caged by Rhys's. His hands were on the wall on either side of her head, his big feet bracketing hers in their fragile satin evening slippers. As she drew a trembling breath, her breasts touched his chest.

'Let me go—you are hurting me.' She tipped up her chin, a mistake. His mouth was just above her own.

'I am not touching you,' he pointed out, his voice reasonable. Only the brush of wine-scented air on her lips betrayed that his breathing had quickened.

Thea jerked up her knee, but he was too close and it merely pushed futilely against his leg. She ducked to get under his arm and he closed his elbows tightly. 'I'll scream,' she threatened.

'I have only to kiss you to stop that,' Rhys pointed

out. 'And do you know what your buck would do after that?' She tried to worm backwards into the unyielding wall. 'He would flip up your skirts and take you here where we stand.' His knee pushed against her, separating her legs. She felt her skirt ride up, felt the pressure of his thigh against her where a flutter of arousal was shameful acknowledgement that her body wanted this, and more. *He can feel how hot I am. How...wet.*

'You do not frighten me.' But he did, she realised. This was Rhys, who would never hurt her, and yet it was also an angry man, aroused by frustrated lust, the violence of that brief fight and anger with her, the cause of all of it.

'Then I am not trying hard enough,' he said and she saw the glint of white teeth as he lowered his head.

As he moved, so did his imprisoning leg. Thea dropped down between his arms, slid against his thighs and then rolled free to scramble to her feet as he turned and lunged for her. 'I wouldn't,' she warned, yanking the long hatpin from her elaborate hairpiece. As she brandished it, the light from the lantern at the end of the alley glinted off the metal.

There was silence, dangerous. The man she had

thought she knew so well shifted on the balls of his feet as though ready to spring, a threatening stranger. *What has happened to us?*

Then Rhys spoke, amusement threading through his deep voice. 'I taught you that trick.'

'I know.' *It was going to be all right. He has not turned into someone else entirely.* 'When I was twelve and that horrible youth staying at the Wilkinsons' tried to pin me against the stable wall. I had no idea then what he wanted.'

'You do now.' Was he really amused or was this simply a trick so she would allow him close again? She wished she could make out his expression. 'I am impressed by your speed, but I wish I could be convinced you could escape another man so easily.' Perhaps his anger had subsided. The fluttering panic under her breastbone eased a little. 'Are you going to put the skewer away now?' Rhys asked. 'You could kill someone with that thing.'

'It was instinct, I would never have used it on you.' Thea jammed the pin back in and tried to sort out her emotions. Rhys had ruined her evening, had completely overreacted and had unsettled her to an alarming extent. But he had rescued her from the importunate rake and by doing so had spoiled his own evening. She supposed they were even.

'You would not have had the chance,' Rhys said, coming closer.

'I do wish you would stop looming over me like that.' They might be even, but she was having to hold on hard to her self-control. Rhys had meant to frighten her and, although she would die rather than admit it, he had succeeded and that was infuriating. And he had aroused feelings she simply did not want to acknowledge. 'Oh, Lord, my new gown.' She brushed at the skirts with all the force she could not apply to boxing his ears. 'At least the ground is dry.'

'If you allow me to walk you home in a ladylike manner, I will show you how to use your hatpin for self-defence without littering the streets of Paris with wounded admirers. Which does not mean,' he added as they crossed the road behind the Louvre, 'that I'll tolerate you putting yourself in a position where you might need it again. Do you understand me?'

'Yes, Rhys, thank you,' Thea said, striving for meekness and managing to sound at least biddable, she supposed. The flare of temper had subsided, but her heart was hammering and her blood seemed to be singing in her veins. It was the same way she felt after a long, hard gallop across coun-

try, or when she heard a beautiful piece of music…
and yet, different. She was restless, there was an
ache inside. Reaction, she told herself. And physical desire. She discovered that she was, perversely,
happy.

'I am sorry about your singer,' she said. She had
promised not to interfere with his enjoyment, she
recalled guiltily. 'Is she nice?'

'Nice?' Rhys chuckled, amused, it seemed by
the foolish word. 'I have no idea. But she is very
beautiful.'

Of course. Beautiful. Thea felt the champagne
fizz of happiness go flat. For a brief few moments,
veiled, elegantly gowned, she had been fought over
and pressed against a man's body as though he
lusted for her. But, of course, it was no such thing.
Her old friend Rhys had simply been protecting
plain, ordinary Thea who had got herself into a
pickle and had taught her a hard lesson. The air of
Paris must be a drug, making her think she wanted
something that, of course, she did not desire in the
slightest.

'Here we are,' she said as the lamps outside their
hotel came into sight. 'You must promise me you
will not be angry with Hodge. It was all my fault.'

And most of all, my pleasure.

* * *

'Good morning!' Thea sounded quite disgustingly cheerful as she went to the buffet to inspect the chafing dishes.

Rhys scarcely glanced up as he rose to his feet, the French newspaper crumpled in his grasp, then sank back onto his chair to bury himself behind its pages. 'Morning.'

He was not good at mornings and especially not after a restless night filled with highly charged, and highly confusing, erotic dreams. For some reason the woman he had been chasing, futilely, had brown hair, not blonde, and as he reached for her over and over again he was shaken by feelings of unfamiliar guilt.

In broad daylight the dreams blurred into a half-remembered, discomforting muddle that he was doing his best to forget. He had completely overreacted with Thea last night; he could see that now in the bright light of morning. He could have rescued her from the importunate stranger and packed the lot of them back in a hackney carriage and brought his own evening to its probable outcome. As it was, he found he could not regret the missed encounter, which was strange.

His mood was not helped by Hodge, who started

nervously every time Rhys spoke and obviously found it hard to believe that he was not about to be instantly dismissed for allowing Thea to go to the Palais Royale. As if the man had a hope of stopping her once she got an idea into her head.

'More coffee, Rhys?'

'Please.' With half his attention he was conscious of her bustling about while he wrestled with smudged newsprint and colloquial French. A waft of fresh coffee, the clink of china, the rustle of fabric as Thea settled herself at the table, a faint drift of subtle rose scent.

Rustling? Scented? Thea? Rhys folded the newssheet and laid it beside his plate so he could study her. The soft mouse-brown hair was gathered into a neat arrangement of plaits and pleats, her hazel eyes regarded him with slight wariness and small pearl earrings dangled from her lobes. Her face, which was developing a puzzled frown as he stared, was the familiar oval, unadorned by so much as a smudge of lamp black or a grain of rice powder.

And yet…she was curiously *soignée*. The French word, one that he would never have thought of before in connection with Thea, swam up from somewhere and he realised it was perfect. She was groomed, elegant and perfectly…plain. If plain could be applied to the soft gleam of fine wool cloth, to the narrow edge of Brussels lace around the muslin fichu at her neck, the glow of the little pearls. Or creamy skin that was developing a blush as he stared.

Under his scrutiny she shifted slightly and there was that soft rustle again—silk against linen, he guessed. Good Lord, what was she wearing under that elegantly simple morning gown?

'You have been shopping,' he accused. It was bad enough having to make conversation at breakfast without being confronted by a disturbingly different Thea.

Thea rolled her eyes. 'You know I have. You saw one of the evening gowns last night.'

'I was in no mood to notice anything but your hatpin,' he growled.

'I left home with the smallest portmanteaux I could find and only two old gowns. I have bought two morning dresses, three walking dresses, two evening gowns, several pairs of shoes and all the, um…associated linen.'

'Just linen?'

A dimple appeared at the corner of her mouth,

unfamiliar and utterly feminine. 'You cannot believe the luxury of silk petticoats.'

'No, I cannot,' Rhys said repressively, as much to his own imagination as to her. 'You look extremely...elegant.'

'Thank you.' Thea reached for the butter, apparently unflustered by the compliment. 'I came to the conclusion when I first came out, and Stepmama was making such a fuss about my looks and figure and everything else, that frills and ornament do not suit me. I am never going to be pretty, but I knew I could achieve *elegant* if I put my mind to it. And I confess to loving luxury. Beautiful fabrics, well-made clothes, soft leather gloves and shoes, lovely scents and soaps...' She gave a little wriggle of pleasure and applied herself to her omelette.

'How did you find so much in only one day?' *How did you turn from a tomboy into such a feminine creature? But she is still plain,* he argued with himself. *No, she isn't...exactly.* He struggled to superimpose this elegant creature onto his image of Thea.

'Ready-to-wear gowns seem to be much more easily obtained in Paris than in London. Not everything has been delivered yet—some had to be altered slightly—but I am not out of the common way in any dimension, which appears to help.'

Rhys took a tactical mouthful of coffee to avoid any form of comment on Thea's *dimensions*.

'The only thing I am not happy with is the riding habit. It was foolish of me not to pack my own.'

'You are unlikely to do any riding.' Rhys, on the other hand, was strongly considering hiring a hack and removing himself from the chaise as much as possible. If he'd had sisters he would have been better fitted to deal with this, he acknowledged. But the only women he spent any time in private with were from the muslin company and that was no help at all in negotiating the shark pool of life with an unmarried, virtuous woman who was not related to him.

'No?' She wrinkled her nose, the expression so at odds with her ladylike appearance that Rhys laughed. Yes, *his* Thea was still there. She grinned back. 'That's better! I was thinking how serious you looked. I have spoken to Hodge, by the by. Thank you for not blaming him for yesterday evening.'

Rhys shrugged and reached for the butter. 'I should not have expected him to be able to influence you when you had made up your mind to anything. *I* certainly never could. I have told the hotel to place a large footman at your disposal when you go out. With Hodge, Polly *and* a bodyguard you should be safe from unwanted attention.'

'Thank you.' The smile she flashed at him was warm, with just a hint of mischief. Rhys relaxed. 'I hope you have a very pleasant day today.'

'I intend to visit an antiquities dealer who has a pair of globes that sound as if they would suit the library at Palgrave Hall, then I will do some shopping on my own account—Hodge has recovered sufficiently to observe that his lordship requires at least half a dozen more shirts and several more neckcloths if he is to present even a passable appearance in Paris.'

'And will you see if you can persuade your opera singer to oblige you?' Thea regarded him with clear, innocent eyes above her coffee cup.

'Does nothing put you to the blush?' Rhys demanded hoarsely through a throat full of croissant crumbs inhaled on a sharp indrawn breath.

'I meant oblige with her agreement to travel to England to appear at the Opera House. If you are put out of countenance because of anything else you want from her, well, you told me about her yourself last night,' Thea pointed out prosaically while he spluttered. 'Would you like me to slap you on the back or would a glass of water help, do you think?'

'Thank you, no. I will certainly send her a note of apology for abandoning her so abruptly.' And that was all. Rhys mopped his streaming eyes and attempted to sound repressive. He had been mistaken in finding Thea the slightest bit alluring. The chit was as unmanageable as she had been at sixteen.

Thea pursed her lips over what he suspected was an unrepentant smirk. 'I expect it is the prospect of shopping that puts you in such a grumpy mood—men always seem to hate it.'

'Grumpy!' Rhys dug his knife into the butter and recovered his sense of humour. This was Thea, for goodness' sake. A few silk fal-lals and fine plumage were no reason to get hot under the collar. She hadn't changed in any way that mattered—certainly not for the better—but she *was* in Paris for the first time. 'Shall I get tickets for the opera tonight?'

'For us?' The excitement lit up her face and made him feel like a toad for the way he had reacted the night before.

'Wear something discreet and a veil and we'll

sit in the stalls. No point in drawing attention to ourselves.'

'Thank you.' Thea jumped to her feet and came to plant a kiss on his cheek. 'You are an angel. Now I will go and leave you in peace with your newspaper.'

That was positively sisterly. Rhys turned a page and tried to feel like an indulgent brother. Even so, he was definitely going to ride tomorrow.

Thea gazed out of the window onto the Burgundian countryside. Three days from Paris and Rhys had ridden every mile while she sat in solitary state in the chaise.

It was not as though having the leisure to observe an athletically built gentleman in well-cut breeches was in any way a hardship, of course. Even the fact that the horses available from the posting stations were far below the standard Rhys would normally ride in no way diminished the sight, for it only showed his skill to advantage. As a boy and a young man he had been gangly. Now he had filled out and most of it appeared to be well-coordinated muscle. What did a gentleman do to keep fit, she wondered, other than bed sport? Sporting pursuits, she supposed, firmly instructing her imagination to cover that body with clothing.

A modest gentlewoman would not stare, let alone permit speculation to run wild through her daydreams. Which doubtless meant that she fell far short of the standards of breeding expected of her. Thea contemplated this lowering conclusion for a moment, then decided that she did not care.

Rhys's amorous interest was fixed, as it had always been, on curvaceous, tall, blue-eyed blondes of a coming disposition, and he would be thoroughly embarrassed to discover that his childhood friend had rediscovered the youthful attraction that—thank Heavens!—he had been blind to before.

The problem now was that the innocent adoration of her fourteen-year-old self had been replaced by the more mature understanding of a curious and uninhibited young lady. She understood what her body wanted and she was coming to regret, very much, that it was not going to experience it.

Still, it did no harm to fantasise. She was sure now that she was not going to find a man to love and who would love her in return, which meant she was not prepared to marry, even if Papa did find her and drag her back.

Thea stamped on the stirring of panic and made herself think of the present. If she did not marry, then that inexorably led her to the conclusion that she was never going to know what it would be like to lie naked with a man. She could not find the slightest shame in her for wishing to experience lovemaking, not after her experience with Sir Anthony. But it was certainly inconvenient for her composure that, if she had to choose a gentleman from a fairly wide acquaintance for the experiment, it had to be this one.

The vine-clad slopes of the Côte d'Or rolled past to the right of the chaise. The stop at Beaune for a change of horses had been regrettably short. The town had looked intriguing and the vast, bustling market colourful and exotic, but Rhys wanted to reach Lyon that evening, for some reason. When she had asked him the reason for his haste he'd simply closed his lips into an implacable line and strode off to talk to Tom Felling, the coach driver.

The horse Rhys had chosen at the livery stables was rather better than the previous one, Thea mused, her attention drawn back from the passing scene to the rider on the wide grass verge. He guided his mount to the side to jump a fallen tree and her breath caught at the fluid beauty of man and animal as they cleared the obstacle.

How would his skin slide under her hands—like silk or would it feel more like kidskin? How would his weight be, over her? He was so much larger than she was that it must be a matter of technique, she supposed. How would it feel when he sheathed himself within her? Would it hurt? Probably, it had with Anthony. She was less clear what happened then in bed, when lovemaking was a leisurely matter of mutual pleasure giving—movement, obviously, with that hard, strong body and her own soft, lesser strength somehow finding a rhythm and a unity.

She had seen Rhys naked as a child, swimming in the lake, but a man's body was different. Did he have a hairy chest? Would that chafe against her breasts or tickle? They tingled at the thought. She would run her fingertips through—

'Whoa!' From behind, Tom Felling shouted at his team. The chaise juddered and skidded as the postilions reined back their horses and Thea jerked her attention to the window at the front and the view beyond the be-capped boys and their waving whips.

A *diligence*, one of the lumbering French stagecoaches, had overturned, its bulk teetering over the deep ditch that bordered the road. In the road half a dozen passengers seemed stunned with shock and the driver and guard were struggling with the team as they thrashed in panic in the tangled traces.

Thea pushed open the door and jumped down as Rhys dismounted, shouting at the postilions, 'Hold our horses. Felling, go and help them free the team.' He saw her. 'Thea, get back in the chaise, this is no place for you.'

'I will do no such thing. There are people hurt.' She ran to help a stout woman to her feet, then pulled off the fichu around her neck to hold to the forehead of a slender young man who was slumped against the bank, blood pouring down his face. *This is no time to have missish vapours about blood*, she told herself firmly, swallowing hard.

'It is just a cut,' she began in English. 'They always bleed dramatically from the head. Oh, *pardon, c'est—*'

'I am English,' he said faintly and lifted his hand to hold the pad in place. 'Thank you, ma'am. I will do well enough. Please, see if anyone else is in need of your help.'

A young woman was screaming, in shock more than pain, Thea thought as she ran to her. Then she saw the girl was pointing a trembling finger towards the wide ditch. *'Mon fils, mon fils!'*

The *diligence* had been stopped from sliding down only by the spokes of one broken wheel and a scrubby thorn bush growing up from the side of the drain. It was slowly collapsing under the weight, the wheel making ominous cracking noises.

For a moment Thea could not see what the girl was panicking about, then she heard a faint wail and saw movement from a bundle of white cloth in the mud, directly under the collapsing carriage.

'Rhys! There is a baby!'

'I see it.' He slid down into the ditch, ducked under the edge of the coach and braced his back to it, his feet dug into the bank. The cracking stopped, but how much longer could he hold it? Thea scrambled down at the other end and crouched to look. The veins stood out of Rhys's forehead, his hands were white where the load pressed down, his body was bent double like Atlas under the weight of the globe. She wriggled closer and grabbed for the baby in the narrow space.

'Get out,' Rhys hissed between gritted teeth. 'I don't know how long I can hold this.'

'You can hold it,' she said, utterly confident as she got onto her stomach and wormed closer. This was Rhys: in that moment she trusted him to hold the world up if lives depended on him. Her fingers touched, gripped, pulled. The baby howled as she dragged him towards her. The wheel slid down with a jerk, Rhys cursed, shifted and it stopped.

There was movement at her feet, someone trod on her leg, apologised in English. 'Sorry. Can you slide out under me?' It was the injured Englishman, supporting the other end of the coach.

Thea wormed her way back with all the speed she could muster.

'She's out!' the Englishman shouted as hands reached down to haul her and her burden up the bank.

'Then roll free, this is about to go,' Rhys called, his voice strained to the point of being almost unrecognisable. 'On my mark. One, two, three—'

The young man landed in an ungainly heap in a patch of nettles as Thea thrust the baby into the arms of its sobbing mother and the *diligence* subsided into the ditch with the sound of splintering wood. 'Rhys!'

It seemed to take minutes, not seconds, to reach the side of the coach he had been supporting. Now he lay clear of it, on his back in the mud, eyes closed, hands bleeding, face white. Thea hurled herself down beside him and pressed her ear to his chest. Surely he hadn't broken his neck?

Under her hands she felt him drag air down to his diaphragm. Not dead, then. 'Rhys! Rhys, wake up.'

'Thea?' He seemed to come to with a jolt and she scrambled to her knees as he reached for her, his eyes opening wide and dark in his pale face, his grip on her wrists painful. 'You aren't hurt?'

'No, just terribly muddy. I thought you were under that when it fell.' She collapsed back onto his chest and hugged as much as she could of him.

'Mmm,' Rhys murmured. 'Much as I appreciate being cuddled, I prefer not to be sinking into the mire at the same time. I seem to be squashing a frog.'

'*Idiot!* I thought… I feared…'

'Don't you dare cry on me,' he said mildly. 'How do you think I felt when I saw you wriggling into that death trap, you madcap creature?'

Thea got to her feet, trying not to tread on him. He was battered enough without squashing what breath remained in him. 'Well, who else did you think was going to go in?' she said belligerently to cover her reaction. 'The passengers were too shocked or too large. Are you hurt?'

Rhys sat up, winced and uncoiled himself from

the ditch. 'Other than feeling as though our esteemed Prince Regent has been sitting on me, and kicking while he was at it, I am perfectly all right.'

Thea repressed the urge to fuss. 'I'll see how the Englishman is, then. He had a nasty cut to the head before he joined us in the ditch.'

She found him retrieving his baggage from the piles strewn along the road. 'Sir? Should you be on your feet?'

He had tied her fichu into a lopsided bandage which gave his pleasant, regular features an alarmingly piratical cast at odds with his severe pallor, and he was moving with great care as though all his joints hurt. Which, she supposed, they did.

'Ma'am, I thank you for your concern. They tell me there is an inn a mile or so along the road. I will find myself a room there.'

'At least allow us to carry you that far. Tom!' She gestured to the coachman who hurried over. 'Place this gentleman's luggage up behind the chaise.'

Rhys made his way towards them through the French passengers who were sorting themselves out amidst much weeping and waving of arms. No one appeared seriously injured.

'My lord, this is the gentleman who supported

the other end of the coach. He needs to get to an inn where he can rest.'

'The lady is too kind, I trust I do not inconvenience you? My name is Giles Benton. I should have a card.' He dug into his breast pocket and produced one.

'The *Reverend* Benton,' Rhys looked up from his study of the rectangle of pasteboard. 'I am Palgrave.'

'My lord. I recognise you, of course, from the House....'

'Never mind the politics. And call me Denham,' Rhys said, offering his hand. 'May I present my cousin, Miss Smith.' He blandly ignored Thea's raised eyebrows, opened the door of the chaise for them then swung up on his horse, calling instructions to the postilions.

Now she was closeted with an Englishman, one who was a gentleman and a vicar to boot. He was probably even now working his way mentally through the *Peerage* and coming to the conclusion that the Earl of Palgrave had no cousins named Smith, certainly not young female ones without a wedding ring on their finger. If his mathematics was any good, he was putting two and two together and coming up with a thoroughly scandalous six.

But what other option did they have but to take him up? They could hardly leave him bleeding by the roadside. For the first time since her flight Thea faced the fact that a scandal would be humiliating, sordid and decidedly unamusing.

Chapter Nine

Thea took a deep breath and willed herself to calm. Panicking would only make her appear self-conscious and that would raise Mr Benton's suspicions about her scandalous status, even if he had none now.

She cast a harried glance out of the window at Rhys, who at least seemed capable of sitting a horse without collapse, and studied her new companion. 'You are travelling far, sir?' That was a safe sort of question and put the focus on him.

'To the Mediterranean coast.' He smiled. 'I have no very clear destination. I am taking advantage of the recent peace to indulge myself with a journey south to the sun before I take up a new position.'

'A new parish?'

'No. After I was ordained I realised I was not cut out for the ministry. I desired to put my talents, such as they are, in the service of the reform of society. I have taken a post as secretary to Lord Carstairs.'

'He has interested himself in the abolition of slavery, has he not?' It was a cause she had read much about, much to the disapproval of her father, who had interests in the West Indies. 'It must be a great satisfaction to assist in that endeavour.'

'Yes, of course, I should have realised you would be knowledgeable on the subject,' he said, puzzling Thea. But Mr Benton swept on before she could query it. 'He is also interested in prison reform, and his wife, Lady Carstairs, is active in advancing the education of women. I hope I may make some contribution to all three causes. I was very fortunate that my elder brother, Lord Fulgrove, knows Lord Carstairs well and was able to recommend me to him.'

'Lord Fulgrove?' Thea faltered before she could gather her wits.

Mr Benton shifted on his seat. 'But do I not know you? I thought your face familiar, but I cannot place... I know, I have seen you talking to my sisters Jane and Elspeth in the park.'

Thea stared at him, struggling to find something intelligently evasive to say. 'I have met them a few times.' First the risk of scandal, now the danger that word would get back to Papa.

'I shall make a point of telling them how you aided me,' Mr Benton said. 'I write to them almost daily. They will be delighted to know their friend Miss Smith is such a Good Samaritan.'

'Ah. I, um… We have arrived at the inn. It seems exceedingly shabby.' She lowered the window as Rhys walked over. 'I do not like the look of this place. See how dirty the windows are, and the yard is full of rubbish.'

'Indeed, the merest country drinking house and none too well equipped for travellers by the look of it.'

'We cannot abandon Mr Benton here.' The sooner they parted company the better, but she could not allow his health to be jeopardised to conceal her guilty secrets. A blow to the head was potentially very serious, and he had lost a lot of blood, even before his heroic efforts with the *diligence*. 'He is travelling south. We can carry him to Lyon and find a doctor to attend to his head.' She turned to study his pale face. 'I fear you may require stitches, sir.'

Both men began to speak, but Polly, opening the opposite door to place a small bag on the floor, cut across them both. 'Here's the bag with the medical supplies. Mr Hodge thought the gentleman might need a fresh bandage, Lady Althea.'

Mr Benton shot Thea a glance and closed his lips firmly in a gesture that spoke far louder than any words. Rhys rolled his eyes upwards. 'Devil take it.'

Thea looked from one to the other, her heart sinking. He was a clergyman; he would not condone what he thought to be immorality. 'May I trust your discretion, Mr Benton?'

'This is an elopement, I collect?' he enquired stiffly. 'Naturally, it is none of my business.'

'No, we are not eloping!'

'Perish the thought,' Rhys added with what Thea felt was unflattering emphasis. 'I am escorting Lady Althea to our godmother, Lady Hughson, in Venice. We are childhood friends.'

Mr Benton's poker face softened into a smile. 'Lady Hughson? I know her well. What a relief! I should have realised nothing untoward was happening after observing your gallant and selfless actions at the scene of the accident. I do apologise! Lady Althea…?'

'Curtiss,' she supplied, her conscience giving her a decided pang. They might not be sinning in fact, but her imagination was scandalous enough to condemn her in the eyes of any minister. 'Because circumstances have led us to travel in a manner which is so open to misunderstanding, I hope you will understand if I ask you not to mention that we met along the way.'

'But of course,' Mr Benton assured her. 'My lips are sealed.'

'In that case,' Thea said, 'I will dress your head with a proper bandage and then we will be on our way to Lyon. Lord Palgrave, would you be so good as to have the sleeping couch put in place for Mr Benton? I am sure he should be lying down.'

'By no means, Lady Althea,' he protested. 'I assure you I will be quite well sitting up—and in any case, I should be travelling with your servants in the coach, should I not? After all, a lady alone in a chaise…'

'I have been travelling in the chaise with Lord Palgrave for most of this journey,' Thea said, unwinding the makeshift dressing from his head. 'I may as well be hanged for a sheep as a lamb. Besides, I doubt the presence of a clergyman will harm my reputation.' She peered at the cut. 'The bleeding has stopped, and I will not risk starting it again by washing your head with the water from this dirty inn. If you will just sit quite still…'

By the time they reached Lyon at seven o'clock that evening Rhys was convinced that he would never get off the horse, let alone walk to his bed-chamber. The bruising and strains from holding up the coach had coalesced into one blaze of pain, and his hands, cut and pierced with splinters, were cramped on the reins.

'Hodge,' he called as the valet stepped down from the coach, 'see her ladyship and Mr Benton into the inn. I need to talk to Felling.'

He waited until they had vanished through the impressive front door of the Chapeau Rouge before he called to the coachman, 'Tom, come and give me a hand, I'm damned if I'm going to fall flat on my face in front of a gaggle of French ostlers.'

It was inelegant and exceedingly painful, but they managed the manoeuvre with a lot of swearing on Rhys's part. 'Say nothing to her ladyship or that maid of hers, do you understand?'

'Yes, my lord. You need some liniment on your back, I reckon. Got just the thing in my baggage.'

'Horse liniment? Do you want to take the skin off my back, man?'

'If it'll do for your thoroughbreds, I reckon it won't do you much harm, my lord,' the coachman said. 'But they'll be getting a doctor to the other gentleman and he'll prescribe some fancy French potions for you that'll set you back a bit of gold, I reckon.'

'Hot bath is all I need,' Rhys muttered. It took him the width of the courtyard before he could walk with the appearance of ease, but he managed the stairs and found Althea and Mr Benton in the private salon he had written ahead to reserve.

They were, it seemed, on first-name terms already. 'The landlord has sent for a doctor and is making up the spare bedchamber in this suite for Giles. Is it not fortunate that they gave us such a spacious one?' Thea did not turn round as she attempted to press Benton into a chair while she stayed on her feet. 'Giles, it is foolish to stand on ceremony. You must take care and, really, I am such good friends with your sisters that you may treat me quite as one of them.'

Rhys cast a swift glance at Benton, whose faint air of dizziness seemed to owe at least as much to the effect of being organised by Thea as it did to his head wound. Or perhaps, he thought, narrowing his eyes at the other man, it was more than that. *Thea, enchanting a clergyman? Surely not.*

'What are you laughing about?' Thea demanded, her attention still on her patient. Apparently his huff of amusement had been audible.

'Just relief at the thought of a hot bath. I'll see you both at dinner,' he added, and caught sight of his own grey face in a mirror. Lord, he'd better be out of there before she noticed he was looking like death warmed over.

'Your chamber is here, my lord.' Hodge at least had the sense not to exclaim at the sight of him until the door was closed behind them. 'I'll send the doctor to you when he arrives.'

'Certainly not. There is nothing wrong with me that a good soak and basilicum powder will not put to rights. Which is probably more than can be said for that coat,' he added as Hodge eased him out of it and then held it up to inspect its battered back.

The sting of the hot water had made him hiss between his teeth as he lowered himself into it, but half an hour's soak had loosened the abused muscles, and he felt rather more human when he climbed out of the tub and wrapped a vast bath sheet around his waist.

Hodge began to dab cautiously at his back with a towel while Rhys hitched one hip on the edge of the table and contemplated his bruised and splinter-stuck hands. 'I need a needle to get these out, Hodge. Can you find one?'

'In my baggage next door, my lord. I won't be a moment.'

The door behind Rhys opened and he added, 'Tweezers might be a good thing, too.'

'Rhys Denham! Look at the state of your back!'

'I can't, can I?' he said reasonably, without turning. 'Thea, you should not be in here. I am not dressed.' In fact, he was damn near naked. Rhys reached for a towel to toss around his shoulders.

'Don't do that,' Thea said sharply. 'It needs dressing properly. Why on earth didn't you say it was this bad?'

'Hate fuss,' Rhys muttered. 'Will you please—?'

'Hodge, kindly tell the doctor to come in here as soon as he has finished stitching Mr Benton's head.'

Rhys took a deep breath. Unfortunately, getting the man out of the room was essential before this went any further. 'Hodge, go and see if you can assist Mr Benton.' He waited until the door was closed behind the valet before he added, 'Thea, go away.'

'You always were dreadful about admitting you were sick or hurt,' she said, deaf to both orders and propriety. Rhys heard the rustle of her skirts and then a towel was pressed gently over his back. 'I'll just get this dry and then you can get half dressed at least before the doctor comes in.'

He should get up and put her outside, but, clad in only a thin towel, Rhys had no confidence in maintaining even a vestige of decency. 'If I promise to let the doctor see to my back, will you leave?'

'Of course.' Thea came round to face him, her eyes sharp as she studied his naked torso. 'Your front does not appear to be injured.'

Rhys clutched a towel to his chest before she saw his nipples tightening. He did not dare look down to see how effective the towel around his waist was at concealing his sudden arousal. 'All I need is a light dressing on my back,' he began, but she reached out and took his hands in hers.

'Oh, look at these! How could you have held the reins? I will get a needle and some tweezers and take those splinters out while the doctor sees to your back.' To Rhys's enormous relief she released him. 'I'll leave you in peace to put your pantaloons on and come back when he has finished with Giles.'

'Thea, has no one told you that a young lady should faint before mentioning a man's nether garments?' Rhys demanded as she bustled away. He was not certain whether he was more relieved that she had taken no notice of his near-naked state—let alone the effect she was having on him—or whether he was indignant at being bossed around by her. The temptation to get up and let his draperies fall where they might was considerable. That would stop her ever trying such tricks again.

'Of course,' she said with a gurgle of laughter. 'Oh, poor Rhys, am I embarrassing you?'

'Shocking me, more like.' But she had gone.

It was quite obvious that she regarded him in no other light than the friend of her childhood. Grown-up to be sure, but no more to be treated with reserve than his fourteen-year-old self had been.

The only positive aspect to this trusting innocence, he concluded as he reached for his trousers, was that he was alone in the unfortunate physical attraction that being close to her provoked. If she felt the slightest awareness of him as a sexual being she would never be so open and so unselfconscious.

* * *

The doctor was ushered in ten minutes later. Monsieur Benton needed only a little rest. He had not even felt it necessary to bleed him. Ah, but *monsieur le comte* required a dressing on those abrasions and to rest for two or three days.

'Be damned to that,' Rhys said in English and was tutted at by Thea, who sat in front of him wielding a darning needle and tweezers to efficient, but painful, effect on his hands.

'Do listen to reason,' she scolded, her eyes fixed on what she was doing.

Rhys tried to sit still while the doctor prodded his bruised back and fixed his eyes on her bowed head, the neat centre parting of her hair and the intricate twists that secured it. *How long is it?* he wondered. *If I pull out those pins...*

Thea was still lecturing. '...or I will tell him to bleed you. Besides, Lyon looks delightful—what is the rush to get south?' She did not wait for his reply. 'May we suggest to Giles that he travel with us? I do not think he should travel on the *diligence* until he is well again, do you?'

Rhys almost told her that his vehicles were neither a public carrier nor a mobile hospital unit, then bit his tongue. 'You like him?' he asked warily.

'Very much. He is intelligent and good company and he was very brave back there on the road. Not as brave as you, of course,' she finished, matter-of-factly.

'Thank you.' She thought him brave? He had acted without considering the dangers because it was obvious what would happen if he did not stop the vehicle's slide downwards. A flutter of something absurdly like pride surprised him. *Popinjay*, he reproved himself. A gentleman simply did what was necessary without having to think about it, that was all.

But Benton, who'd had the opportunity to assess the dangers, and who was hurt into the bargain, was obviously a man of courage and resolution. *And good birth, even if he is a younger son.* An idea, probably absurd, was beginning to form. Thea ought to be married to someone of her own choosing. The man should be someone of principle who would value her for what she was, not for her connections and wealth. The nonsense about wanting to fall in love was just that, nonsense, and she would realise it soon enough once she found someone congenial and eligible she could trust. Someone who would steady her wild starts.

Rhys would give Benton some subtle encouragement. It was, if he said it himself, a brilliant plan. Thea eligibly, if not spectacularly, married, no risk of scandal—Godmama could put it about that Thea and Benton had met when Thea was staying with her in Venice—and the fact that she had travelled there so scandalously would be conveniently hidden.

The doctor finished and Hodge ushered him out. Thea dropped her tweezers on the table and peered at his hands closely. 'There! That should do perfectly,' she exclaimed, tipping her head back to study his face. 'And just what are you looking so smug about, my lord?'

'Just relief that it is over.' Rhys tried to turn the smirk into something innocuous. Relief no one was prodding his injuries any longer and relief that, as Thea said, he always had a plan.

Chapter Ten

'And you will rest for at least two days?'

Rhys gave a heavy sigh. Thea watched him suspiciously. He sounded as though he was reluctantly allowing himself to be persuaded. 'Two nights, certainly. And you and Benton can explore the city, if he feels well enough. I'll spend tomorrow lying down,' Rhys added. 'I'll probably go mad with boredom, but it is no doubt sensible.'

That was so unlike Rhys. Perhaps he really had changed with the years, for she would have sworn he would do anything rather than admit to weakness.

'Giles says his headache is better already and the doctor does not think he has a concussion, so if you do not need us, it will be amusing to explore.' She reached for a towel and tried to pat his hands dry.

Rhys twitched it out of her grasp. 'Don't fuss,

Thea. I'm indestructible—you should know that by now.'

And yet you meekly agree to rest? 'Don't say that and tempt fate.' She met his eyes, saw thoughts there she could not decipher and felt the colour rise to her cheeks. 'I am sorry I burst in here when you were…had just got out of your bath. I had no wish to put you to the blush.' Rhys raised one eyebrow and she laughed. 'I suppose managing that is quite a challenge! But I made you uncomfortable, I know that.'

It had certainly made her uncomfortable. The shock of seeing his elegant, muscled back, and then the realisation of how much those vicious bruises and splits across the skin must hurt, had left her dizzy with a mixture of desire, horror and admiration for Rhys's stoicism.

Thea got up and walked across to the bed where his shirt was laid ready. She found she was shivering. Perhaps it was delayed shock after the accident, or perhaps the realisation of just how much danger they had been in under that carriage. She let her fingertips trail over the soft linen. Yes, both those things, but most of all, the impact of finding herself alone with Rhys when he was almost naked.

'You had better put this on. I'll help you so you do not dislodge the dressings.' She gathered it up in her hands as fiercely as she gathered her self-control and turned, her expression schooled into the one of slightly harassed practicality she knew he'd recognise.

Rhys still sat on the edge of the table, which brought them almost eye to eye. He bent his head for her to drop the shirt over, then threaded his hands into the sleeves, a little clumsy because of the strapping. For some reason that made her vision blur with sudden tears. *I might have lost him.*

Thea swallowed and reached to straighten the collar where it had rucked up at the back of his neck. With Rhys so close she could feel the warmth of his skin against her chest, see the laughter lines at the corner of his eyes, paler against his faintly tanned skin. What joys had caused that laughter? And what concerns had etched the faint lines between his brows and at the corners of his lips? Rhys had an entire, adult life she knew nothing of. Her fingers brushed the ends of his hair as she fussed with the collar.

Her composure seemed to unravel as though he had tugged a string, and yet he had not moved or spoken. 'I was worried about you,' Thea said abruptly. Before she could think she was clinging to him, her arms tight around his neck, her face buried in his shirtfront. 'I'm sorry,' she mumbled into the cloth. 'But when the *diligence* collapsed I thought you were still under it.'

Rhys closed his arms around her body and held her close. *It must hurt him to hold me so,* she thought, her senses filled with the scent of his damp skin, the Castile soap he had used in the bath, the smell of the liniment the doctor had applied. She felt him rest his cheek on the crown of her head and closed her eyes.

When he spoke softly against her hair it was as though his voice resonated through to the soles of her feet. 'You told me, when you were burrowing through the mud beneath my feet, that you trusted me to hold it up.'

'I did. For as long as there was anyone under it, I knew you would, somehow. I knew I was safe, and the baby, too. But when we were out...'

'Hush now.' Rhys rocked her back and forth, gentler than she could ever remember him being. All her will-power seemed to ebb as his tenderness sapped it. She would weep in a moment, and she had to be strong. 'We are all safe. Don't think about what might have been or you will have nightmares.'

'I know.' Thea sniffed, determined not to let him see how affected she was by the touch of his body, the strength of his embrace.

She felt his mouth move against her hair and knew he smiled. 'Don't you go crying on me now, Thea.'

'I'm not.'

'You are sniffing.' He chuckled. 'Any other woman I have had in my arms would die rather than do anything so prosaic.' *Any other woman would be in his arms because he desired them.* 'No other woman I can think of would be so brave. All right now?'

'Mmm.' She loosened her stranglehold on his neck and leaned back against his linked arms to look up into his face, almost undone by that tribute. She had thought him angry with her, or, at the very least, that he had considered her foolhardy. She blinked back unshed tears, glad now she had not given in to them. 'Thank you.'

His lips were very close to hers. How had that happened? His breath was sweet—coffee and honey—and his lips were parted, his eyes intent and bright. She swayed closer as he lifted one hand to her hair, fumbled for the pins. What was he doing? His cut, bruised fingers lacked finesse, strands catching as the pins fell to the floor with tiny metallic sounds, and she felt the whole elegant construction unravel before the sliding weight was caught up in his palms.

'Soft, brown, scented silk,' he murmured.

'Rhys?'

'Thea.' She saw the movement of his throat as he swallowed and his voice roughened as he said, 'I wanted to see what it was like down. It is lovely, a living thing.'

'Mousy,' she protested.

'Pretty mouse.'

She took a deep breath and realised that she had been holding it ever since he had touched her hair. *What is happening? One of us has to be sensible.* 'I think we have both had a shock today and probably we are not ourselves. Perhaps we should lie down before dinner.'

For a moment she saw the thoughts behind his eyes quite clearly. He had interpreted that as an euphemism, believed for a moment that she was suggesting they lie down on his bed and… *Please.* Had she said that out loud?

Then Rhys's face became an expressionless

mask. She stepped back and he opened his fingers, letting her hair fall around her shoulders.

'That is a good idea.' Rhys said. 'Will you give Hodge whatever orders you think best about dinner? Tell him I am going to rest now and will not need him until just before it is served.'

'Yes, of course.' Thea stooped and raked together the little pile of pins, swinging the mass of hair over her shoulder. *Pretty mouse... What is this? Is he flirting because there is another man with us now? Men are so foolish like that, so possessive and territorial. Oh, Rhys.*

What would he have done if she had not stepped back, if she had lifted her lips to his and claimed a kiss?

He stood when she got to her feet, but did not turn as she left the room. Thea made herself walk with dignity, not take to her heels and flee as every instinct of self-preservation screamed at her to do.

Dinner was oddly unsettling. Perhaps it was because she had never eaten with Rhys in company like this. It felt as though they were a couple entertaining a guest, and that was too close to her foolish daydreams to be comfortable. Thea compensated by paying most of her attention to Giles, on whom a rest and the attentions of the doctor had worked wonders.

No one, Thea decided as they exchanged impressions of Paris, would think he had been in an accident, hit on the head and half squashed under a stagecoach. He must be tougher than his slender frame suggested.

'Is your post with Carstairs a permanent position, Benton?' Rhys asked during a lull in conversation while the soup tureen was removed. He was a trifle paler than usual, and his hands were disfigured by the emerging bruises, but otherwise he seemed recovered. Perhaps she was imagining the strange watchfulness in his demeanour.

'Yes, to my great good fortune. I spent some time assisting him last year, so he knows I will suit.' Giles passed Thea the butter.

'He will be an influential patron. Do you have ambitions in politics yourself?'

'I hope for a seat in Parliament in a year or two, if I can convince his lordship and the party that I would be an asset. As you know yourself—'

'Oh, let us not discuss me.' Thea could have sworn Rhys threw Giles a warning glance. What was that about? 'And you will reside in the household?'

Thea shook her head slightly, but Rhys did not seem to notice. Really, he was interrogating poor Giles as though interviewing him for a position!

'I have my own small town house, although Lady Carstairs has made a suite available for me in both the town house and at their country seat.'

'How wonderful that both Lord and Lady Carstairs have such similar interests,' Thea remarked before Rhys could enquire how much Giles was being paid or something equally intrusive. 'So many couples in society appear to be completely distanced from each other.'

'And that is a bad thing?' Rhys enquired. 'Most marriages are ones of convenience, not of shared interests. Or passions,' he added sardonically. 'I would not expect a wife to want to live in my pocket.'

'I do not agree,' Thea retorted. 'That is another reason why I will not marry without lo—without affection. Do you not agree, Giles?'

'I am completely in accord with you, Althea. Take the question of prison reform, which greatly interests Lady Carstairs...'

Ten minutes later, when the servants came in to clear for dessert, Thea realised they had been in earnest dialogue the entire time. Giles had tried to draw Rhys in from time to time, but, after a few near snubs, had apparently accepted that he did not want to talk about social policy.

Guiltily she glanced across at Rhys and caught him with a look almost of approval on his face. It was odd, because Rhys must be completely bored by the conversation. As soon as he saw her watching him he raised a brow and assumed such an expression of innocence that she almost burst out laughing.

He was up to something, the rogue—she remembered that look all too well. But what could he be plotting? A mystery. She contented herself with giving Rhys a reproving shake of the head. 'Is there any shopping we can do for you tomorrow? Giles and I intend to visit the cathedral and then explore the town.'

'And the shops by the sound of it.'

'But, Rhys, this is *Lyon*. Silk! Surely you do not expect me to ignore the finest silk in France, if not in Europe?'

'I expect Benton to return virtually on his knees, staggering under the weight of your purchases.' He addressed Giles earnestly. 'I recommend you take at least one sturdy footman with you unless you wish to set back your recovery by days.'

'I will follow your advice, Denham, but I confess to finding industry of any sort of interest. I intend to take notes while Lady Althea makes her purchases.'

'I would have thought you better employed advising her on the best green to suit the colour of her eyes,' Rhys said, surprising Thea into silence and earning a startled look from Giles.

After Rhys's haste to reach Lyon, he had slowed their journey to what seemed to Thea to be a crawl by contrast. At first she could not understand it, but after the first day from Lyon, as they set out for Valence and she quizzed him about it, he confessed with reluctance that he was feeling sore and battered and preferred to take it easy.

'If you did not ride, you would be more rested,' she said, wishing she dared ask him to let her check his back, or call the doctor. This willingness to admit weakness was so unlike Rhys.

'You want me to act as gooseberry?' he enquired.

'Whatever do you mean? You are most welcome to ride in the chaise! I hardly feel that I am on such terms with Giles as to lead you to think you would be intruding upon anything.'

'Whoa!' He held up a hand to ward off the vehemence of her protests. 'I am not suggesting you have set up a flirtation with Benton and require a chaperon.' He studied her face and Thea felt her colour rising under the scrutiny. 'Hmm…on second thought, are you perhaps protesting too much?'

'Ridiculous man,' Thea muttered. 'Of course I am not flirting with Giles, merely enjoying his conversation and company. I do not flirt and, even if I did, Giles is too serious for that. Thank goodness,' she added.

Giles was indeed rather serious and, although intelligent, he lacked Rhys's sharp wit, but she was coming to like him very much. But surely neither man thought she was *falling* for Giles? She shot Rhys an anxious look from beneath her lashes. How could any woman fall for Giles Benton when there was Rhys Denham riding beside their carriage? Though she could hardly put forward that argument.

'You are blushing,' Rhys remarked. 'I will say no more. I have no wish to squash up in the chaise with you. The couple I was referring to are your maid and my valet—I foresee a wedding in the offing. At least, I trust one will be forthcoming.'

'Polly and Hodge? My goodness.' How had she not seen that developing? 'It would probably be a good idea if they were not alone for so long, in that case.' *Hypocrite. Why can't my maid enjoy a flirtation—it is what I want for myself after all. Flirtation and rather more.* But how reliable was Hodge where women were concerned?

'You may go and chaperon them if you wish,' Rhys said with a shrug. 'But I prefer the fresh air. Besides, my back may be stiff, but the exercise is good for it.'

Rhys's teasing made Thea self-conscious for a while, but Giles appeared not to find any awkwardness in being alone with her, and the unrolling countryside and the drama of the Rhone flowing beside the road were so engrossing that she forgot to be distant with him.

'*À Valence le midi commence,*' Giles said as they clattered though the gates of the town. 'That is all I recall from my lessons, I am afraid, but it is true— I think we are finally in the south. Look how shallow the pitch of the roofs is now—no need to shed the snow here.'

'And the air is warm, even though it is evening.' They climbed down and waited for the coach to pull up alongside in the inn courtyard. Thea drew a welcome breath of warm, scented air deep into her lungs and watched Rhys with what she hoped was well-concealed anxiety, but he swung down out of the saddle without any sign of discomfort.

'I cannot wait to explore,' she said as he walked across. 'There is the river and a Roman amphitheatre….' The joy of this freedom to experience new things, to form opinions, to share impressions, made her feel like a hot-air balloon, soaring free. *I am never going back, I am never going to accept I am fit for nothing but blind convention and obedience.*

'Fascinating, I am sure, but I have a letter of invitation from an old friend of my family, a French *émigré* who returned once things became stable. I was going to drop in and see if I could take pot luck on dinner. Why don't you and Benton explore the town this evening?'

'Of course, if Giles would like to do that.' Thea did her best to sound enthusiastic, but it was a disappointment. She and Rhys never seemed to spend any time together now. Since Paris, he had ridden, and it was almost as though he was using Giles as an excuse not to be alone with her.

But she had promised not to expect to be entertained, not to want to be taken about in the evening. No doubt Rhys was delighted she had some company and a reliable escort.

'If I could have a word with you before you go out, Denham,' she heard Giles say as Polly came up with her dressing case.

'Let us go in,' Thea urged her. Probably Giles wanted to discuss paying his share of the expenses. He had mentioned it in the carriage and she knew he felt awkward about accepting Rhys's hospitality to this extent. She just hoped Rhys had the tact to allow him to pay a share.

Giles was unusually silent that evening as they made their way along the riverbank under the spreading lime trees. Thea hugged her shawl tighter around her shoulders against the cool breeze from the water and hoped Rhys had not snubbed Giles's efforts to pay his way. Perhaps she should say something. 'Rhys can be a trifle…lordly,' she began and then wondered how to go on.

'I have not found him so,' Giles said. 'He has surprised me by how encouraging he has been.'

Thea had not noticed any encouragement. Perhaps the two men talked into the night after she had retired. 'Indeed?' she said with what she hoped was an encouraging intonation.

'Normally I would not presume...certainly not after such a brief acquaintance.' He stopped mid-sentence in front of a bench. 'This may be too soon and yet... Perhaps you could sit down, Althea. Let me brush these dead leaves away.'

Mystified, she did as he asked, although a hard wooden bench after hours sitting in the carriage was not what she had hoped for. 'Is there a problem? Forgive me for mentioning it, but is it money that is concerning you?'

'Money?' He seemed completely thrown off his stride. 'No indeed. I am more than capable of maintaining a wife and a household. As well as my salary I have a private income sufficient to keep a separate household from Lord Carstairs. Lord Palgrave was quite satisfied about that.'

'A wife? Lord Palgrave satisfied?' A horrible sinking feeling took possession of Thea's stomach. There could be no mistaking Giles's intent: this was a proposal of marriage. How on earth had she not realised Giles had become so attached to her? And how, without wounding him, was she going to get out of this?

Chapter Eleven

'Why, yes, a wife. Let me start again. I am making a dreadful mull of this,' Giles said with a rueful smile. 'Lady Althea, you cannot be unaware of the esteem in which I hold you. Both you and Lord Palgrave have shown me the greatest trust in admitting me into your confidence, and I am aware of your difficult circumstances.'

'My—?'

'You having left home without your father's consent, I mean.' He cleared his throat and embarked on what, through her state of befuddlement, she supposed was a prepared speech. 'My birth, although not the equal of yours, is respectable. I believe my prospects are good, and you already know my sisters.' He went down on one knee and took her unresisting hand. 'Lady Althea, will you do me the honour of becoming my wife? I will ensure that not the slightest scandal attaches to your name as a result of this journey and—'

'No! I mean… Mr Benton. Giles. I regret if anything I have said or done has aroused expectations which… I am sorry. I hold you in the highest regard and I am sensible of the honour which you do me by your proposal.' *That is what one says, isn't it?* 'But I cannot accept you. Do, please, get up. Look, someone is coming.'

A couple were strolling along the bank towards them, a small dog at their heels. Giles sprang to his feet and assumed a rapt interest in the water tumbling over rocks at the waterside while Thea fiddled with her reticule and tried to make sense of what had just happened.

As soon as the couple had passed she asked, 'What led you to imagine I would accept a proposal of marriage? I realise my behaviour in travelling alone with you in the chaise is unconventional, but I hope I have done nothing to give you the impression that I expected a display of…affection or that I consider that you have in any way compromised me.'

'Certainly not.' Giles looked appalled. 'Your deportment has been, in every way, that of a lady of breeding. But I am aware of your circumstances, and Lord Palgrave was so encouraging when we spoke of this—in fact, he urged me not to waste time in securing your affections.'

'*Lord Palgrave?* Rhys encouraged you to propose to me?' *How could he?* Thea felt quite sick. *He wants to get me off his hands so badly that he would thrust me into the arms of a virtual stranger?* 'Lord Palgrave has no right to speak for me.' Somehow she kept her voice steady. 'He is no relation of mine and certainly no trustee or guardian. He knows little of my mind or he would understand that I will only marry when I fall in love with a man who can love me as deeply.'

She stood up. 'Please, will you walk me back to the inn, Giles? Your heart is not engaged in this, is it? I would not hurt you for any consideration.'

He shook his head as she took his arm. 'My deep regard, but, no, not my heart. That, I hoped, would follow our union, which I saw as a most advantageous one for both of us.' He sounded subdued, but not, thank goodness, hurt, Thea thought.

'Then no harm has been done.' *Except for my trust in Rhys.* 'Can we put the awkwardness of this behind us and return for dinner, do you think?'

'Of course.'

They walked back in the gathering gloom. Giles,

like the gentleman he was, made light conversation on indifferent topics. Thea responded automatically while all she could think was, *How could he? How could he fail to understand me so very badly?*

Rhys strolled into his bedchamber, tugged off his neckcloth and stretched with a certain degree of caution. Not too bad—his muscles responded almost without a twinge now. He contemplated ringing for Hodge, then dismissed the idea. Let the poor devil sleep—whomever's bed he was in. Who was he to spoil the man's fun, if he was getting any?

Sharing a couple of bottles of good Burgundy and the old *vicomte*'s brandy had left him feeling more mellow than he had since Thea had reentered his life. Cunning old devil, to hide it behind a false wall in the cellar before he fled the country.

He took off his coat and threw it over the wing chair that stood with its back to him in front of the hearth. It was flung back at him with considerable force.

'How could you?' Thea erupted out of the chair and swung round to face him, her index finger pointed to jab, painfully, at his breastbone. 'How—could—you? I trusted you, Rhys Denham.

I thought you were my friend. I thought, Heaven help me for being such an idiot, that you still had a trace of sensitivity and sympathy somewhere under that expensive tailoring.'

Another sharp jab and Rhys stepped back, mind working in frantic calculation. He could hardly pretend he had no idea what she was talking about. Somehow Benton had rushed his fences, managed to make a mull of a perfectly simple proposal and apparently it was all his fault.

'Stop poking me,' he protested mildly. 'It hurts.' Strategic retreat to the other side of the bed seemed advisable, but Thea stalked after him.

'Good. Excellent, in fact. I am delighted it hurts. If I had something more painful, like a blunder-buss, I would use it. What the blazes did you think you were doing, encouraging Giles to propose to me?'

'Don't swear.'

She bared her teeth at him.

'I thought you liked him,' Rhys protested.

'I do like him. I like your coachman. I like the Archbishop of Canterbury, who is a very nice man. I liked Byron on the one occasion I met him. I even like the Prince Regent because he makes me laugh. It does *not* mean I want to marry any of them!'

'You have to marry somebody.' Rhys wondered whether vaulting across the bed would be undignified or cowardly. Probably both, he decided with regret.

'No, I do not! Why did you do it?' Thea demanded, toe to toe with him now. 'I told you my plans—why did you have to go and incite poor Giles to propose to me?'

There were tears sparkling in her eyes, catching the candle flame. Rhys hoped they were tears of anger. 'I told you why I think this scheme of living by yourself is a bad idea. You would be much happier with a husband who shares your interests, your social circle. Benton will probably end up a government minister one day. He's well bred, has excellent connections, enjoys a comfortable private income as well as his salary, he's hard-working—' He broke off when she did not reply and just stood there, her mouth pressed into a hard line. He had a horrible feeling that was all that prevented it from trembling.

'Thea, for goodness' sake, say something.' It was so long since he had seen her this upset, and never because of something he had done. He felt a toad, despite his good motives. And he realised with something like horror that he was becoming aroused. Her eyes were sparkling, her bosom was heaving, the colour stained her cheeks and all that passion was directed at him. She was no longer ordinary little Thea. What she was, he had no idea, except that he wanted to have her under him so badly it was painful.

'Giles is everything you say. I cannot marry him.'

'Why?' he flung at her, furious that she made him feel bad in so many ways. 'Because of this idiotic *love* you are cherishing for some man long ago in your past?'

'No. Not that. I know that is impossible, otherwise I would never have allowed myself to be so foolish as to think I could marry Anthony.' She dragged the back of her hand clumsily across her eyes and his heart turned over.

'What is it, Thea?' Rhys made himself gentle his tone. 'Why won't you let a decent man make you secure and happy?'

'Because…because as well as not loving him, I do not *desire* Giles. There! You would have it.' Thea turned on her heel, marched back to the cold hearth and stood staring down at the jug of flowers that stood on the flagstones.

'Desire? Oh, for goodness' sake, Thea.' Exasperation won over compassion. 'What do you know about desire? A sheltered virgin—'

She muttered something, then lifted her head and stared defiantly back at him. 'I am not a virgin.'

'Not? That bastard Meldreth ravished you?' For a moment a wash of red coloured his vision. 'When I get back to England I'm calling him out and I'll make the swine sorry he was ever within a mile of you. I'll castrate—'

'I was willing,' Thea said and sat down in the wing chair, her back straight, her hands folded in her lap as though perfect posture would make this conversation somehow less shocking. 'I thought I was going to marry him and I wanted to know what it was like to make love, so when it was obvious that was what he hoped, I agreed. He did not ravish me.'

'I see.' Rhys told himself that she was an adult, that she had a right to make her own decisions about things like that. He picked his way carefully into his next sentence. 'Just because you experienced pleasure with Meldreth does not mean that you cannot experience it again with another man. Benton, for example…' The thought, he realised, made him queasy.

'Pleasure?' she exclaimed. 'What pleasure? It

was thoroughly *un*pleasant. He is selfish, clumsy and has the finesse of a bull at stud.'

'I see.' Somehow he had to make this right, although shooting Meldreth because he was a poor lover was hardly honourable, not if she had consented.

'And then he had the nerve to say I was frigid!' She sniffed. 'Have you got a handkerchief?' Rhys produced one and she blew her nose. 'Thank you. I had read all about it—sex, I mean. I know what happens, I know it should be pleasurable for the woman.' Thea swept on, ignoring his faint moan of protest at these confidences. 'I am *not* going to find myself married to a man with whom I cannot enjoy making love.'

Thea making love, Thea studying an erotic text she had somehow got hold of, Thea's slender pale body writhing on cool linen sheets, that soft brown hair fanned out around her. Thea.

Rhys got a grip on himself and cleared his throat. Fleeing the room was not an option. 'Perhaps if Benton kissed you, you would feel more attracted,' he suggested. *What am I saying? I want her.* Thea shot him a withering look. 'Look, you think you know about desire, but, after all, you have only read about it. You might not be a virgin...' *Oh, good God,* I'm *blushing now. Ten years of sexual experience and this girl—woman—is putting me to the blush.* Doggedly he ploughed on. 'A woman needs arousing, and Meldreth is obviously an insensitive boor.'

'I know exactly what it is to desire a man physically.' Thea's face was as red as he suspected his own was.

'Who?' he demanded. *Another money-grubbing rake trying to seduce her?* She turned her head and stared out of the window, her lower lip caught hard between her teeth. 'Tell me, Thea.'

'You.' It was a whisper.

'What did you say? Don't mumble. For a moment I thought you said it was me.'

'It is. I do. I don't want to, for goodness' sake! It crept up on me,' she added wildly. 'Like a cold. You know how it is. One day the back of your nose feels odd and the next morning you are sneezing and then you've a sore throat and before you know it, you have a streaming cold.'

'Desiring me is like catching a cold?' What the devil had been in that brandy? This had to be a bad dream.

'It is about as welcome,' Thea snapped. 'You hold me. You wrap yourself round me at night on the boat. You rescue me from that rake, looking all masterful, and you were so strong and heroic at the accident and then you sit around with no clothes on and cuddle me.'

She glared at him as though he had drowned a basketful of kittens, Rhys thought, unable to take in this stream of accusations.

'You ride all day looking magnificent and you are so heroic and strong.… Do you wonder a poor female falls for you? Yes, that's better, stand there looking like a stunned cod, I don't want you at all when you look like that.' A choked laugh escaped her as she walked unsteadily to the window.

'Are you saying you have fallen in love with me?' Rhys sounded utterly incredulous.

'No, of course not.' *I haven't fallen. I was there years ago.* 'I am saying I desire you. That I want to make love with you.' Thea slapped the flat of her hand against the wall in frustration with herself. How had she stumbled into this—and how on earth was she going to get out of it?

'I want us to go to bed,' she added with desperate honesty. He would throw her out of the room in a moment, or the floor would open up, or lightning would strike. Something would save her from the looming humiliation of his rejection. 'Have sex,' she said, just in case Rhys had not entirely grasped the enormity of what she was saying. 'You may laugh now. I realise perfectly well that I am not the sort of woman you desire.'

There was silence. No natural disaster occurred to save her. Thea stared blankly out of the window and waited for Rhys to laugh. He would not take her at her word and mock her, of course not. Rhys, whatever else she felt for him, was her friend. He would turn it into a joke, pretend he thought she was teasing him. Yes, Rhys would think of something tactful and they could pretend this had never happened.

'There's coincidence for you,' Rhys said. 'Or fate? I didn't believe in fate, but here it comes and slaps me in the face.'

'What do you mean?' Thea made herself turn and look at him. He no longer looked stunned. He was studying her with rapt attention, his face starkly beautiful in the candlelight, his mouth, so often a hard line, relaxing into a sensual curve.

'I mean that I desire you. That I want to make love to you, go to bed with you. Have sex with you. Interesting coincidence, is it not? Damnably awkward, of course. But interesting.'

'You... You're drunk,' Thea said, suddenly certain. Relief swept through her. If she could get more brandy into him, he might, just might, wake up in the morning convinced he had imagined the whole episode.

'I am not.' He shook his head. 'Just a trifle mellow, nothing like far enough gone to think this is a dream when I wake in the morning, which is what you are hoping, is it not? I'm sorry, Thea, but we are just going to have to deal with this.'

'How?' She wanted, so much, to sound calm and sophisticated. The word escaped in a bat squeak.

'We could pretend it did not happen, but I would know and you would know and every time we looked at one another there it would be.' Rhys walked away to the far side of the room, leaving the path to the door clear as though giving her room to escape. 'Or we could act on it. Make love. See if we get it out of our system.'

'But I—' Thea found her feet had rooted themselves to the wide chestnut floorboards. 'What if I became pregnant?' *What am I saying? I should say no and leave this instant. I should not be thinking of problems that might arise if we do make love!* 'But there are ways to avoid that, aren't there?'

'There are and, believe me, I'd use them. Nothing is infallible, of course,' Rhys said slowly, 'but there is always marriage.' He did not appear to notice her wince. 'You have been reading somewhat widely for an unmarried lady, have you not?'

'And talking to married friends,' Thea admitted. 'Rhys, it is all right, you do not have to make me feel better by pretending to want me. I know I am ordinary and mousy and not…alluring. Not what you are used to, in fact. If you had not made me so angry and hurt by encouraging Giles to propose, I would never have lost my temper and told you how I feel. I can pretend this never happened, I really can. You do not have to be kind.'

'Kind?' Rhys ran both hands through his hair. 'Making love to you, Thea, would be many things. Kind is not one of them.'

'But you do not want to marry me, do you?' she ventured. Better to get that firmly out of the way. 'I do not want to marry you, of course,' she added hastily in case he misunderstood.

'Good God, no!' He looked at her face and backtracked rapidly. 'I mean, I would be the worst sort of husband for you. I want… I *need* a wife who won't interfere with me, who won't expect me to fall in love with her, or dance attendance on her. I want, to be frank, a well-bred, well-dowered, moderately intelligent mother for my children and chatelaine for my homes. I'd make you miserable.'

And I, you, apparently. 'You do not want to find someone like Serena?'

'A deceitful, faithless little madam who expects every man for a mile around to worship at her pretty little feet? No. I want a wife who will be meek, obedient, faithful, slightly dull and perfectly content with comfortable domesticity.'

She must have hurt him so badly, Thea thought with a wrenching sensation of misery. 'Not at all like me and not like Serena, either.'

'Exactly.'

'And I am not at all like the women you usually…I mean I am not blonde, or beautiful or curvaceous.'

'No. But I have discovered to my considerable discomfort that you are entirely and provokingly female and no longer sixteen years old,' Rhys said grimly.

'So what are we going to do?' The suspense was killing her. 'Pretend this conversation never happened or go to bed? Those appear to be the only options.'

'There is a third.' Rhys sat on the end of the bed and dragged his fingers through his already disordered hair. 'I hire another coach and a good driver, some armed outriders and ask my friend the Comte de Beauregard to recommend a chaperon. You can then proceed to Venice with your maid, and Benton as escort, and I will follow along a few days behind. No one will be tempted by anything then.'

That was the best thing, of course. What a relief that one of them was thinking clearly. 'Is that what you wish to do?'

'No,' Rhys said with a rueful shrug. 'But I will do whatever you want. Do you know what that is?' He raised an eyebrow and waited.

Thea stared at the big bed. She *should* say she would go with Giles. She *could* say she wanted to sleep on it and would decide in the morning. With the sense that she stood at a fork in the road of her life, with no idea which path would lead to regrets, she met his questioning gaze. 'Yes, I know what I want to do.'

Chapter Twelve

Rhys stood, the blue of his eyes like the flame deep in the heart of a log fire. 'Tell me.'

'I would like to go to bed with you. Tonight.' Thea felt a trifle dizzy. An abyss was opening up beneath her feet and she dare not look down into it. 'I do not expect anything else, you understand. Not more nights, not to be your lover—your mistress.'

He took the few steps to the door. 'There is no need to think of tomorrow, just tonight. Let me lock this.' The snick of the key made her jump, even though she was expecting it. Every nerve ending seemed to be on the surface of her skin, exposed, quivering in the cool draught from the window. Rhys took the tinder box and lit the candles, and the flare of light deepened the evening shadows into mystery.

'Polly has gone to bed. She was tired and I told her I would not want her until the morning.'

'You are trembling.' Rhys's big hands cupped her shoulders.

'Just shivering. The evening air…'

'Then the sooner we are in bed the better.'

He sounds so calm, so in control. But of course, she told herself, *Rhys has done this many times*. It was not as reassuring as it ought to have been. *He has never done it with* me *before*.

His fingers, healed now, had regained their usual dexterity. The fastenings of her gown seemed to melt away. *He was always good with knots and fishing lines and…* The fabric whispered down and pooled at her feet, and fleeting memories of childhood went with it.

'Turn around,' Rhys murmured.

It should have been easier when she could not see him, but his breath raised the hairs on the exposed skin of her nape and she could hear his breathing almost, but not quite, controlled. That slight betraying catch gave her an unexpected feeling of power and the last lingering fear that he was pretending desire in order to save her humiliation fled.

'Ah.' The bliss of loosened stay laces, the sense of freedom as her corset joined the gown on the floor. Her petticoat followed it, leaving her in chemise, stockings and a blush. 'I find I am shy,' Thea confessed.

'And I find I am somewhat overdressed,' Rhys murmured in her ear.

She had though he would kiss her, touch her, but only his breath stroked her skin. Thea turned. 'Should I undress you?'

'Don't you want to?' There was amusement in his eyes, but not mockery.

'I told you, I am shy.' She had never been shy with Rhys before. Once she could tell him anything, make a fool of herself in his company, call for his help when she was stuck in a tree or shriek with horror when they had been paddling in the lake and leeches had attached themselves to her legs. And Rhys always kept her confidences, never laughed at her. He would rescue her from trees and remove the leeches. Now she felt as though she had never known him at all.

'Don't worry.' He dragged his shirt over his head and sat on the edge of the bed to dispose of shoes and stockings. 'At least you have encountered a naked man before.'

'No, I haven't. Anthony just unfastened his falls

and pushed me onto the *chaise*.' It had almost been exciting at first and then…not.

Rhys stopped with his hands on the fastenings of his evening breeches. 'The man is a clod. Shall I put out the candles?'

Thea shook her head. If this was going to be the only time she made love, then she wanted to see everything, know everything. And she was prepared; she had felt Rhys's aroused body pressed against her in the *chaise* on the ship.

Rhys pulled off his breeches and stood there, a faintly quizzical expression on his face as she stared. It seemed she'd had no idea quite what to expect after all.

Oh, my goodness. Thea said the first thing that came into her head. 'I think you look magnificent.' Quite unable to feel shy, afraid or even apprehensive, she reached out her right hand.

Rhys gasped as her grip closed around his erection. 'Thea! Hell's teeth, you are as curious and bold as a cage full of monkeys, you wicked girl.' He wasn't angry; she could tell by the way he hardened still more against her fingers and by the trace of laugher in his voice. 'Let go for a moment and I will take off your chemise and do my share of admiring.'

'My stockings,' she mumbled as the fine lawn was whisked over her head.

'Leave them. They are very arousing.' Rhys sat down on the edge of the bed and pulled her close between his parted thighs before she could realise just how exposed she was or wonder how stockings could be arousing. He held her still with one hand behind her waist and bent to kiss her breast.

The hairs on his legs were strangely stimulating against her bare skin, his lips were warm and sure on the curve of her breast and she moaned softly. *So gentle.* And then he took the nipple in his mouth, sucked, nipped lightly with his teeth and Thea almost jumped out of her skin. She caught his head in her hands and held him close, panting with the shock of the sensation that tugged a response from her womb, her thighs, deeply, intimately…

When Rhys lifted his head she thought she would sink to the floor if it were not for the pressure of his legs and his hand holding her.

He looked up, his eyes dark. 'You are so lovely, Thea. So sweet and so innocent, despite what that oaf did. If I am going to stop, I have to do it now.'

'You cannot stop now,' she gasped.

'I can. Barely. I should.'

'Sooner or later I will find a man to make love to

me, because I am not going to live and die a spinster and not know how it should be. And I would very much rather it was you, Rhys.'

'That, my sweet, is blackmail.'

Thea bit her lip. He sounded so serious. Was she goading him to act against his honour? She would never do that to Rhys. 'I am sorry, it was, was it not? Rhys, you aren't being a rake or a seducer. I am not a virgin. I want this and I understand what we are doing.'

'And the consequences? If I do not prevent you becoming pregnant?'

'It will not happen.' He would keep her safe, she had total trust in him, just as she had under that *diligence*. She placed her hands flat on his chest and leaned in to kiss him, as if that would explain just how deep her trust was.

With a groan Rhys lay back and pulled her with him, rolling until she was beneath him. His face was buried in the angle of her neck, his heart beat over hers and her legs had opened of their own accord to cradle him intimately against the heat at the core of her. It was a kind of perfection, a moment of stillness, poised on the brink of the blissful abyss.

Thea closed her eyes and let herself absorb

every sensation. Rhys's hair smelled faintly of woodsmoke and somewhere he must have brushed against a flowering bush, for a fragrance clung to the cropped curls. His skin was soft and smooth in some places, firm and roughened with hair in others. The weight of him was dominating, and yet he held himself in such control that it was not at all frightening. At the junction of her thighs she could feel the shape of him, beating with a pulse of its own, heating her flesh, moving as it strained against his will, wanting to thrust.

'Ah, Thea.' He lifted himself on his elbows and she opened her eyes to look up into his. 'I never—'

'My lord, are you awake?' A piercing whisper, the rap of knuckles on the door. *Polly?*

They froze, staring at each other, desire fled. 'What do you want?' Rhys snarled. 'What hour is this to be hammering on doors, for goodness' sake?'

'It is one o'clock, my lord. I'm sorry, but I got up to go to the necessary and peeped into Lady Althea's room and she isn't in her bed and it's not been slept in. Where can she be?'

'Blast the woman, she'll start a hue and cry,' Rhys whispered, then raised his voice. 'Perhaps she went into the garden for some air and slipped and hurt herself, or fell asleep. Go down and look, Polly, and be quiet about it, don't make a fuss. I'll dress and come and help.'

'Yes, my lord. But I've told Mr Hodge and the landlady, I was that worried—and Mr Benton woke up, too.'

'Go! And don't wake anyone else,' Rhys ordered. He rolled off the bed and reached for his breeches. 'Confound the wench, she's started a hue and cry. Get dressed, Thea, hurry. The garden slopes up past this window. I'll lower you down—go and find a bench to pretend to fall asleep on.'

It was as though someone had doused her in icy water. The heat of Rhys's body had gone, the enchantment of that perfect sensual moment fled and in their place was the sordid possibility of being discovered in a man's room by a search party.

She whipped her hair into a braid as Rhys tied her corset strings. 'Try to tie it as it was or Polly will notice,' she urged. He tossed her gown over her head and fastened it in urgent silence. 'Find the hairpins, hide them,' she whispered as she thrust her feet into her slippers.

The window had a low sill. She sat on it and swung her legs over, straining to hear. There was the sound of movement and people talking lower down, near the entrance to the inn. Rhys took her wrists and swung her down to the path some six feet below the window, just as he had in those long-ago days when they went scrambling over walls to pick illicit apples. 'Take care!'

Thea crept up through the tangled garden that clad the slope, onto a terrace that, in daylight, commanded a view of the river. There had been a wide bench, she remembered, and groped towards it in the starlight. When she bumped against the cool stone she lay down and tried to arrange herself in a convincing pose for sleep. She realised she was panting and focused on taking deep, sleepy breaths.

'Lady Althea! Thea!' Giles, coming closer...

When she heard footsteps on the gravel she sat up, stretched her arms and gasped with what she hoped was realistic alarm for someone waking up, confused, in the dark. 'Giles! Where are you? What time is it? Oh, my goodness, I must have fallen asleep.'

He came out onto the terrace, his face eerily underlit by the lantern in his hand. 'Past one,' he said as he went down on one knee by the bench. 'Are you all right, Thea? We thought you might have fallen and hurt yourself.'

There were voices farther down, the sound of bodies crashing through the undergrowth. 'I am perfectly all right. How many people are searching? What a fuss—it was only that I was hot...'

'Polly is convinced you have been snatched by bloodthirsty revolutionaries or a gang of ruffians bent on kidnap and ransom. Lord Palgrave suggested we search the gardens first.' He twisted round. 'Here he is.'

'Idiotic woman,' Rhys said, as he strode onto the terrace with Polly and what looked like half the inn's staff on his heels. 'You'll catch your death of cold one day with this obsession with fresh air. Why the blazes didn't you tell anyone you were out here?'

He sounded thoroughly irritable and was probably not having to act in the slightest. If he felt anything like her, Rhys was aching with frustrated desire.

'I didn't mean to stay and fall asleep,' she protested. 'I went out after Polly left me because I couldn't drop off.' That was all technically true, at least, even if it barely touched the real facts in passing.

'You are frozen.' Rhys hauled her to her feet, despite a murmur of protest from Giles. He pulled off his coat and slung it around her shoulders. 'How the hell I let you persuade me to bring you along on this journey, I'll never know.'

Whatever else the onlookers were imagining, Thea doubted they envisaged any kind of romantic tryst. Rhys sounded like a man with a delinquent younger sister.

'And don't start crying,' he snapped.

Thea took her cue and flung herself sobbing into Polly's arms. The more fuss she made, the less likely the maid would notice anything untoward about the way she was dressed. Goodness knew what Rhys had done with her corset strings.

'Don't shout at me,' she pleaded from behind the large handkerchief that Giles had pressed into her hands.

'I'll get rid of the staff,' he said. 'This is turning into a circus.' He herded them before him, leaving Thea, Polly and Rhys on the terrace.

'Go and get warm bricks for your mistress's bed,' Rhys ordered. He prised Thea's arms from around the maid's neck and marched her towards the steps down to the front of the inn. 'Hurry up, girl.'

'Hell's teeth, that was a near miss,' Rhys said as Polly ran off to obey. He tipped Thea's face up and studied it in the light of the lantern he held. 'Are you all right?'

'Yes, of course. You know I don't cry.'

'That isn't what I meant,' Rhys murmured as they walked down the steps.

'I feel… I haven't the words for it, but it isn't comfortable.' Her skin was sensitive, she was unnaturally aware of Rhys's hand on her bare arm, her breasts ached and an insistent pulse beat intimately. She wanted to tear off all her clothes, all his clothes, and wrap herself around him.

'No,' he agreed sombrely. 'I think we scraped through without anyone suspecting, but my nerves may never be the same again. That is not the experience I wanted you to have, Thea, my sweet.'

'I know. And you had better stay angry with me tomorrow.'

'I'll try.' He stopped and pulled her into the shadow of the log store. 'This will probably only make things worse for both of us, but I can't leave you without at least a kiss.'

He was right, it would only make the aching longing worse, but how could she resist? Thea went into his arms and his mouth moved over hers, tender and yet a little rough from frustrated desire. She opened to him and his tongue took possession, its rhythms mimicking the act they had been denied, his hands holding her as though he would never let her go.

It could only have lasted a bare minute. Sixty precious seconds for the kiss she had waited all her life for. Thea stroked the back of her hand down Rhys's cheek. 'I wish...'

'This is where I start shouting at you again,' he said as he caught her fingers in his and kissed the tips before pulling her towards the front door. 'Come on, Thea! If you catch a cold and we are held up here for days, I am not going to be at all pleased.'

The next day Rhys managed to inflict his bad mood on her, their servants and the inn staff until he flung himself into the saddle and cantered off ahead of their little cavalcade.

'Phew.' Giles collapsed back into his corner of the chaise. 'Is Denham's temper always that bad?'

'I don't know,' Thea confessed. 'I have never seen him lose it like that before.' She pondered a moment. 'At least, not since he got into fights when he was a lad, and that was usually because someone was being bullied, or was cruel to animals or something.' She suspected that it went against the grain for Rhys to shout at servants, but it was probably all part of the act.

'Are you well this morning?' Giles regarded her, frowning. 'You do not look as though you slept well.' She grimaced and he hastened to apologise. 'I am sorry. I realise that a gentleman never notices that a lady is looking anything other than ravishing.'

'You are quite correct. I hardly slept a wink.' She had wrapped herself tightly around a bolster and tried to imagine it was Rhys and his arms held her, but it had done nothing to calm the ache of longing or the shock of their near discovery.

'It is doubtless my fault that you could not sleep in the first place,' Giles said penitently. 'If I had not made that gauche declaration, you would probably have dropped off to sleep easily and none of this would have happened.'

Thea snatched gratefully at the offered explanation for her behaviour. 'I confess, I felt very badly about refusing you, but please do not think I found your proposal gauche, simply unexpected.'

'And unwelcome.'

'Never that,' she protested. 'What lady would not be flattered and charmed by a proposal from a gentleman such as yourself? But we would not suit, you know.'

'I would have said we would suit very well,' Giles observed. 'I suspect the problem is more that you know another gentleman who would suit you even better. One who has already secured your heart.'

It was not fair to lie to him and the knowledge that she loved another man must surely be a salve to his pride. 'Yes,' Thea agreed. 'There is some-one.'

'And he does not feel the same way?'
She nodded.

'A man who has known you so long that he fails to see you as you are now, I suspect,' Giles continued. 'Someone who has hurt you by the way he has changed, perhaps. He does not understand your need to be loved, so he tried to arrange a suitable marriage for you. His temper is not as you remember it, either—'

'Stop!' Thea regarded him with something like horror running through her. 'You think… You suspect I am in love with Rhys?'

Chapter Thirteen

'I mention no name and I would never do so. Nor would I give anyone the slightest hint that is what I conjecture,' Giles said calmly.

'Thank you.' Thea turned from him and stared out of the window, struggling to find some composure. If Giles was so clear-sighted, who else might suspect her feelings? *Please, not Rhys,* she prayed. She thought she had convinced him that what she felt was simple desire. What would he do if he believed her to be in love with him? Shun her company? Insist she marry him out of duty after last night? Tell Godmama? He would be kind, of course, and pitying. That would be worst of all.

'Has he…has he asked you whether you have made me a declaration?'

'No, we have hardly had a chance for private speech.' Giles leaned across and patted her hand.

'He may be in such a temper because he thinks you might have accepted me. It sounds irrational, but if, having done what he thought was best for you, he then discovered he was jealous, it reveals he has deeper feelings for you than you suspect.'

He sounded so pleased to have discovered a possibility for hope that it hurt to disabuse him of the notion. 'I told him last night,' Thea said baldly. 'I am sure he will have recovered his temper by luncheon. He is…fond of me, of course, and feels responsible. That is all.'

'If you do not mind me mentioning it, I find it strange that, given your shared interest in social reform, he is so reluctant to discuss it.'

'Rhys? Social reform? He has no interest in that, I am sure. Certainly, he is no High Tory and, despite his spending so much time in town, I believe he is an excellent landlord, but beyond that—'

'You do not know how important he is to the reformers' cause? Why, Lord Palgrave always supports every vote and speaks with passion and clarity of all those subjects you and I have discussed.' Thea simply goggled at him. 'And beyond that, he is the man that the party leaders send to, shall we say, persuade the doubters and the troublemakers. He has, I understand, the knack of getting his own way. They call him Hermes.'

'The messenger of the gods?' Yes, Rhys would be very good at persuasion and, when that did not work, even better at domination. And he had discouraged Giles from discussing it with him in her presence. Thea frowned. She recalled Rhys's jeering remarks when she confessed she had not thought through her plans for charitable works. She had skimmed over the Parliamentary reports in the papers too often, or she would have seen his name. It made her ashamed to think she had dismissed him as simply a pleasure-loving aristocrat. She should have known the adult Rhys would care as much for the underdog as the boy ever had.

This conversation, with its layers of deceit, was becoming too complex for either safety or her peace of mind. 'You have the road book—tell me, which is the next town of note we will encounter?'

Rhys dismounted at their luncheon halt and watched Giles Benton assist Thea from the chaise. They seemed to be on perfectly good terms, despite her refusal of his suit. It had been a mistake to try to matchmake, and Thea had been hurt by his lack of understanding, that was obvious now he was sober. The fire of unsatisfied desire had finally left him with nothing but an edgy awareness of her and a dull ache he was trying to ignore, which was probably a suitable penance for his meddling, he reflected as he studied Thea from a distance.

She looked unwell this morning. Her face was pale and there were smudges under her eyes, which were heavy with lack of sleep. He just hoped it was frustration that had kept her awake and not regret.

He should be repenting last night's actions, but he could not find it in himself to be sorry that he had discovered this passionate, sensual Thea. His childhood friend was still there, he thought, recalling the way she had launched herself into space from the window, trusting him to hold her safe as he always had during their ramshackle adventures.

She was independent, caring, reckless—and she knew herself too well. Thea recognised she was unsuited for the tight boundaries of marriage. To force her into them with the wrong man would be to kill that spirit.

What a contradiction she was, he thought, as she followed Benton into the shade of an arbour outside the inn, laughing at something he said. The reckless child somehow coexisted with the elegant young lady. The plain child was still plain, yet transformed into tantalising femininity. He had been stupidly unimaginative, assuming only conventional good looks gave a woman true beauty. For the first time since she had thrown his coat back at him in his room, Rhys smiled.

Thea saw him, waved, and the last of his ill humour, real and assumed, dropped away.

Benton, having settled her on the bench, strolled over and joined him as he went into the inn to order their meal. 'I've a fancy to ride this afternoon,' the other man remarked as the landlord went off to relay their requests to the kitchen.

'I doubt this place has riding horses for hire.' Rhys leaned back against the counter, crossed his ankles and moved his shoulders in a pleasurable stretch.

'I thought we might change places for a bit.' There were definite undertones of an order in the pleasant voice.

'Did you, indeed?'

'I have quite recovered from my head wound and I would appreciate the exercise and fresh air,' Benton said, and added, without changing his tone, 'and I think some bridge-building between you and Lady Althea might be in order.'

Rhys stared at him. The reticent, polite clergyman was showing an unexpected set of teeth. 'The devil you say!'

'You and I both made an error yesterday—you in thinking that Thea would marry where she does not love and me for proposing to her when I had no reason to suspect she favoured me,' Benton remarked calmly. 'She could probably do without my company for a bit, and that will allow you to make your peace.'

'I need to do that, do I?' Rhys swivelled to face the other man and unclenched his hands, which had balled into fists at his sides. For a moment he had thought Benton was hinting that he knew last night's events had been a farce.

'I think so.'

Rhys studied Benton's thoughtful frown. No, he was too straightforward to throw out hints.

'Thea hasn't slept. She looks unhappy.' Benton picked up the glass of red wine the innkeeper had put before them the moment they walked through the door and held it up to the light, squinting at the colour as he spoke. 'She does her best to hide it, of course. A very remarkable young lady. Some man is going to be very lucky to win her heart.'

'Yes,' Rhys agreed as he took up his own glass.

A pity some undeserving idiot had already got Thea's heart and had no idea what a treasure he held unawares. 'All right, you take the horse this afternoon, but I warn you, the stupid thing is afraid of goats.'

The food that was brought out to them was simple but good. Thea breathed the herb-scented, dry air and leaned back against the upright of the pergola that supported a trellis of vines over their heads, filtering the sunshine through to dapple them with shadows. A lad came out and flicked a printed cloth over the table, then laid it with platters of bread studded with olives, goat's- and sheep's-milk cheeses, air-dried meats redolent of garlic, more olives and a pitcher of wine.

They all ate well, but conversation lagged. There was nothing she wanted to say to Rhys in company, she and Giles had talked themselves out, there was a faint air of tension between the two men and the effect of a disturbed night had dried up even a well-bred young lady's resources of small talk, she discovered. Their staff, cheerfully ensconced around another table, had no inhibitions, laughing and chatting and, from what Thea could hear, teaching the post boys some English cant terms.

When she came out of the inn after refreshing herself she found Giles mounted on the horse, which was demonstrating a skittish dislike of the flock of hens that scratched in the dusty road. Giles, who did not seem to have Rhys's skill on horseback, was cursing mildly as the animal backed and fussed.

'I thought you said it was goats it objected to,' he called to Rhys, who was standing by the step of the chaise to help her up.

'Those are the first chickens we've been close to,' Rhys said with a grin. 'I'd take care with cows and sheep, too, if I were you.' He followed her into the carriage. 'He would ride.' He shrugged.

'Are you all right?' she asked.

'I am fine.' Rhys shut the door and leaned back in the corner, apparently in order to study her face. 'Giles thinks we need to talk.' When she did not answer he added, 'He is probably correct, although I must admit, talking is not what I would prefer to be doing.'

As if I need reminding! To be alone like this with Rhys, surrounded by windows and perfectly visible to Giles as he trotted alongside, was more difficult than she had imagined it would be. With an instinct not to throw fuel on the fire, she ignored the end of Rhys's remark and asked, 'What does he suggest we should be discussing?'

'He says I should be apologising for urging him to propose to you, and I think he is right.' He reached to take her ungloved hand in his. The touch of his bare skin on hers sent the fine hairs shivering erect all along her arm. 'I am sorry, Thea. I should have listened when you said you did not wish to marry without love. I decided that I knew what was best for you because I was worrying about your future and, when what seemed like the perfect man for you dropped at our feet...' He grimaced. 'I had never suspected myself of being a matchmaker.'

Her hand was still in his. *No one can see,* she told herself. 'Many people matchmake,' she said, returning the pressure of his fingers to take the sting out of her words. 'Everyone feels it acceptable to have an opinion about an unmarried woman's future.'

'I suppose it is because the position of women by themselves is so precarious. Insufficient money to maintain respectable standards, or a loss of reputation, and the downward slide is rapid.' He shifted to sit shoulder to shoulder with her and their clasped hands rested on her thigh.

Thea let herself lean very slightly into him and enjoyed the tingle that the pressure of his solid body sent fizzing through her.

'If women had a better standard of education and were trusted to manage their own affairs, then it would not be such a problem,' he added, startling her. Then she recalled Giles's revelation that had become lost in the shock of discovering that he had guessed her feelings for Rhys.

'Why have you said nothing about your work in Parliament?' she demanded. 'Giles told me that you are a valuable supporter of all the progressive legislation, that you are instrumental in persuading, or silencing, the doubters and those that try and obstruct change. Tell me, *Hermes*, why you let me think you indifferent to the suffering of others so that I misjudged you?'

'I did not want to turn your tête-à-tête with Giles into a general conversation. I was matchmaking, remember?'

'I wish you had told me. I should have known that you would have supported such causes.' She glanced sideways and saw that she was making him uncomfortable with her praise. *Good!* 'And tell me, while I am chiding you, why did you say you did not expect a wife who shared your interests? You would not expect her to want to live in your pocket, you said. Was that more flummery?'

'No, it was the truth. I told you what I wanted—a good, domestic wife. I do not want shared passions of any kind—in the bedchamber or in beliefs.'

'Oh, Rhys.' He made her want to weep. 'That is so sad. Think what you will be missing.'

'Drama? Tantrums? Jealousy? Constant demands on my time and attention? Arguments about politics over breakfast?'

'And what is so wrong with that? Not the tantrums and jealousy, of course. If you love someone and they share your beliefs and enthusiasms, surely it would be wonderful.' *You and me in harmony, working together for important goals, passionate together in bed at night...*

'I told you, I have no intention of marrying for love.'

'You will be an unfaithful husband, then? You will keep a mistress?' If only he could see what he was depriving himself of, how much richer his life would be if he could only believe that he could love and that it would be returned. If he could believe that a woman might be faithful to him.

'Certainly not. I did not say I would marry a

woman I found unattractive. I will be swearing to be faithful, and I will hold to that vow.'

Thea fixed her eyes on the vineyards they were passing through and fought to keep her temper. She believed Rhys when he said he would be faithful to his wife, which meant that he was intending to squander all that passion within himself on a tepid relationship with a woman who would never know what it was to be truly loved. As he would not. His courage was invincible, it seemed, except in this one thing: he would not risk his heart again, even if that meant settling for the safely mediocre.

'I can hear your thoughts, Thea.' He sounded amused, but she did not turn to see if he was smiling. 'You are a true romantic.' She hunched a shoulder in a pettish refusal to engage with banter and, as if in response, he opened his hand, pressing until her own palm lay flat, his still on top, long fingers threaded through hers. She became aware of a subtle pressure as the pads of his fingers pressed lightly in a rhythm she could not quite catch. It was as if a big cat, claws sheathed, was gently kneading her thigh.

Does he know he is doing that? It made it rather hard to breathe, that rhythm. Thea began to count in her head. *One, two, in, out. One, two.*

'I am surprised, you being the romantic you are, that you would contemplate becoming my lover,' Rhys said. 'Is that not a betrayal of your true love?'

Breathe. 'I know a lost cause when I see it,' Thea said, her voice steady. The pressure on her leg had become a series of short, stroking movements, moving the fine lawn of her chemise back and forth over the bare skin beneath, the silk of her petticoat sliding against the thin fabric of her gown. The friction made a soft whispering sound, almost too faint to hear.

'You meet him, then? Or was that just a figure of speech?'

'I see him occasionally,' Thea admitted incautiously. 'We do not mix socially.' The pressure of Rhys's fingers was making it hard to think. She pulled her hand away and realised too soon that doing so left his big hand firmly on her thigh. He began a slow caress down as far as her knee, and then up, her skirts riding with the movement. 'Rhys!'

'Do you not like it? Am I tickling you?'

'No. I am not ticklish.'

'You are, unless my memory is very far at fault.' Rhys's chuckle brought her round to glare at him. 'Relax, Thea, I am not going to tickle your ribs in a chaise in broad daylight.' Somehow his hand had curved to cup the top of her leg and his fingertips were caressing the inner surface. The chemise had ridden up and there was only fine lawn and thin silk between his hand and her skin.

Her breath was coming short now. She turned her head on the squabs so she was looking out of the window again, the perfect picture of a well-bred lady interested only in the passing scene.

'*Rhys.*' She should move. She should slap his hand away. This was broad daylight on a public highway, for goodness' sake! His hand felt wonderful. Sure, confident, skilled in administering this focused sensual torture.

'I am thinking how I would like to caress you when we are naked in bed again,' Rhys said. She shot him a startled glance, but he was turned towards the window on his side. To anyone looking in they would appear detached, conversing lightly on matters of no importance.

'I will start with your toes, I think.' He sounded thoughtful. Her toes curled in the tight little nankeen boots she wore. 'Then I will kiss all the way up to the back of your knees. I wonder if you are ticklish there. Are you, Thea?'

'I do not know,' she managed to gasp. His fingers

were brushing high to the junction of her thighs now. She pressed them together and somehow that only made the heat and the throbbing worse.

'We must find out.' That wicked chuckle again. 'Then I will lick and kiss and nibble my way along here.' One finger traced a wandering path from her knee up the quivering length of her thigh to the point of the delicious discomfort. 'To the delta of Venus.'

'Delta?'

Rhys placed both thumbs tip to tip, then joined his forefingers into a triangle. 'The Greek letter delta, that mound covered in curls that hides the honeyed secrets of a woman's desire.' Thea bit down on a moan. 'Then I will part those soft white thighs and kiss—'

'Kiss?' It was more of a squeak than a word. 'Rhys, if you do not stop this minute I am going to… I do not know, but I should not be doing whatever it is in a chaise!'

He lifted his hand and caught hers. 'You are right, of course. I do not think I can stand it, either—see what you have done to me.' He laid her unresisting hand against the falls of his breeches, then groaned as she reflexively tightened her grip on the blatant erection that pressed itself into her fingers.

Thea snatched her hand away, face burning, insides quivering with mingled desire and terror. 'Is this *normal*?'

'Perfectly. What we are feeling is simply desire, what any man and woman who are sexually attracted feel. Normal, healthy and decidedly uncomfortable under the circumstances.'

'Well, there is nothing to be done about it here.' Thea retreated into her corner and crossed her legs. It did nothing to subdue the desire to throw herself on Rhys's chest and kiss him senseless.

'There is, if you were a little less innocent. Don't look at me like that, I promise to behave. And I also promise,' he added grimly, 'to find a way to be with you tonight if I have to feed that maid of yours a sleeping draught to do it.'

'As long as she does not have to sleep in my dressing room, or on a truckle bed in my bedchamber, then I will tell her I do not want to be disturbed until morning and lock the door,' Thea said firmly. 'And you must come to me.'

'But of course,' Rhys agreed. 'A gentleman can do nothing else.'

Chapter Fourteen

Polly put down the hairbrush and began to tidy the small disorder on the dressing table.

Now, how to convince her not to come into my room tonight without sounding suspicious...?

'Will you be requiring me again this evening, my lady?'

Thea looked in the mirror and saw the maid was positively blushing. 'I do not think so. I was going to read for a while before I went to bed, but I doubt I will stay up long.' The clock outside on the landing of the top floor of the inn struck ten o'clock. 'Why, Polly? Are you tired, too?'

'No, my lady. I thought… That is, Mr Hodge suggested… There's a fair down by the waterside. I'd like to go and see it.'

'With Hodge.'

'Yes, my lady.'

Goodness, Rhys had been right after all. My maid and his valet. 'Are you and Hodge courting, Polly?'

'I think so, my lady. Do you mind? I mean, I don't know what you think about followers.'

'Hodge is not so much following as travelling with us, isn't he?' Polly giggled at the feeble joke. 'I have no objection, although it really is a matter for Lord Palgrave, as he employs you both. Here, take this in case there is anything to tempt you.' She handed the girl the loose change that lay on the dressing table. 'Have a good time and be back by midnight. I will lock my door as there are other guests on the floor below us, so do not disturb me when you return, will you?'

'Oh, thank you, my lady! I won't disturb you, I promise.' Polly folded away the last items of clothing, turned down the bed and positively skipped out of the room.

Everything had conspired to smooth her path this evening. Their rooms were spread over the topmost floor of the inn, with no other guests on that level. They were spacious and well appointed, but there were no dressing rooms, so both Hodge and Polly had their own bedchambers at the far end of the corridor, while Rhys's was separated from her room by what Polly told her was the large linen store. Giles was on her other side.

Thea had pleaded tiredness after dinner so she could retreat and not have to sit making general conversation while Rhys looked at her, his lids heavy over those hot blue eyes. It had been bad enough over dinner, but she was quite certain she could not remain calm with nothing to distract her.

When would he come? She studied her reflection in the glass, her confidence diminishing by the second. What on earth was it that Rhys found so desirable about her? Perhaps she should snuff out some of the candles....

Their rooms were quiet and faced the back of the inn, not the yard or the busy street. The silence was broken by a dull thump from outside as though something had fallen. Thea caught her night robe tight around her and went to ease open the shutters onto the balcony. Was that a faint curse from somewhere outside?

The moon was half-full, the sky clear and, as she glanced up, she caught her breath at the blaze of stars. Then a gleam of white to her left caught her eye. 'Rhys!' He was standing on his own balcony's parapet and by his foot was a black hole where a stone should have been.

'Damn thing fell off,' he whispered.

'Go back, then, it isn't safe,' she hissed back. 'Come in through the door, for goodness' sake!'

'Less chance of being seen this way.' He shifted his balance and jumped the four feet to the intervening balustrade and then down to the balcony itself.

Thea removed her hands from her mouth where she had clamped them to hold in the scream and peered at the stonework. 'This looks in very bad repair.'

'Stand back.' Rhys climbed onto the edge, and the stone beneath his feet rocked.

Thea fought the instinct to try to reach for him and retreated to the far side. Rhys jumped, the stone teetered but stayed put and he landed and jumped down with perfect grace.

'You idiotic man,' she scolded.

'I thought it would be a romantic gesture.' He held the shutter for her, then followed her into the room. 'Is the door shut? No?' He strode across and locked it.

'Romantic? You don't have a romantic bone in your body.' Thea plumped down on the dressing-table stool and tried to recover her breath. 'I thought you would fall off—and a mangled lover at the foot of the wall is not at all romantic.'

He grinned, unrepentant, and began to brush dust and lichen off his evening breeches, which were all he appeared to be wearing apart from his shirt, open necked. 'I should have put riding breeches on,' he observed. 'Lord knows what Hodge is going to make of these.'

'He has gone to the fair and taken Polly. Did you realise?'

'It was my idea.' Rhys looked smug. 'I suggested he might like the evening off and he jumped at the chance. He even managed to keep a straight face while remarking that Polly might welcome the outing.' He strolled towards her with what seemed dangerously like a prowl. 'Why are we bickering about the way I arrived here and discussing our servants' love lives, Thea?'

'Because I am frightened,' she admitted. Where had that come from? She slid round to the far side of the stool.

'The other night you were lying naked in my arms.' To her intense relief Rhys leaned against the bedpost. 'I do not think that fear was uppermost amongst your emotions then.'

'You are not mellow with red wine and I am not

angry now,' Thea explained, as much to herself as to him.

Rhys smiled, lazy, dangerous and yet somehow reassuring. 'We do not have to do anything.'

Thea flickered a glance at the arousal that his thin evening breeches were doing nothing to disguise. 'You are hardly going to be pleased about that.'

'Thea.' His voice was suddenly rough. It was not anger, but surely it could not be emotion? 'We are friends. Old friends. I have never made love to an unwilling woman and I am not going to start with you. This is about what you want. If you do me the honour of lying with me, I will do my best to make you happy and I know it will give me great pleasure. But if *your* happiness requires me to go out of the door now, then that is what will happen—with no ill feeling.'

'Not back along the balconies?' Something bubbled inside her, something close to happiness tinged with the traces of that fear. But now it only gave the happiness a sparkling, dangerous edge.

'If my lady commands.' He had seen the change in her eyes; she did not have to tell him.

'I think the door, later,' she conceded. 'I buffed my toenails.' Rhys's eyes crinkled into a smile. 'I do not know why, because I really did not understand what you were talking about in the carriage.'

'Then let me show you. Stay just where you are.' He straightened and dragged off his shirt, then his breeches.

Oh, but he was magnificent. She remembered the lanky boy swimming in the lake in his drawers and just had time to wonder where all that elegant muscle had come from before he was kneeling at her bare feet.

'And very pretty toes they are, too.' He lifted her right foot and the flounces of her night robe fell back, pulling the nightgown with it to bare her leg to the knee. When he sucked her toes into his mouth and did outrageous things with his hot, wet tongue, she did not giggle or shriek, only reached wildly for the edge of the dressing table and held on. And then he did as he had promised, and his tongue trailed up her calf to circle her knee before he switched legs, and her other foot was left tingling.

'I have never been so shocked in my life,' Thea panted. She had to say something, do something...

'In which case,' Rhys said as he got to his feet and scooped her up in his arms, 'you haven't been trying hard enough. Now for those deliciously ticklish bits.' He laid her on the bed, her garments bunched into a mere froth of inadequate coverage at the top of her thighs, and bent her right leg.

Those broad shoulders pushed her legs apart so she could do nothing but sprawl shamelessly as he explored the delicate skin behind her knee. It wasn't ticklish; it was bliss. Wicked, wicked bliss. None of the books she had studied so surreptitiously had said anything about knees!

And then, before she could recover herself enough to understand what he was doing, his mouth was buried in the curls at the junction of her thighs and his tongue had slipped into the secret folds. All she could do was fist her hands into the bedcover and try to stop herself lifting up to wantonly press herself against his sinful, clever mouth.

One moment she was consciously fighting for control, the next something took her, took charge of her body, her mind, her soul and swept over her with an irresistible force. She heard a scream and felt Rhys move, there was a moment, or perhaps an hour—an entire night?—of dizzying pleasure and then she was wrapped in Rhys's arms, his body hot and hard and strangely gentle as he held her.

'Oh,' she said. 'Oh.' There were probably words,

but she had no idea what they were or what language she needed to say them in.

'Thea,' Rhys said, his voice strangely husky, and then his weight was on her and she felt him nudging between her thighs, and she opened to him and tried to breathe as he pushed into her. So slow, not like Anthony's painful, impatient thrust. Gentle, smooth, inexorable. He was very large and it was not exactly…comfortable. She shifted instinctively, tilted her pelvis and heard him groan against her hair and, strangely, that gave her confidence.

There was discomfort. Her brain told her it was pain as he stretched and filled her, yet her body told her it was not. Her body welcomed it, sang with delight, arched against him, tightened so that the pain should have become worse, but instead became simply pleasure, shimmering through her muscles and veins, driving her thoughts into abject submission as they tried to tell her this had been an unpleasant experience before.

But that was not Rhys. She caught at the vanishing thought and sought for his mouth. *There. Kiss me. At last. Oh, kiss me. I love you….*

His body arched over her, muscled, hard, tense to breaking point, every sinew, it seemed, straining. Thrust and withdrawal, thrust, in a rhythm of spiralling tension and pleasure. Their skin was slicked with the heat of effort and the warmth of the night and her nostrils were filled with his masculine scent and what she hazily realised was the musk of their lovemaking.

She needed to be closer to him somehow, anyhow. Thea curled her legs around Rhys's hips and he cried her name and held still for a second like a hawk poised to plunge. The strange tightening, spinning sensation swept through her again as he thrust and his mouth found hers. Thea was distantly aware of him leaving her and cried out in protest. And yet, as she lost herself utterly, she felt Rhys holding her, surrounding her, kissing her. *I love you.*

Rhys stirred and drifted up to consciousness. He had been here before, his arms around these soft curves, his nostrils teased with the scent of rose and this warm, sleeping woman. But this time they were not on a makeshift bed on a ship and this time he did not have to conceal the all-too-evident fact that his body was ready and eager to make love to her. Rhys smiled into the darkness and nuzzled the soft skin below Thea's ear.

She mumbled something and wriggled more

firmly into his embrace, but she was clearly still asleep. Faintly the sound of the church clock striking four drifted through the latticed shutters. There was a perceptible lightening at the window.

Time to go. He would have to wake her so she could lock the door behind him. The temptation to slide into her, wake her that way, was considerable. And inconsiderate, Rhys realised. He had no right to assume Thea would want to make love again. Her curiosity had been satisfied and, very likely, that flare of desire for him had been quenched. For him it was going to take some time to get the need for her under control if Thea decided that enough was enough.

Could they go back to the way they had been before? No, because that had been founded on his lamentably slow realisation that his childhood friend was a woman now. So what next? Rhys indulged himself by running her hair through the fingers of his left hand, the one that was free and not under Thea's ribs, fingers curved around her breast.

They could continue with this and it would become an *affaire*, or they could stop now, and find a way of coexisting until they reached Venice. Was that possible? Rhys had never been friends with a mistress and had never had to live in close proximity with one after the relationship had ended.

But he could not compare this to those past liaisons. Those had been, at heart, a business matter. True, he had done his utmost to give pleasure as well as gold, but it had still been a transaction. And this? Honest mutual desire, as simple and as fiendishly complicated as that. Because he had taken the innocence of a respectable lady, never mind that she had not been a virgin. To all intents and purposes Thea had never made love before, and she could have gone to a husband's bed with a very good chance of him never realising that someone else had been before him.

Now, not. Although, knowing Thea, he thought she would carefully explain to the man that she was not an innocent before matters progressed as far as a proposal. And then the proposal would not be made unless the suitor was head over heels in love with her and, given that she was hardly going to find herself courted by some idealistic nineteen-year-old, that was not likely to be the case. Grown men had more sense than to fall in love.

He should, he knew perfectly well, offer her marriage. And he could imagine, with a searing clarity that brought him thoroughly awake, what Thea would say to that. He had shaken her faith in him quite far enough by thinking she would accept a *suitable* marriage to Giles Benton. She wanted to marry for love, and she expected him to understand and support that.

It was a relief, of course. Thea was far from the placid, domesticated, undemanding lady he needed to marry. House, home and children would not be enough for her. She would demand to be involved—when she was not doing something outrageous like reading unsuitable books or climbing trees. That would be fine while they agreed. But when they did not? When that enquiring mind of hers decided she was not happy with one of his opinions or decisions? Would she then be wishing she was not tied by vows and friendship?

But the biggest barrier of all was that she expected to be loved, and he could never feign that besotted state—she would see through him with one sharp glance from those clear hazel eyes. He did not know how to make that unquestioning surrender any longer, and Rhys found he could not bear the thought of hurting her.

'Wake up, Thea,' he murmured into her ear.

She stirred and then, without saying anything,

wriggled round in his arms and kissed him, finding his mouth, it seemed, by blind instinct.

Rhys fought the urge to follow where that kiss was leading. He lifted his head. 'Sweetheart, I have to go.'

'Not yet.'

Her hand slipped down between their bodies and Rhys groaned. Four warm fingers and an erotically enterprising thumb closed around his erection. 'Thea, if I don't go out of the door now it will be the balconies later.'

That worked. Thea rolled away. 'You are not risking breaking your neck again.' She slid out of bed, groped her way across to the shutters and opened them, letting in the faint grey light of dawn to bathe her unashamed nakedness. 'Brrr. It is cold out here.'

'Then get back into bed.' Rhys winced as his feet hit chilly boards, but he pulled on his breeches and found his shirt as briskly as he could, trying not to look at the pale dawn ghost that was Thea as she flitted about the room setting things to rights. 'Or put on your robe and slippers.'

To his secret disappointment she pulled her nightgown over her head. 'I'll get back into bed when you have gone,' she promised. When he padded over to join her by the door she put her head on one side and laughed, clapped her hand over her mouth to stifle the sound and stood there, eyes twinkling at him.

'What?' He knew he sounded grumpy with the sheer effort of not throwing her back onto the bed and having his way with her.

'You look like a tomcat going home after a very wild night on the tiles,' Thea said, and reached up to stroke his hair into some kind of order.

'Well, and so I am.'

'At least you did not yowl at the moon.'

'Oh, I did,' Rhys said with a grin and bent to brush his lips over hers. 'Inside I was making enough noise to have every boot in the neighbourhood thrown at me.' He eased the door open and checked the corridor, then slid outside and shut the door before she could reply and make him laugh even more than he was tempted to do now. Tomcat, indeed!

He reached his room without so much as seeing a sleepy-eyed boot boy. What would be heaven, of course, would be a wife for duty and Thea for fun. And passion. And something else he could not quite put his finger on. Friendship, he supposed.

Rhys threw off his much-abused clothing and got

between his own chilly sheets. The bed needed to look slept in, so somehow he was going to have to try to sleep.

Chapter Fifteen

Thea shook out the bedding to remove any betraying jet-black hairs, remade the bed then got in to toss and turn it into a convincing state. That took ten minutes in all. After a further two hours tossing and turning she sat up and ran her hands through her tangled hair in exasperation.

What idiocy had made her think that one night in Rhys's arms would be enough, that she could keep the memory like a pressed flower in an album to be taken out and sighed over in pleasant reminiscence? All she had achieved was to make her long for him more, with the added torment of now knowing exactly what she would be missing every night for the rest of her life.

And he will be married to his dull, respectable wife and it will be positively sinful of me to feel jeal-

ous of her. Why did I assure him one night would be enough and that I would not ask for more?

It was all very well and good being undemanding and honourable and doing everything to make him not feel he was under any kind of obligation but… No, she had been right. The only thing worse than not having Rhys in her bed would be him being there, but knowing it was out of pity.

There was a faint scratching at the door. 'My lady? Are you awake?'

Thea opened the door to find Polly beaming with good humour. 'Would you like your breakfast in your room, my lady?' She came in and flung the shutters open. 'What a glorious morning it is! We don't get sunshine like this in London, that's for sure.'

'Breakfast here would be excellent, thank you, Polly.' And would have the advantage of giving her some time before she had to face Rhys under Giles's perceptive eye. Possibly she could manage not to blush like a peony when she was dressed.

'Not that it's much like a proper breakfast. The food's all right over here—better than I thought it'd be—but there's nothing to set a body up for the day in those mimsy little pastries, now is there?'

After countless breakfasts with her father demolishing bloody beefsteaks and fried eggs, Thea was grateful for chocolate and croissants and some fresh fruit. 'It suits me very well,' she said. 'I'll have my washing water first, though.'

'You've had a restless night,' Polly observed, flapping the bed into some sort of order as she passed it. 'And you've put your foot right through the bottom of this sheet, my lady.'

'Oh, dear. I must make sure it is added to the accounting.' She escaped behind the screen to hide her scarlet cheeks. That must have been Rhys.

'Did you have a pleasant evening at the fair?' she asked when, washed, dressed and feeling rather more composed, she sat down at the little table on the balcony. It was a miracle that Rhys hadn't managed to demolish that on his way to her room.

'It was lovely, my lady. I bought ever such a pretty lace trim for my Sunday best and a handkerchief and some soap. And there were swings and jugglers and a fortune teller.'

'And did you have your fortune told?'

'John…Mr Hodge, I should say, teased me until I did. But he had to come in with me or I wouldn't have been able to understand a word!'

'Sit down and tell me what your fortune is to be,' Thea urged.

'Ooh, my lady, thank you. Well, I'm to meet a dark man with grey eyes who is good with his hands and much travelled and we'll fall in love and live happily ever after and have three children. What do you think of that, my lady?'

'That possibly it was being translated by a dark man with grey eyes?' Thea teased.

'Could be, my lady.' Polly's pink cheeks dimpled into a smile. 'Not that I mind him taking an interest, mind you.'

'You will be careful, won't you, Polly?' *And who am I to lecture?* 'I'm sure if anything should… Well, you know what I mean. I am certain his lordship would insist on Hodge marrying you, but it isn't the way you'd want to start married life, is it?'

'Don't you worry, my lady,' Polly said. 'I don't believe in letting a man take liberties. A girl loses all her mystery if she does that, my sister Bethan says. You give them what they wants and then they don't want it anymore, she says. And she landed herself an attorney's clerk! A little kiss is all John Hodge is getting until I've got a ring on my finger.'

'Very wise,' Thea said as her stomach took an unpleasant swoop downwards. Is that what would happen now? Perhaps she had only been a novelty for Rhys, and the attraction he had felt for her would evaporate now there was no mystery about the woman she had grown up to be. Perhaps, in the cold light of day, he would think less of her, believe her wanton. No, surely Rhys would not be that hypocritical.

'Is your sister's a happy marriage?' she asked, and stirred another spoonful of sugar into her chocolate for courage.

Polly shrugged. 'There's money enough and he's kind to her and the kiddies are healthy. I'd not be surprised if he doesn't stray now and again, if you take my meaning.'

'So it wasn't a love match?'

'No. Our Bethan's got her head on the right way round. She set out to catch the best man she could, provided she liked him well enough.'

Love matches would be different, Thea told herself. If a man loved a woman he would not think worse of her the next day if she slept with him. *But Rhys does not love me, not that way.* All the warm, happy, sensual glow that had been with her since Rhys's departure ebbed away, leaving her apprehensive and shaken.

What did I think, deep down, was going to hap-

pen? she asked herself. *That Rhys was going to wake after a night in my arms and realise he loved me passionately?* She hoped that was not the case. At least expressing desire frankly was the sort of thing an independent adult woman might do, but to daydream about fairy-tale endings was uncomfortably like her youthful yearnings.

'Shall I lay out your green walking dress, my lady?' She had been so deep in her troubled thoughts that Polly had already found her clean linen and was standing waiting to help her with her stays.

'Yes, please.' Another day in the chaise with either Giles and his uncomfortably perceptive gaze for company, or the agony of being with Rhys, on public display and unable to touch him, let alone ask how he felt about her now. 'No, put that back, Polly. I have an idea.'

'Are you riding today, Denham?' Benton pushed back his chair from the breakfast table and stood up.

'Hmm?' Rhys yanked his thoughts back from their review of last night's delights. 'Riding? Yes, I thought I would.' Thea might need a while to feel comfortable alone with him, and he could well do without the strain of sitting next to her in the chaise, unable to do any of the things that he would find himself aching for.

'In that case, I think I'll see if the landlord can hire me a horse.' Benton went out and Rhys drained his coffee while he tried to make up his mind how to approach Thea. She might well be regretting what had happened last night, in which case he had to make her feel confident that he would not press her for any further intimacy and that no one would ever know what had transpired between them.

On the other hand, she might want to continue their liaison, but would probably be far too shy to say so—especially after she had assured him that she expected nothing more from him than one night.

And what did he want? Well, that was easy— what he *wanted* was to continue as her lover. Her untutored, sensual, generous response to lovemaking had delighted and shaken him. To explore with her all the other delights that bed sport held would be intensely pleasurable.

But. But he had been careful last night. Every time they made love, however carefully, there was some risk of pregnancy and of discovery.

And how could he be certain she would tell him the truth about what she wanted? If he made it clear he wished to continue as her lover, she might very well feel obligated to agree, and, being Thea, would put a very good face on it. Would he be able to tell if her agreement was genuine?

Rhys stared into the muddy dregs at the bottom of his cup. They seemed to have a lot in common with his thought processes. This was why he wanted a placid, emotionless marriage. No anxiety about hurting another person, no fear of them hurting you.

What he ought to do now was clear—never mind what he wanted. He should not make love to Thea again. In fact, he should pretend it had not happened. Then she would not feel pressured. And if the worst did happen, then surely he could rely on her to tell him that she was with child?

That thoroughly straightforward conclusion was curiously unsatisfying. *Do your duty,* Rhys told himself. Even that thought did not produce the immediate sense of purpose and contentment it normally did. For a ridiculous, self-indulgent moment he imagined life with Thea, then gave himself a brisk shake. This was the sort of emotional muddle he was intending to avoid. He pushed back the chair and went to pay the reckoning, the warm afterglow of sexual satisfaction ebbing with unpleasant finality.

The stable yard seemed full of horses. The post boys were supervising the four being hitched to the chaise, Tom Felling was arguing about the shoes on one of the animals the ostlers were trying to harness to the carriage and Benton was mounted, holding the reins of two other horses.

'They tell me the lady has ordered this one.' He gestured towards a neat grey bearing a side saddle. 'And then they ran off before I could tell them they had made a mistake.'

'No mistake.' Thea walked past Rhys to take the reins. 'Will you give me a boost?' Her smile was just the same as it always was, her gaze meeting his with perfect frankness.

Last night might not have happened, Rhys thought with a flash of what he recognised as hurt pride. *Damn it!* Then he saw the shadows under her eyes and the way her smile wavered as he stared at her, and he made himself smile.

'Yes, of course. That is a charming habit.' He cupped his hands for her booted foot and tossed her up. The mare sidled, but Thea had the reins competently in hand.

'It is French,' she said with a rueful twist of the lips. 'Their gowns are fabulous and their fashions always ahead of ours, but their tailoring is not as good as London tailoring. This is meant for parading in a park, not for the hunting field, I fear.' She gave the exaggeratedly long skirt a dismissive twitch. Yes, now that he was looking for it he could see the constraint behind the facade.

'Even so, the effect for the spectator is most pleasing.' Rhys mounted, one eye on the grey. He would have much preferred to try the animal out himself before he let Thea near it. And was this wise, in any case? After all, she had been as near a virgin as made no difference, and perhaps she'd be more comfortable in the chaise.

'Are you sure you should be riding this morning?' he said, low voiced, as he brought his own bay alongside her. 'Should you perhaps be resting?'

Thea gave a snort of laughter. 'What a poor honey you must think me if you do not believe I can manage a strange horse, Rhys. You taught me to ride, remember?'

'Astride, when you were six,' he protested.

She lowered her voice, 'Or perhaps your male

pride is dented because I am not prostrate with, er…emotion?'

'Thea!' Well, that answered that! Whatever she was feeling this morning, it was not shyness or an excess of sensibility. Even so, she was somehow not quite herself.

'I am tired of being shut in the chaise.' Her voice rose and Rhys saw she controlled it with a conscious effort. 'The weather is beautiful, the scenery is so new and different and the air smells delightful. I want to enjoy it.' She nudged the grey into a walk and the three of them rode out of the yard side by side.

'Where are we?' she asked. 'I never thought to ask last night.' From her calm expression and downcast lashes no one would have guessed that the reason had probably been nothing to do with tiredness and everything to do with nervously anticipating an amorous encounter.

'Just north of Montélimar.' Rhys relaxed, the grey was well behaved and Thea was obviously more than competent in the saddle, even if her attention was not fully on the horse. 'I was aiming for Orange tonight and that is only thirty-five, forty miles. Do you want to see anything in Montélimar?' he asked Benton, who shook his head. 'Then we will buy some of the famous nougat for Thea on our way through.'

'It isn't me who has the sweet tooth,' she retorted. 'It was always you who stole the fudge if Cook did not hide it well enough.'

'I am prepared to admit I would like to try nougat,' Benton interjected. 'Shall we canter?'

Thea urged the grey on and left them in a cloud of dust. Rhys let Benton chase after her and held his horse back to a more controlled pace. What had he expected this morning? That Thea would send him some unmistakable signal that she wanted to continue as his lover? Or an equally clear signal that she did not? He had not thought how tricky this would be, or how difficult it must be for her to make either inclination clear.

He must take the bull by the horns and broach the subject, making certain he gave no indication of his own wish. To put her under any sort of pressure ran counter to every instinct he possessed as a gentleman. And his instincts were usually to be trusted, he thought, recalling how reluctant he had been to bring her with him on this journey. If he had not, if he had been sober enough to find a sensible solution to her problems, then in a year or two they would doubtless have met again, both of them married to highly suitable spouses. And then his blood would not be running hot with desire for a woman who was better fit for marriage to some scholar or explorer or eccentric reformer. *And then I might get some sleep at night,* Rhys thought and urged his mount into a gallop.

'I am blissfully sticky and far too full,' Thea remarked, and sucked her fingers in a manner she knew full well was unacceptable in any lady over the age of six. Across the table in the private parlour Rhys gave a slight shudder. It must have been too hoydenish even for his tolerance. Giles, armed with a thick guidebook, had gone out to scout around the sites.

The atmosphere was strained, or perhaps it was simply her own shyness. What did one say the day after the first time one lay with a man? Or did one say nothing until you were in bed again? If that ever happened. She watched Rhys out of the corner of her eye as he sat checking the route map spread out before him and the notebook he had weighted open under the pewter sugar basin. His mouth was closed in an uncompromising line and he had not looked her straight in the eye since they had arrived, dusty and a trifle saddle sore, at the best inn in the centre of Orange.

Thea sat up straight and gave her fingers one last wipe with her handkerchief. She was a grown-up woman who had taken a lover; it was simply a matter of having a frank, adult conversation about who was sleeping where tonight. 'Um…' *Oh, for goodness' sake! That was hardly a sophisticated opening.*

Rhys glanced up, then must have seen something in her face that made him put down his pencil and give her his undivided attention. 'Yes?'

And that was hardly an encouraging response. 'Last night—'

'Thea, you do not need to be in any way concerned that I will take last night as a *carte blanche* to impose on you again.'

'You did not impose,' she protested. 'I asked you.'

'I know, but I mean, in future.' He looked about as eager as a man discussing an invitation to a three-hour poetry reading. 'You were curious and we had behaved in a manner calculated to inflame anyone's passions. I hope that at least it has removed any dread of the act that Meldreth's actions gave you.'

'Of course,' Thea agreed, finding the syllables stuttering on her tongue. 'Certainly it has.' The subtext to his words was clear enough to read. He was her friend so he had not wanted to snub her when she asked, he was concerned that she had been left with a horror of intercourse after Anthony's clumsy wooing and he had been sufficiently aroused by the situation to find it no actual hardship. If Rhys had wanted to make love with her again he would have kissed her the moment they were alone, would have told her—even if it had been a lie—that she had been wonderful last night, would have acted, in other words, like a lover.

'Thank you,' Thea said and rose to her feet. 'I am truly grateful for the care you took of me. No, please don't get up. I must go and ring for a bath or I will ache all over tomorrow!' That was really a very convincing little laugh, she congratulated herself as she left the room. It was strange how tired she felt, but that was due to spending the day in the saddle, no doubt. And she felt queasy. But that was an incautious indulgence in nougat.

Bother the dust, it seemed to have got everywhere, even into her eyes. Thea stopped outside her own bedchamber door and groped for a handkerchief to catch the solitary tear as it began to trickle down her face.

Stop it, she told herself. *You had one night of complete bliss, you slept in his arms, you will remember it always. Now have some pride or he will guess you are within a hair's breadth of going on your knees and begging him to make love to you again.*

Thea scrubbed at her face, forced a cheerful expression onto her face and pushed open the door. 'I absolutely must have a bath, Polly, or I will be as stiff as a board in the morning.'

Chapter Sixteen

At least Giles had not noticed anything amiss, Thea thought as she shaded her eyes against the bright morning sunlight and listened to him expounding on the history of the Arc de Triomphe. Rhys appeared to be genuinely engrossed. *And why should he not be?* she chided herself. *He is an intelligent and cultured man, and to view sites such as this is one of the reasons a gentleman embarks on the Grand Tour.*

'It was built to commemorate the conquest of the Gauls by Julius Caesar,' Giles explained. 'The detail shows his superiority in both land and sea warfare, as you can see from the anchors and ropes here and the prisoners on the other side of the arch.'

Thea told herself to stop moping and take an interest. 'Through here?' She walked into the shade of the massive central arch.

'They are in a state of nature,' Giles called after her. 'You may not wish—'

Having seen Rhys in such a state she was hardly likely to be outraged. 'I am certain the cultural and historical significance outweighs any scruples of that kind,' Thea said, and wondered if she had caught the fleeting glimpse of a smile on Rhys's lips.

She studied the battered carvings with a purely intellectual interest, she assured herself, although it was hard not to reflect how much more beautiful Rhys's body was than anything the sculptor had depicted.

When she strolled back to the other side both he and Giles had pocket sketchbooks in their hands. 'May I see?' *Rhys sketching?* 'But these are very good! I had no idea you could draw.'

'I took it up at Oxford. There was a group of us who were interested. It made a focus for walking holidays. I am competent, that is all. Benton has a much surer touch.'

Giles handed her his book readily. He had obviously studied more than Rhys and the standard was more than amateur, but somehow it seemed academic and lacking in the life that Rhys's rapid sketches held.

'You have a real talent,' she praised.

'Thank you.' Giles smiled diffidently. 'You should join us. We could acquire some watercolours and we could all work together.'

'Me?' Thea laughed. 'I cannot draw, let alone paint in watercolour.'

'You are too modest! I thought all young ladies learned as a matter of course.'

'Thea turned her drawing master grey,' Rhys remarked. 'Our godmother always engaged one for the summer when we stayed with her. He would have a gaggle of intense young ladies around him like a duck with ducklings—and Thea would be out in the middle of the lake in the rowing boat or up a tree or persuading the grooms to let her try out every horse in the stables.'

'You sound disapproving. You always encouraged me at the time.'

'I was no more sensible than you were,' Rhys said with something of a snap. 'Or should I say that boys have no concept of the attributes a young lady needs to acquire to fit herself for her future role in life.'

That was clear enough, Thea thought as she handed his sketchbook back to Giles with a smile that seemed to be frozen on her lips. *I was fun to*

*play with when I was a tomboy—now I am a hoy-
den, unfit for a respectable marriage.*

'I have saved the best until last,' Giles remarked
as he slid the book into the pocket in his coat-tails.
'We have seen the cathedral and the arch, now it
is time for the Roman theatre. We must walk back
through the old town, but it is not far.'

He offered his arm to Thea, who listened with
only half an ear to his explanation that the hill in
front of them was the old castle of the princes of
Orange. Behind her she was conscious of Rhys's
footsteps on the cobbled pathway and imagined
his eyes on her back. Imagined his thoughts and,
worse, his regrets.

Even so, the sight of the theatre stopped her in
her tracks and knocked any other thoughts from
her head. Battered red sandstone towered up like a
cliff face, pigeons wheeling across its facade from
the niches and cracks that studded it.

Giles was talking about the emperor Augustus
and ten thousand spectators and something about
acoustics, but she was still gawking at it and hardly
listened as he led them inside.

'If you climb the steps to the seats at the back,
we can try the sound,' he said with enthusiasm,

urging Thea and Rhys forward across the semi-circular area. 'Be careful, the stone is very worn.'

'We had better do what our tutor tells us,' Rhys remarked, low voiced. 'Give me your hand—these are very uneven.'

In the heat, neither of them was wearing gloves. *More hoydenish behaviour on my part,* Thea thought bitterly as Rhys's grip tightened and her heart began to pound. The steps between the tiers of stone seats were broken in many places, so they had to climb from seat to seat. After the first few, with Thea grabbing desperately at her skirts to stop them riding up with the height she had to lift her leg, Rhys simply dropped her hand and boosted her from one to the other.

His hands were sure and firm around her waist and he was so close her senses reeled with the scent of hot man. If she closed her eyes, she could imagine herself back in his arms, imagine the musk of their lovemaking.

'I should have insisted we stop so you could have a glass of lemonade before embarking on this,' Rhys remarked. 'And I ought to have warned you to put on sturdier shoes.'

His words were so alien to the remembered sound of his voice, the gasped words of passion, the groan deep in his throat when he thrust deep into her, that Thea opened her eyes, lost for a moment. Below her on the dusty theatre floor was the small figure of Giles, pacing to and fro. The stone tiers of seats fell away like a crumbling mountain slope and above her the swifts dived and screamed in the hot blue sky.

'Steady!' Rhys caught her by the arm as she swayed. 'I thought you were fine with heights.'

'I am.' She shook off his restraining arm. 'I was dizzy for a second, that is all.' She had been remembering passion and intimacy and desire. Rhys had been thinking about lemonade and practicalities.

'We had better sit down, in that case. I will signal to Benton that we are ready for him to begin.'

'What is he going to do? He will have to shout if we are to hear him here.'

'Listen,' Rhys said. 'I have heard of this.'

And then Giles spoke. He was not shouting, or even speaking loudly, she realised, entranced. His voice reached her as clearly as though he was standing just in front of her and speaking conversationally. 'What is he saying?' It was Latin and she could read that a little, but she had never heard it spoken.

'It is from Caesar's *Gallic Wars*,' Rhys said. 'Trust Benton not to spout poetry.'

'The triumphal arch put him in mind of it, I suppose. How intimate it sounds.' How would she feel if it was Rhys down there speaking verse, something romantic? This place was magical—surely he felt it?

Rhys got to his feet and walked off around the arc of the seats, head tilted as he listened. 'Interesting effect. I don't understand the science. I must read up on it.'

Obviously he did *not* feel the romance. Thea slid to the edge of her perch and dropped the few inches to the next seat, sat and repeated the process. It would do her walking dress no good at all, but it was better than having Rhys's hands on her, so practical and impersonal. Touching her, being close to her, did not affect him at all, it seemed. Thank goodness she had said nothing to lead him to think she wanted to resume their intimacy.

'That was fascinating,' Thea said enthusiastically when she reached Giles, who came up the bottom steps to help her. She turned and looked up to where Rhys was silhouetted against the sky. 'Are you coming down?' she said, half doubting her words would reach him.

He waved, but then sat down and held up his sketchbook.

'We will see you at luncheon?'

Rhys made a gesture that seemed to encompass *perhaps* and *don't wait for me* and *goodbye.*

'What about you?' Thea asked Giles. Really, with the bright smiles and the air of unconcern she was managing to summon, she was missing a promising career on the stage. 'I would like to go and look around the shops this afternoon, but I can take Polly with me. You will want to explore and sketch, I am sure.'

'If you are sure?' Giles offered her his arm and they turned and left Rhys on his lonely eyrie.

'Oh, yes. I saw some delightful printed fabrics and there are lavender oils and soaps…. I will be in terrible trouble with Rhys for buying more things, I have no doubt, but the temptation is too great.' Her laughter would reach him up there, she was certain. He would know she was quite unconcerned.

Thea came down to breakfast the next day to find the two men making somewhat stilted conversation over wide cups of milky coffee. She paused, unseen just before the doorway, and listened.

'But you obviously want to push on to Avignon

now and I want to spend some more time sketching here.' That was Giles.

Rhys made a sound that might have been agreement.

'How long do you intend to stay in Avignon?' Giles asked.

'A few days. I want to buy wine to be shipped home, see the sights, visit the dealers for artwork. Then on to Aix and down to Toulon to take ship around the coast to Genoa. What are your plans?'

He sounded a trifle cool, Thea thought. Had he and Giles somehow fallen out?

'I will spend a few more days here and then go directly to Arles. I intend on making my way to Marseilles and after that I will take ship along the coast to Viareggio and then inland—Lucca, Florence, Rome.'

'You are leaving us?' Thea entered the room and both men rose with a scrape of chair legs on the terracotta tiles. To be alone with Rhys would be blissful, and yet Giles's company had kept her anchored in the real world, a bulwark against losing herself utterly to hopeless dreams.

'I think I must. It has been delightful to journey with you and I am deeply in your debt for rescuing me at the roadside, but we all have our own route to travel now, do we not?'

Was she imagining he put some emphasis on the last, innocuous question? Warning or encouragement, she could not tell. 'We will miss you,' Thea said warmly.

'We will, indeed,' Rhys added, and to her relief he sounded regretful and not as though he was anxious to see the back of Giles.

Polly packed away the lengths of charming printed cloth in rose and gold, green and blue, and found corners for soaps and oils and Rhys had nothing to criticise when the vehicles were loaded and they rode away from the inn.

It had been hard to say goodbye to Giles, although they promised to write. 'Keep faith,' he murmured as he kissed her cheek. 'Hold on to that love.'

Thea turned and waved one last time, and then urged her horse up to keep pace with Rhys. He was quiet, and she wondered at it. Did he dislike her kissing Giles? Or perhaps he regretted the other man's departure and had valued a buffer between himself and her.

But she could not read his mood and he had very

little to say to her at all, beyond perfectly amiable commonplace remarks. 'Are you sure that wide-brimmed hat is sufficient shade from the sun?' he asked as they emerged from the cover of the town walls. 'The sun is getting very hot now and you will complain if your nose becomes pink!'

'Quite sure. And I have taken a leaf out of your book and found a linen jacket to replace the woollen one with my riding habit.' Rhys looked casual, relaxed and altogether edible, Thea thought. His hair was overlong now, for Hodge appeared to have no influence with the scissors. His skin was tanning golden in the sun, unlike poor Giles, who had turned pink and freckled, and he had changed leather breeches and his wool coat for heavy cotton and linen.

There should be a law against men with muscled forearms like that taking off their coats and rolling their sleeves up.

'Very sensible,' he commented on her jacket. 'We have no need to hurry today at all. Avignon is a very short journey, so we can linger over luncheon in the shade or explore anything along the way that takes our interest.'

Thea smiled and agreed and assured herself that this calm friendliness was what was prudent, was what she wanted—and was what she had told Rhys she expected. It was beyond foolish to feel as though she had been spurned, that her heart was breaking, that she was a hundred times unhappier than she had been before, when Rhys was simply a dream she had resigned herself to losing.

An hour later the sun was bouncing off white limestone, the road was dusty and the air was heavy with the scent of thyme, lavender and a dozen herbs Thea could put no name to. The buzz of the cicadas had gone from strange to irritating to simply part of the atmosphere and everyone had lapsed into a state of relaxation that would have scandalised polite London society.

Rhys had shed his coat and neckcloth and was letting his horse walk a zigzag pattern from one patch of shade to the next. Hodge and Polly had abandoned the inside of the coach and were perched up on the box with Tom, staring round as they fanned themselves with their hats and passed a flask of what Thea hoped was lemonade from one to another. Rhys had sent the chaise with the post boys, impatient with the strange dawdling of the English, on ahead to advise the landlord of their arrival in time for dinner.

Beside them the Rhone wove its slow way in intricate braids separated by sandbanks and islands, some wooded with scrubby trees, others bare. 'Phew.' Thea took off her hat and fanned her flushed face with it. 'That water looks tempting.'

Rhys had turned off the road and was splashing along the shoreline. 'I was thinking that.' He sounded himself again, relaxed and cheerful. 'We need a sheltered branch where there is no current—the main channel is not safe.'

'We are going swimming?' Thea urged her mare down to join Rhys. The horse went down on its haunches as it slid over the low bank of rounded river pebbles, sending driftwood shooting in all directions. 'Wonderful! All we need is one of these side channels where there are some bushes for changing.' Thea craned her neck. 'Look, that's perfect, just ahead. The water is flowing enough to prevent it stagnating, but there are no swirls and currents. You men can go behind those low willows and Polly and I can use these rocks.'

'Men, my lady?' Tom pushed his hat back on his head and scratched his ear. 'I don't rightly hold with getting wet all over. Soaks in, if you ask me. Ain't healthy.'

'Very well, you may water the horses, then sit

under a tree in the shade and relax while the rest of us swim.'

'What, like at the seaside, my lady?' Polly sounded shocked, but she looked at the water with longing. 'We haven't got any bathing machines.'

'We don't need them.' Thea kicked her foot free of the stirrup and slid down. 'We go in wearing our shifts and the men—' she stifled a giggle '—the men will wear undergarments.'

Rhys was already out of the saddle. He tossed his reins to the coachman and sat on a boulder to pull off his boots. 'I'll try it first and make certain it is safe.'

He was rolling down his second stocking before Thea realised that Polly was tugging her arm. 'My lady! His lordship is taking his clothes off!'

'Goodness, yes, so he is. Behind the bushes with us, Polly.' She did not even try to pretend to herself that in her mind she was back all those years ago when the children had splashed and tumbled in and out of the lake without a care in their innocent heads except for what would be said about their sodden clothes when they got home for dinner. She had been watching Rhys with a very adult yearning and it would *not* do.

'Quite safe!' he called. 'Sandy bottom, gentle

flow. Come on, Hodge. We'll swim down a bit and leave the ladies some privacy.'

'Ladies,' Polly said with a giggle. 'Fancy his lordship calling me a lady.'

'We're all the same under our clothes,' Thea said, helping Polly with her buttons. *All cats are grey in the dark and one woman between the sheets is much as another, no doubt.* She had tried not to think where Rhys had got his bedroom skills from and now she gave herself a brisk mental shake. 'Just leave your chemise on. They'll dry quickly enough on the bushes afterwards.'

She peeped around the bushes. Two dark wet heads bobbed at the other end of the channel, both tactfully facing downstream. Tom was already asleep, propped under a spreading willow. 'Come on, Polly. Can you swim?'

'No, my lady, but I'll just bob about, like.' They tiptoed into the water. 'It's cold!'

'Better once you are right in.' Thea took a run and ducked under. 'Lovely,' she called as Polly bravely followed suit. Then they were both splashing and laughing and the men turned cautious heads to make certain they were safely immersed.

Don't look, don't imagine. Once they would have been diving, catching each other by the ankle, playing and teasing. But not now. Thea turned onto her back and floated, feeling the sun warm on her front while the water beneath was chilled and refreshing. She closed her eyes, paddled vaguely with her hands to keep station and let her mind go blank.

'Beware, here comes Ophelia,' a voice said by her ear and she sat up with a start, forgot where she was and promptly sank. It was deep here, her feet did not find bottom, but she opened her eyes in the brown gloom and swam confidently upwards. Legs, pale, with paler cotton drawers plastered to them by the current, loomed into sight. They trod water and then there was a convulsion as the man upended and dived down. *Rhys.*

He saw her, reached out, but she made a little gesture of reassurance and broke the surface, spluttering. 'The current is faster than I thought,' she called to the other two, who were gazing tactfully in the other direction.

'Rhys?' She looked around. No sign of him. Thea splashed round in a circle, treading water. *Cramp? A snag of dead branches? Clinging weed?* She was about to dive under when hands took her around the waist, tossed her upwards and she fell back with a great splash and a shriek.

'You wretch,' she spluttered, dragging wet hair out of her face.

'Pax,' Rhys called. He had taken refuge behind Hodge.

'Coward!'

'I know where I am safe.' He was grinning like the boy she remembered from so long ago and her heart contracted with love for him and with nostalgia for a time when all was innocent and uncomplicated.

She realised, with a jolt, that she was happy. Whatever had passed between them, however much she might love him in vain, she and Rhys were back on their old terms of friendship. 'I have a long memory,' Thea threatened, trying hard not to laugh as she swam back to Polly as decorously as she could manage.

'Snails in my slippers?' Rhys called after her.

Thea rolled onto her back and assumed her best society expression and voice. 'You may have reverted to thirteen years of age, Rhys Denham, but I have put no snails in slippers since I was eight.' That reduced even Hodge to hoots of laughter and Rhys… It was clear Rhys attached no importance to their night together.

Chapter Seventeen

It had been almost time for the evening meal when they finally arrived in one of Avignon's smarter hostelries, close by the Porte du Rhone. They'd still been rather damp about the underwear and decidedly relaxed.

'The proprietor obviously thinks the circus has come to town,' Thea remarked as they met in the hallway an hour later. 'Either that or he will expect all English visitors to arrive removing water weed from their hair.'

'The place is like a morgue,' Rhys complained. He had been looking forward to dinner, to enjoying good food and wine while watching Thea laughing. She seemed to have recovered her poise after their reckless interlude, and it was good to have her so comfortable with his company again. He only wished he could put it behind him so easily, but desire was not to be suppressed.

'I was told it was clean and comfortable,' he grumbled now, focusing on that and not on the memory of her slim waist as he had caught her in the water, as near naked in her clinging shift as made no difference. There had been a moment as their eyes had met, the second before she hit the water, when he had imagined he'd seen a yearning as intense as his. *Wishful thinking.*

'It *is* perfectly clean and well appointed,' Thea pointed out.

Rhys felt a perverse desire to disagree. 'I suppose it is a superior establishment, but I do not fancy eating my dinner in a private dining room that looks as though it was decorated for one of the gloomier popes.'

'I was forgetting that the popes were here for some of the Middle Ages.' Thea tucked her hand into his elbow and he had to consciously keep himself from squeezing it against his ribs. 'Were they gloomy?'

'Probably not. There's a very splendid papal palace and acres of vineyards—I would wager they had rather a good time.'

'I wonder what the music is.' Thea went out to the front terrace and Rhys followed her.

'There is a festival, *madame.*' The proprietor

came through the doors as she spoke. 'One trusts the noise will not disturb you.'

'It sounds delightful. Will there be food down there?'

The man looked down his nose. 'Rustic fare, *madame*. The eating places of the townspeople, vendors with stalls. Wine sellers.' He made a very Gallic flicking motion of dismissal with his fingertips.

'Sounds excellent,' Rhys said. 'We will eat out. Hodge!'

'My lord?' The valet emerged from the shadows.

'Tell Polly and Tom we're going down to the fair and you can all have the evening off. All right?' He raised an eyebrow at Thea.

'That sounds wonderful. I would like to try the local food.' She adjusted her shawl over her shoulders, took his arm again and made for the steps.

They strolled amidst the old stone buildings, gilded by the setting sun, then wove their way through narrow alleyways and across tiny squares, headed for the music and then followed the smell of roasting meat. The Place du Palais had three great fires that had obviously been nursed since early morning—a whole ox, two sheep and three pigs were turning on spits with waiters hurrying to and fro between them and the tables grouped around to form impromptu eating places.

Other stallholders shouted their wares from boards laden with pies, breads, salads, sweet-meats and fruit. Down the middle of the long open space, dodging the cursing waiters and tripping each other up, a group of men were laying boards over the cobbles.

'A dance floor. What fun.'

'You want to dance?' Rhys asked with a sinking heart. He danced out of duty, because it was expected of a gentleman, and he always felt a fool promenading about, despite being assured by any number of young ladies—with much fluttering of lashes—that he was an excellent dancer.

'I love to dance,' Thea said firmly.

They strolled around the *place* amidst the ladies in their local traditional costume, skirts wide with frothing white petticoats, lace in their headdresses and at cuff and throat, the men with coloured waistcoats and wide sashes. One side was dominated by the Palais des Papes, more a fortress than a religious building, Rhys thought.

'This one,' Thea decided and stopped by a group of tables, each topped with a spotless chequered cloth, some red and white, some blue and white.

'See how busy this is, which should mean it is good. It is not too near the fires and there is a table here with a good view of the dance floor.'

Rhys pulled out chairs, settled Thea at the table and clicked his fingers for the waiter. 'Bring us a good selection of what you would recommend. And as for wine, a Châteauneuf-du-Pape.'

The waiter suggested adding some of the local *crémant*. 'As sparkling as the *demoiselle*'s eyes, *monsieur*,' he said, and hurried off.

'I cannot wait,' Thea said. 'Good food, wine, music, dancing. Bliss. You do dance these days, don't you, Rhys?'

'Not if I can help it, no,' he responded. His mood had soured again with the waiter's mildly flirtatious comment about Thea's eyes. He wanted to be at that little table over there, half-hidden by a drapery of creepers, not here, on display. He wanted to feed her titbits of food, to watch her eyes sparkle with the wine, to hold her hand under the table and steal kisses. And then they would dance, but not in this square under the stars, but in his bed, which was wide and plump with snowy sheets and a goosefeather mattress and the dance would be the ancient pavane of loving...

'Oh. Of course, I expect you do not care for it anymore.'

Her face fell as if he had snubbed her and he supposed he had. How not to hurt her? It was like picking his way across a scatter of broken glass, barefoot with his eyes closed.

'I never did.' Rhys found it impossible to keep the edge out of his voice. 'Serena cared for it, so I danced, that is all.' Now he really had cast a damper over the proceedings. Thea bit her lip, upset, he supposed, that he should mention that name. 'I have little talent for it,' Rhys added, striving for a lighter tone.

The musicians started to group together, fiddle players, drummers, various woodwind players and one with a strange device that they guessed was a hurdy-gurdy. Couples were coming onto the dance floor, girls giggling and pretending reluctance, young men in their best suits, swaggering and showing off, older couples, stocky and more sombrely clad, but moving together with the ease of long acquaintance.

'*Madame?*' A pleasant-faced, stocky young man stopped at the table and bowed. 'You would care to dance? If *monsieur* permits?'

Thea jumped to her feet, took the stranger's hand

and left without a glance back at Rhys. He heard her laugh as they took their places in the lines of men and women and say something to the pretty girl on her right. Then the fiddlers stuck a chord and they were off, weaving and spinning, promenading, a human plait.

She turned wrongly, bumped into two other women, righted herself and they laughed good-naturedly, turning her back into the measure. Now the women were waving neckerchiefs over their heads. Thea tugged the lace fichu from her shoulders and used that. She looked beautiful, Rhys thought. Graceful, happy, full of life and enthusiasm, her face transformed with a flush of colour, a wide smile.

When the dance ended, her partner brought her back, bowed and went to the next table in search of another girl. Thea sat down, fanning herself. 'That was such fun!'

Before she could sit down another man approached, bowed. *'Madame? S'il vous plaît?'* He was tall and dark and even Rhys could appreciate that he had looks that would set any woman's heart aflutter.

Thea darted a glance at Rhys. Not asking permission, that was certain, and yet there had been something in her eyes…. Yearning? For what?

He was still puzzling when she turned to the Frenchman. '*Merci, monsieur.* You do not mind, do you, Rhys?' Without waiting for an answer she took his arm and they went back to the dance floor.

'Mind?' Rhys snarled under his breath. *I'll tear his head off if he so much as puts a finger wrong with her.* He glowered at the colourful scene. The dancers were turning, then the women spun beneath their partners' upheld arms. Thea was smiling up at her Frenchman, chatting despite the speed of the steps.

Rhys splashed out more wine and slid farther down in his chair, the glass cupped in both hands, shoulders hunched. He was perilously close to sulking, he told himself. It was bad enough to do something so juvenile, but worse when he wasn't at all sure what he was sulking about.

Thea returned at last, with a small group of eager young men, all pressing her for a dance. And this time she did not so much as glance in Rhys's direction.

He dumped the glass on the table, levered himself out of the chair and strode over to meet her. 'This dance is mine.'

Thea did not take kindly to being ordered about, he knew that of old, but he was determined to win this. He was not going to watch her laughing up into another man's face, happy and carefree. She was damn well going to suffer trodden toes with him.

'I would love to!' Her smile took his breath and Rhys struggled for some poise as she turned to her followers with a pretty apology in French. 'Thank you,' she murmured as she slid her hand into his. It felt small and delicate. Puzzled, Rhys glanced down at her. This was Thea, with confident, strong, long-fingered hands—what was the matter with him? Her immaculate coiffure was coming loose and tendrils of hair curled and fluttered on her brow, which was slightly damp from her exertions.

Desire burned through him like flames licking along his veins, and yet all he wanted was to hold her and keep that smile on her lips, that sparkle in those hazel eyes. The band struck up a lilting air and couples turned into each other's embrace.

'A waltz,' Thea said. 'How dashing. I do not believe the patronesses of Almack's have presented you as an eligible partner, my lord.'

'I am willing to risk the scandal if you are,' Rhys offered, and gathered her firmly into his arms, all sweet curves overlying a lithe strength that only emphasised her femininity. His bad mood vanished like smoke.

Thea looked up, her face serious. 'We have already risked it. And yet... we dance.' There was no regret in her voice, nor teasing, either. Her eyes were soft and held the smile her lips did not. Rhys moved without conscious thought into the opening steps of the dance, feeling that he had been punched in the gut and had no air in his lungs. Could she mean what he thought she meant?

'I would very much like to be that scandalous again,' he said when he had found his voice. 'But I can well understand if you do not. Forgive me for—'

'Yes,' she said.

'Yes?'

'If you truly want to.' He must have looked incredulous, for she shook her head and smiled, despite the blush that was turning her cheeks rosy. 'I said I had no expectations beyond that one night, and I would hate it if you felt obliged by gentlemanly scruples to return to my bed.'

'Gentlemanly scruples should keep me from it,' Rhys said wryly, knowing that nothing on earth was going to do that now. This was madness, but madness with a term to it. How long before they reached Venice and a return to sanity? Two weeks, perhaps. He wanted to invent diversions, convince himself that reaching Venice should involve going via Rome, Naples, Sicily. But he could not. It was not fair to Thea; it was not fair to himself.

'It will not change anything, will it?' she asked now. 'Our friendship, I mean. I felt I had lost you, these past years.'

'You had,' Rhys confessed. 'I think I had lost myself, too. I should have realised that I did not need to cut off the whole of my past simply to leave behind one part of it. Now we will not lose each other again, whatever befalls us. We will write, often, I hope.'

Thea quirked an eyebrow. 'Until your marriage. I doubt your wife would look kindly on a correspondence with an unmarried female.'

His wife. That theoretical, nebulous lady. Rhys knew he had lost sight even of her outline these past few days. All that remained of her was an arid list of requirements. Arid, but safe. Sensible. He'd think of her again once he had left Venice. 'Yes, of course. But you may be back in London by then. We will meet.'

Thea across a dance floor in the arms of another man. Thea married, perhaps. Thea in another man's bed. Or unmarried, available, but not to him because he had married some near stranger with good bloodlines and a placid temperament.

'The music has stopped.'

'And you may stop laughing at me, you provoking chit.' Around them couples were smiling. Some ladies even appeared to be regarding them with a sentimental sigh. 'For goodness' sake, they look as though I've gone down on one knee in the middle of the dance floor, just because I kept turning for a few bars!'

'About a minute, actually. The French are romantics,' Thea said with an abrupt return to her prosaic tone. 'Come and have your supper. It will get cold.'

Of course Rhys cared for her, Thea thought as she picked up a spoon and delved into the first of the interesting platters before them. And he loved her as a friend and, miraculously, he desired her as a woman. But he did not want *her*, not as a wife, not as a lover for ever. *We will write*, he had said. And when he was married no doubt she would be invited to dinner and to parties at his town house or to stay at the Norfolk estate.

It had been foolish to mention his marriage. What had she expected? That he would drop to one knee, as he had joked just now, and declare that he had been blind, that he had loved her all along and they must marry at once? He was treating her precisely as she had asked. She would be delivered to Godmama, much educated in the sensual arts and with her heart in tatters, for now she knew the adult man as a friend, and a lover and a companion, all day and every day. She would know him as well, if not better, than a wife.

Rhys reached towards the plate of cheese-and-herb pastries. 'Oh, no, you don't, that's the last one.' Thea pounced on the remaining flaky morsel. It melted on her tongue, an instant's pleasure. That was what she must do, live for the instant. Then, when Rhys had left, she would rebuild her life with all the courage she had. *As if he had died.*

They finished the food with sighs of mutual pleasure, then fell silent. Or possibly Rhys was simply distracted by the subtle assaults he was launching on her composure. His arm lay warm across the back of her chair and his thigh touched hers beneath the cover of the cheerful tablecloth. Both limbs were an incitement to lean into their strength; both promised a leashed power that made her shiver with anticipation. From the slight curve of Rhys's lips she knew he could feel that tremor.

'Shall we go?' Rhys stood and Thea looked up at him, tall, dark, broad-shouldered, somehow un-mistakably English against the golden stone, lit now by flickering torches. Desire quivered through her as he took her hand and then trapped it hard against his side as she came to her feet. *I will be-come addicted to him,* Thea thought with a sud-den plunge into despair. *I will be like a laudanum user, only half-alive without his touch. If I was strong, I would tell him no. This should end here. But I will not.*

They turned at the mouth of a dark alleyway to look back at the festive scene. 'There are Polly and Hodge, dancing.' Rhys pointed at the two figures, Polly, lively and laughing, and Hodge, upright and respectable as ever, even in the midst of a country dance, a great grin on his face.

'At least they are happy.' She spoke her thought aloud and Rhys looked down at her.

'And you are not? Ah, Thea...' He stepped back into the darkness and pulled her into his arms. 'Tell me what you want.'

Chapter Eighteen

'Tell me what you want.'

This was the moment to be strong and sensible. The moment to tell him it was a mistake, that they should resist this attraction and to leave him quite clear that her actions were simply driven by sexual desire.

But if to love was to be weak, then so be it. She would have to find her strength soon enough, because she would not wallow in despair and loss. After Rhys she would rebuild her life, but she had perhaps two weeks to give him everything but the words.

'I want to be with you. I want to make love with you again. I want to spend the night in your arms.' It felt sinful and wonderful to be like this in the open air, in a dark alley in a foreign city pressed against the aroused body of her lover.

'That seems clear enough.' Rhys's voice rumbled in her ear as she pressed her cheek to his shirtfront. He turned and she was trapped against the wall. 'I tried this in a Paris alleyway and got threatened with a hatpin for my pains.' There was laughter in his voice and a husky anticipation of passion. 'I wanted to kiss you then. What will happen if I kiss you here?'

'Try.' Thea put her arms around his neck and ran her fingers into his hair, closed them tight and pulled his head down.

It must have hurt, but he simply growled, deep in his throat. 'You want to play rough games, do you?'

She was not certain what he meant, but it sounded…exciting. 'Yes,' she managed to get out before Rhys's mouth crushed down on hers. He lifted her, his hands spanning her waist, and raised his leg so she was riding his thigh, her feet off the ground, her back to the wall, her full weight bearing down on the point where her body ground against his.

Rhys slid one hand between them to cup her breast, his fingers teasing at the nipple through the fine fabrics until somehow he freed it from the constriction of her stays.

Thea moaned against his mouth as his tongue plunged in, filling her with the taste of him. His fingers rolled and pinched the hard peak past the point of discomfort into a thrilling, shocking dazzle of excitement that flashed like lightning to her core. It was uncomfortable, exciting, wild. The wall was unyielding, his body as hot and as hard as the stone. She tried to move, to rub against the hard muscle of his thigh to reach for the pleasure that seemed just out of reach. She felt full, swollen, wet down there. 'I need...' she panted.

'Tell me.'

'I need to move.'

'No. I am in control here.' He left her nipple, slid his hand down, bunched up her skirts and pushed his fingers between his own leg and the swollen folds that ached for him. 'Is that what you want?'

'Yes. Rhys...please.'

Then he touched her, one long, sliding stroke perfectly placed, and she shattered, sobbing, limp in his arms.

'Can you stand?'

Thea found herself with both feet on the ground, Rhys still holding her pressed between his body and the wall. 'I think so.'

'Good. I cannot see our host approving of me

sweeping you through the front door and up the stairs in my arms.' He eased away and took her arm.

'A pity, it would be so romantic.' She sighed with pure contentment, all her dark worries fled. 'The darkness and the starlight. These ancient buildings, the warm air and the scents. The music…'

'Venice will be more so. Gondolas and beautiful palazzos reflected in the canals.'

Venice would be wonderful, and it would be the end. Once she was safe with Godmama, Rhys would leave. There would be no romance in Venice, only safety. Safety from a drab half-life, safety from the pain of being with Rhys. 'I am resolved to enjoy every moment as I live it,' Thea said, pushing the thoughts away. 'Tonight, teach me to make love to you, Rhys. Show me how to give you pleasure.'

'You already do.' His voice was husky.

'You are being careful with me, I know. Show me, Rhys.' She sensed both his arousal and his reluctance to what? Shock her? 'It excites me to think of touching you. I want to drive you wild.'

'Continue talking like that and you will have succeeded. Talking is even more powerful than thinking, sometimes.'

'We're here.' Thea made herself walk sedately up the steps to the front door. *'Bonsoir, monsieur.'* She nodded to the proprietor. 'I'll retire, I think, my lord,' she added to Rhys, 'and leave you to your brandy.'

'Goodnight, Lady Althea.' She heard him talking to the Frenchman, discussing Cognac. When she reached the landing she picked up her skirts and ran to her chamber. There was something she had bought in Orange, just for Rhys, never thinking he would see it.

She had bathed before they went out, so now she threw off her clothes and sponged herself all over with the tepid water on the nightstand, dabbed rosewater behind her ears, between her breasts and behind her knees. The nightgown she had bought slid over her curves like the water of the Rhone had done that afternoon, silky, fluid, semitransparent, honey coloured. Her hands went to the pins holding her hair up and then left them. Rhys liked to take it down; she had learned that already.

What else might he like? She was going to find out and the waiting was killing her. Thea paced back and forth, the new silken gown swishing around her ankles. Would he like it? The *vendeuse* had assured her it would bring any lover to his knees.

The sharp intake of breath behind her was all the warning she had that Rhys was in the room. He closed the door and leaned back against it. 'Is this my birthday?' He fumbled behind him with none of his usual coordination and managed to turn the key in the lock. 'You no longer believe you are plain, do you, Thea?'

'I am not beautiful. Rhys, you do not have to flatter me—it is more than enough that you desire me.'

He pushed away from the door and began to walk towards her, shedding clothes as he came. Neckcloth, coat and waistcoat fell to the floor. 'No, you aren't beautiful.' He heeled off his shoes. 'You are extraordinary.' He dragged his shirt over his head and dropped it. 'You leave me speechless,' he said as he unfastened his breeches and kicked those and his stockings out of the way.

Thea swallowed at the sight of all that male magnificence right in front of her. 'Your body is communicating quite adequately without words,' she managed. His erection stirred as if it had a life of its own. 'But you had best find the words to tell me what to do.'

'Explore. You have me at your mercy, do what you will.' His eyes were half-shut, his hands fisted at his sides, his chest with its light pelt of dark hair rising and falling with his breathing. 'Men are very visual animals—we are aroused by what we see. And our minds are aroused by what we hear,' he added, his gaze fixed on her lips. 'And what we imagine.'

So much control and so much banked heat. What would happen if she forced him to even exert even greater control? Thea padded forward and threaded her fingers into the hair on his chest. Rhys lifted his hands. 'No, don't touch, leave them by your side. I am exploring.'

To her surprise he obeyed, even when she raked her nails lightly over his nipples and he growled, deep in his throat. A big cat, provoked, she thought, hardly daring to breathe.

She slid her hands down, over the rippling, corded muscles of his stomach, across to his flanks, down his thighs, ignoring the reflexive thrust of his hips that demanded she touch him where he most wanted. 'Lie down on the bed. Face down,' she added and was rewarded by the flare of curiosity in his eyes.

Still in the silken nightgown Thea climbed onto

the bed and straddled his thighs. She leaned forward and palmed his buttocks, intrigued by how hard the muscle became as it tightened under her hands. She slid them up, her thumbs following the groove of his spine, stroked them over the scars and healing bruises from the accident. 'Where do you get all this muscle from?' she asked, bending low so her nipples touched his back through the silk.

'Riding, sparring, fencing, swimming.'

'I am taking off the nightgown,' Thea murmured. She stroked it down his back and over his buttocks, and his hands fisted in the thick white cotton of the bedspread. 'Now I am taking out my hairpins and letting down my hair.' She knelt up and bent to sweep it across his shoulders, up and down until he shivered beneath her, muscles bunching with his effort to stay in control.

'What are you doing now?' Rhys rasped when she sat back to recover her breath.

What would drive him wild? Dare she? Thea murmured, 'Touching my breasts.'

Rhys rolled faster than she could react. Thea found herself pinned beneath him, staring up into dark blue eyes burning in a face stark with desire. 'You are more provoking than the most skilled courtesan could ever be. It is all instinct and honesty with you, isn't it? No wiles, just natural, sensual skill.'

'Skill?' she faltered. 'But I don't know what I am doing.'

'You are driving me wild, that is what you are doing.' He caught her wrists and held them one-handed above her head so he could nuzzle her breasts, use teeth and lips and tongue.

'I was…exploring,' Thea gasped, writhing against his hold on her wrists, 'and you stopped me. Next time I will tie your hands to the bed head with my stockings and then I can do what I like.' Rhys went very still. 'Would you dislike that?'

'I have never wanted to lose that much control,' he said slowly and ran his tongue over his bottom lip. 'But perhaps…'

'It excites you.' Thea arched up against the rigid evidence of just how much.

'*You* excite me.' He dipped his head to brush his cheek, rough with the evening regrowth of his beard, over her sensitive nipples. 'You could probably suggest making love in a bath of cold custard and it would be arousing, you witch.'

'I don't think—' Thea broke off, panting, and

curled her legs around his hips. 'I don't think they make custard in France.'

'Crème anglaise.' Rhys gasped and eased into her on one long stroke, hot and hard and over-whelming.

'Whipped cream,' she murmured against his mouth as she rose to meet him. 'Chocolate sauce...'

'Thea.' Rhys dropped his forehead to hers and held himself still. She could feel his heart ham-mering. 'If you mention one more sweet, slithery foodstuff or item of underwear or thing to tie me to, then I am going to lose control completely.'

'Warm strawberry jam, corset strings, bed posts,' she whispered as she twisted to curl her tongue into his ear. 'Oh...Rhys!'

An hour later Thea snuggled up against him, sleepy, satiated, warm. Rhys *had* lost control and had been hard, urgent, almost desperate, which was very satisfying. And then, of course, he had to make up for it by making slow, tender, exqui-sitely careful love to her. It seemed incredible that she could excite him so, could satisfy him. Could even, she thought with a sleepy smile, shock him a little. What would it be like to have that big, beautiful body helpless while she investigated what pleased him?

'I can feel you smiling.'

'I was thinking that if I tied you up I would never dare untie you.'

'I will teach you knots so I can free myself and you can have a head start. Now go to sleep before I give in to the temptation to kiss you all over— and you know where that would lead.'

Three days later the landlord was standing on the steps of the Porte du Rhone, surveying their cavalcade of chaise, coach and two riding horses with the smug air of a man who had just received a substantial payment.

Thea felt subdued, but Rhys seemed even more so. *How strange—we've been so happy here. Perhaps it is simply sadness to be leaving that makes us both so serious.* Rhys said nothing, simply tossed her up into the saddle and mounted himself, but when they had left the city and taken the road south-west towards Aix, she challenged him, 'Why the frown, Rhys?'

'That was an idyll—now we are back to reality.'

And very scratchy and real it felt, too. But what was the matter with Rhys? She was the one who was in love, the one who was fighting the entire time to keep her fears for the future under control. Strangely, they seemed to get worse the farther away from England she travelled.

'If you are going to be so bad-tempered, I could wish Giles back!'

'Regretting you did not accept his offer of marriage?'

'For goodness' sake, Rhys. Of course not. But he is a friend.'

'Rather more, I think.'

'He is a clergyman, even though he does not minister. I found him easy to confide in.'

'What? You confessed all to him, did you? Did he give you penances for your sin of sleeping with me?' He looked like thunder. Sounded like it.

'No! Certainly not. I was able to talk to him about something else that was on my mind, that is all.'

Rhys's saturnine expression deepened. 'Your mysterious love? Is it on your conscience that you make love with me while you have those feelings for another man?'

Thea knew she was blushing; she could feel the heat mount up her throat to her cheeks. What could she say? *You and he are the same man?* 'You are jealous, that is all,' she shot back. If she feigned temper, that would explain her flushed face. The mare she was riding skittered sideways, unnerved by whatever she could feel along the reins.

'Watch your horse,' Rhys snapped. 'Of course I am not jealous. What need have I of jealousy?'

'And what does that mean, pray? That no one would bother with me or that you are such a superior specimen of manhood that you cannot conceive of a female straying from your side? Oh...' She realised what she had said as soon as it escaped her lips. Rhys's face was expressionless, his eyes fixed on the road ahead. Only his horse's sudden toss of the head betrayed that his hands had tightened on the reins.

'I am sorry. I did not think. Serena...' Her voice trailed away as she lost herself in a morass of words, none of which would call back the ones she had spoken.

Rhys dug his heels in and set off down the road at a canter. 'Come,' he tossed back over his shoulder. After half a mile he reined in and waited for her. The following carriages were out of sight. 'Listen to me,' he said without preamble. 'I trust you, Thea. You do not lie, you do not dissemble and you do not flirt. Other men most certainly would want to take my place, but you would not encourage them. That certainty does not mean that I enjoy the thought that you share secrets with another man, however innocently. I am possessive and you will have to accept that.'

'I did not mean to—'

'To allude to Serena. I understand that. When she ran off with Paul I felt betrayed and used. What I did not feel, I realised once I had sobered up, was heartbroken. I did not love Serena. I am not jealous of Paul and I do not think he *took* her from me. I think she was always his and they used the fact I was dazzled by her for their own ends. Is that clear?'

'You did not love her?' Thea realised she was staring blankly at him. 'You never loved her?'

'I thought I did. I was young, idealistic and in lust. If I had been a little wiser in the ways of women, I would have tumbled her in the summer-house and then, no doubt, the truth would have come out with a slapped face from her and a punch on the nose from Paul. Serena was never going to put herself in a position where she might betray her lover with more than a few sweet words and batted eyelashes in my direction.'

'You think they were lovers?' Thea felt as though

the ground had trembled. Rhys had never been truly in love with Serena? 'What happened to them?' No one had spoken of the pair since that day, not in public and not to her. But Rhys would know, surely?

'I have no idea.' He looked out indifferently over the rolling countryside, dotted with olive trees, rising to the blue hills beyond. 'I told you, I did not care.'

'If you had loved her, you would have cared,' Thea murmured, thinking aloud.

'Exactly.' Rhys's sharp ears had picked up her words. 'That is what convinced me I did not. Now, have I shocked you, you little romantic? I know you think I have been nobly bearing a broken heart and an undimmed image of my golden-haired love all these years.'

'But you *do* believe in love.' Desperate to convince him, Thea leaned out of the saddle and put her hand on his arm. 'The very fact you recognised that you did not feel it for Serena proves it. Rhys, don't you see how much happier you would be if you married a woman you loved, rather than settled for a loveless marriage of convenience?'

'Love led Serena and Paul to betray those who loved and trusted them. They could, for all they knew, have broken me. That is an emotion that is selfish, weakening, dangerously sentimental.'

'Sentimental?'

'Serena no doubt told herself that she was making sacrifices for love, that love is too grand a thing to allow considerations of trust and honour and decency to stand in its way.'

'You cannot blame love for that, only the character of the person who loves....' But he had spurred the horse on, leaving her mouthing her beliefs to the hot, scented air. *Oh, Rhys. You let me dream and now you are going to break my heart.*

Chapter Nineteen

Thea cantered after Rhys, but made no attempt to ride through his dust cloud to catch him. Twice she saw him rein in, turn and stand in his stirrups as if to reassure himself that she was still there, then he cantered on.

She had made him *feel*, she realised. For a contained and self-controlled man such as Rhys, that was probably an unforgivable sin. Now she understood why he wanted a marriage with no emotions attached and why the rumours were that he was rake, a man not to be trusted to give anything more of himself than what a mistress might expect. And he had been avoiding the marriageable girls, the ones he would have to choose from sooner or later if he continued in his determination to marry with his head and not his heart.

There will be two of you unhappy, Thea thought

when at last she saw his bay gelding tied up in the shade outside a wayside inn. *Why not marry me? At least you can trust me. At least you desire me. At least we are friends.*

She slowed the mare to a walk while she digested that thought. *Marriage? Don't be a fool. What are you going to do? Propose to him and ruin your friendship for ever?* As she came closer, Rhys got up from a bench under the vine-covered pergola that stretched along the front of the building. He had been slumped, long legs stretched out, hat discarded beside him.

He strolled across to take her reins, the blue eyes half-closed against the sun, that sinful mouth relaxed into a smile of welcome. Thea was not fooled. He helped her down and, as her body slid down the length of his she looked up, trying to read his eyes. They were implacable, closed, private. Friend or no friend, lover or not, she would get no closer. She had dragged secrets from him, feelings that he had never wanted to speak of, and now he was on his guard. Rhys would no more marry a woman who laid open old wounds, as she had done, than he would forgive Serena for her betrayal.

'Wine or lemonade?'

She saw there was a table under the arbour. Pitchers, glasses and dishes of olives were already set on it. 'Lemonade, please.'

'Have we just had our first lovers' tiff?' Rhys enquired as he handed her the glass of cloudy white liquid,

'Rather more than a tiff, I think,' Thea said coolly. She was not sure she was ready to forgive him, although what his crime was, she was not certain. Making him love her? Breaking her heart? He was not responsible for either. Never having loved Serena? There was still a shameful glow of pleasure deep inside at that knowledge. For being so pig-headed over his own happiness? Yes, that was probably it.

'I do not enjoy having the scabs torn off old wounds,' Rhys said. He lifted the wine pitcher, then put it down again and poured himself some lemonade. 'I prefer to let them heal in peace and quiet. Of course, if you want to tell me all about your lost love, then I will let you probe my wounds all you wish.'

'Thank you, no.' Thea put down her glass and ran a finger down the moisture on the outside, chasing droplets until they pooled at the base, staining the table with a dark patch. 'I will put away my scalpel. Truce?'

'Truce.' He lifted her wet fingers and kissed them. 'Here come the carriages.'

They rode slowly through the starkly beautiful countryside all day, amongst fields of lavender and groves of olives, past stone farm buildings that seemed carved from the rock itself, where barking dogs on long chains made their horses shy. The sky was cloudless and eagles soared, their mewing cries plaintive in the hot air.

Aix-en-Provence was, to Thea's eye, more elegant, more formal and more modern than Avignon. It was a university town, Rhys explained as they strolled along the fashionable Cours Mirabelle under spreading plane trees with the splash of fountains all around them.

Thea wore the best of the half-dress gowns she had bought in Paris with a lace scarf from Lyon thrown over her hair. The town felt so elegant that dressing up for it seemed only right, and Rhys, resplendent in black breeches, dark blue swallow-tail coat and gleaming white linen, had obviously felt the same.

'Where are we going?'

'To a café called Les Deux Garçons. It was opened just before the Revolution and apparently has managed to survive as the place to see and be seen. I thought we would eat at the hotel, but that you might like some refreshment now.'

He was more formal somehow, as though the wicked lover had become a respectable escort. Thea put aside naughty thoughts of silk stockings and bed heads; one glance at Rhys told her that he was going to want to be in total control of events that night.

He was relaxed, charming and—what was it he had called himself? Possessive, that was it, Thea decided. She was flattered that he appeared to find it necessary to guard her quite so carefully, as though the sight of her might cause a stampede of amorous French admirers. A passing gentleman had only to meet her eye, doff his hat and then glance at her companion to hurry on.

'Is there some signal between men that I cannot read?' she asked him, a silver spoon loaded with a luscious confection of cream, fruit and fragile pastry halfway to her lips. 'You have just routed those young gentlemen with one look.'

'Students.' He caught her eye and smiled. 'I told you, I am possessive.'

'But how do you do it?' Thea persisted. Rhys looked at her, all the amusement gone from his face as he lifted one eyebrow fractionally. Thea's pulse leapt. 'Goodness! I can almost hear the clash of antlers.'

'You compare me with a rutting stag, do you?'

'Mmm.' Thea licked the cream from the spoon very slowly, her eyes locked with Rhys's. 'Are we very far from the hotel? We walked around in a circle, I think.'

'Ready for dinner already, despite that confection?' He glanced at her lips. 'You have a tiny smear of cream, just there.' He brushed it with his finger and then licked the tip.

'No, I don't want dinner. I want you.'

The blue fire flared in his eyes. 'I keep thinking you cannot arouse me any more than you do, Thea, and then I find I am wrong.' He gestured for the waiter. 'But how do you intend to distract your maid from the fact that there is a man in your bed?'

'By having the foresight to tell her that I would not need her until I finally retired for the night and suggesting that she and Hodge go and explore the town and have their evening meal out.' Thea gathered her shawl and reticule and stood up. 'I gave her the money to pay for it. She was delighted.'

'And you are smug.' Rhys dropped a kiss on the end of her nose. 'Excellent.'

* * *

Nothing was said, and yet the pace of the journey had slowed. Thea knew that Rhys had intended, that night in Avignon, to be in Venice within the fortnight. Now it had taken them a week to reach Toulon, three days to find a boat that he was prepared to accept, then another week around the coast to Genoa. Rhys had found something to explore at every cove, every village, every little port.

'It is as if time has stood still.' Thea leaned on the ship's rail and watched the scattered lights twinkling like stars along the darkening coastline. Out in the bay the sea was studded with bobbing lights: the fishing boats were at work. 'Where are we?'

'Italian coast somewhere,' Rhys said vaguely. He dipped his head and nuzzled beneath her ear. 'Genoa tomorrow, impatient one.'

'I am not impatient.' She shifted to give him better access. 'Not to arrive, anyway.' This was like a honeymoon, a romantic, sensual, idyllic journey, first through beautiful countryside, now on a placid, gentle sea, every day sunlit with the coast slipping past, every bay and headland a new kingdom to explore.

Thea had given up caring that Polly and Hodge knew that she and Rhys were lovers, just as she closed her mind to the fact that the maid and valet were, too, despite Polly's stated resolve not to give him more than a kiss. They were all adults—besides, she was certain the two would marry just as soon as they arrived somewhere with an Anglican clergyman.

Her mind, distracted by Rhys's mouth on her skin, drifted back to where that chain of thoughts had begun. Honeymoons ended in a married life together—this one would end in separation. A phrase came to her. Was it a song or a poem?

'Rhys, where does the line, "Journeys end in lovers' meeting", come from?'

'What made you think of that? It's Shakespeare. The clown sings it in *Twelfth Night.*' He hummed a few notes. 'We performed it at Eton. Let me see if I can recall it.' When he sang his voice was a rich, clear tenor. Thea realised she hadn't heard him sing since he had been a youth.

"Trip no further, pretty sweeting,
Journeys end in lovers' meeting—
Every wise man's son doth know.
What is love? 'Tis not hereafter;
Present mirth hath present laughter;
What's to come is still unsure:

In delay there lies no plenty,—
Then come kiss me, Sweet-and-twenty,
Youth's a stuff will not endure.''

'Then come kiss me,' he repeated. 'Kiss me, sweeting.'

What is love? The words echoed in her head as she went into his arms. *'Tis not hereafter.* It would last, this loving, only until Venice. That was why Rhys was dragging out the journey, because he was already anticipating its end. She might daydream—his mind was quite clear.

'There it is—Venice. Magical,' Rhys murmured. A heat haze hung over the lagoon, blurring sea and sky, water and mud bank. In the distance, the mirage of the city shimmered, floating.

The small boat that they had taken from the coast skimmed over the water, the men bent to the oars, their efforts scarcely seeming to move them over the vast liquid expanse.

The carriages had been left on the mainland, with Tom to guard them. He was happily ensconced in an inn run by a buxom widow and appeared to be making considerable headway with her, despite not having a word of Italian.

Rhys spread a map of Venice open on his knee and glanced from it to the vista in front of them while the skipper of the boat traced the route with his stubby brown finger.

Godmama had taken a palazzo on one of the canals off the Grand Canal. It sounded impossibly romantic to Thea, who sat, her fingers entwined with Rhys's, and watched the fairy-tale city that marked the end of her fairy-tale journey come slowly closer.

It was all a dream, she thought now. She had a fever, or perhaps had simply not woken up, because this could not be real, could not be the end. Last night Rhys had made love to her with the tenderness of a man parting from his lover for ever. She imagined that a man going out to die in a duel at dawn or setting out on a voyage to the distant Arctic, expecting never to return, might make love like that, as though he was creating a memory almost too fragile to hold. Then, without a word, he had left her and gone back to his own room, something he had not done since Aix, and she had finally allowed herself to weep, silently, into her pillow.

Now the water traffic got busier, the buildings began to loom out of the haze, exotic, like the work of a confectioner spinning architecture out of sugar. Rhys pointed out the Doge's Palace, the massive church of San Giorgio Maggiore, the pillars marking the waterfront of St Mark's Square, but all she could do was stare, unable to focus on one thing out of the shifting scene.

'Santa Maria della Salute,' the boatman said, and they skimmed into a wide canal. Thea unlaced her fingers from Rhys's and stiffened her spine. They had arrived. She was awake, this was real.

'This is the Grand Canal.' Rhys shifted the map on his knee to align it. 'We are almost there.'

Every building lining the canal looked like a palace to Thea. Their walls rose straight from the green water. Gondolas were moored in front of landing stages, small boats laden with everything from barrels to a vast load of hay criss-crossed their path. 'It sounds so different,' she said. 'No carriages, no horses, just people and the lapping of the water.'

'It smells different, too,' Rhys remarked. 'Of the sea and old stone.'

The boat made a sweeping turn into a smaller canal. Walls rose on either side, above them were balconies, now and again stone landing stages jutted into the water, all with their striped mooring poles. *'Ecco, Ca' Riccardo,'* the boatman announced, and brought their vessel alongside a wide platform. In the wall were double-ironwork gates with a courtyard behind them. The boat with Polly and Hodge and more of the luggage came in behind them as Thea schooled her face to show nothing but pleasure. Of course, she wanted to see Godmama again and of course she wanted to be in Venice. Pride kept her from showing any of the other feelings that left her mind dazed with unhappiness and her stomach tense with expected pain.

Hodge pulled the heavy iron ring that hung by the grill. Faintly they heard a bell, then several pairs of feet on stone steps. The grill was thrown open by two liveried footmen, and an imposing, gaunt figure stood in the opening. 'Lady Althea, Lord Palgrave. Welcome to Venice.' He bowed.

'Edgerton!' Rhys ignored the man's bow and shook him vigorously by the hand. 'Good to see you after so many years. I had no idea you had travelled with Lady Hughson. My letter from Paris to say we were on our way has arrived, judging by your lack of surprise.'

It would take more than the unexpected arrival of a few travellers on his damp threshold to surprise Godmama's secretary, Thea thought with a smile.

'Indeed, yes, Lord Palgrave. Allow me to bring you inside.'

They followed him across the courtyard, which Thea supposed served to keep the living rooms well clear of the water in times of flood, up a wide flight of steps and in through imposing wooden doors. It was a palace, she thought, staring around her at the painted, arched ceiling, the high walls, the expanse of inlaid marble floor. Empty, cool, very quiet.

'The salon,' Edgerton said, throwing open yet another set of double doors and ushering them into a lofty chamber with pillared walls, gilded carving and high arched windows, swagged with yard upon yard of crimson brocade. 'I will send for refreshments, but first, I regret, there is a slight problem.'

'A problem you cannot deal with, Edgerton?' As Thea sat down on one of the long sofas, Rhys went to the window and gazed out. 'You surprise me.'

'You are kind enough to say so, my lord. However, this is not a situation I am able to remedy. Your letter arrived and, as her ladyship's secretary, I naturally opened it. Unfortunately, she had left the week before.'

'Left?' Thea stared at him. Of all the things that could go wrong with her plan, it had never occurred to her for a moment that she would not find Godmama here. 'Surely not to go back to England, not if you are still here?'

'Lady Hughson is at present travelling on board the private yacht of Prince Frederico d'Averna.'

'A prince?' Thea said, visions of the Prince Regent swirling through her head.

'Of a very minor principality,' Edgerton said with a faint smile. 'A most amiable gentleman, with a most handsome yacht.'

'It could be an eighty-four-gun ship of the line, for all I care,' Rhys said, stalking away from the window. 'When is she due back?'

'I regret to say that I have no information on that. It could be another month. Or longer. His Royal Highness had the intention of showing her ladyship the island of Sicily, but if the weather remains clement they may well continue around the coast to the Bay of Naples.'

'On board a yacht with a prince,' Thea said faintly. 'That sounds so unlike Godmama.'

'Indeed, Lady Althea.' Edgerton's voice was so dry it would have been used for toast.

'You do not approve of him?'

'I believe he is who he says he is—the introductions were beyond reproach. The vessel is lavishly equipped and appears perfectly seaworthy and well crewed. I have been unable to find anything to the prince's detriment, despite exhaustive enquiries.'

'On whose behalf?' Rhys asked.

'Mine, my lord. I would not countenance Lady Hughson placing herself in such a position with anyone who was not of the utmost respectability.'

'You intrigue me,' Rhys remarked. 'What would you have done if you had found something to his detriment and Lady Hughson did not agree with you?'

'I would have contrived to have the prince removed from her ladyship's orbit,' the secretary said. 'This is Venice after all.'

Thea decided she did not want to know whether the secretary meant murder, kidnapping or, more probably, a nighttime visit from a group of gentlemen with strong persuasive powers.

'How very Gothic of you,' Rhys drawled.

Thea smiled, then realised she was on the verge of bursting out into relieved laughter. No Godmama meant that their idyll was not at an end. She was sorry that Godmama was not there, of course; she loved her and wanted to see her again, but it sounded as though she was having a wonderful adventure of her own.

Then she caught the edge in Rhys's voice and turned to look at him. Whatever he was feeling was not inspiring him to laughter. 'This is a pretty coil,' he said, his mouth a hard line. 'Now what the devil am I going to do with you?'

Chapter Twenty

Thea stared back at him. '*Do with me?* Why, nothing, my lord!'

Now what the blazes is she annoyed about? Rhys suppressed an exasperated sigh. It was he who was responsible for her, he who would have to sort out this mess.

'I can remain here until Godmama returns, can I not, Mr Edgerton?'

'Certainly, Lady Althea. There is a most respectable widow living nearby who has become quite a friend of her ladyship's. I am sure she would be delighted to move here and chaperon you if I were to explain the situation.'

'What situation?' Rhys demanded. One word out of Edgerton that implied that he knew Rhys was anything other than Thea's courier and he would be retrieving his teeth from his gullet.

'That her escort has had to leave Lady Althea here without a female companion,' the secretary rejoined smoothly. 'There is no need for the *contessa* to know that Lady Althea has not travelled with an older woman at her side.'

Rhys felt the flare of temper subside. He knew perfectly well what the matter with him was. Since he had left Thea's bed last night, his conscience, subjected to a thorough dose of reality with the prospect of the end of their journey, was giving him hell.

'That would seem to be the best solution. Thank you, Edgerton.' He raked his hand through his hair and tried to think like a responsible friend and not a frustrated lover. 'I had best remove myself and find some other lodgings. What would you suggest?'

'Oh, no,' Thea protested before the secretary could speak. 'That is unfair. Why not stay here? Your obliging *contessa* does not need to know when we arrived, does she, Mr Edgerton?'

'No, indeed, Lady Althea. And it is normal for ladies to go around the city masked, so you may see the sights *incognita* until Lord Palgrave leaves Venice. And, as you say, her ladyship would wish you both to stay here.'

'You see, Rhys! You would be so much more comfortable here, and I know Godmama would expect it.' To Edgerton Thea's face would reveal nothing more than a concern that her travelling companion was not inconvenienced, but Rhys read a plea and a promise that she put into careful words a moment later. 'I am sure there is a room for you where you will be…undisturbed.'

That was a promise not to come to his chamber at night. Thea was a woman of her word: their liaison had been for the duration of the journey and she was not expecting him to put any greater strain on his conscience by making love to her in their godmother's home. After all, last night she had done nothing to keep him at her side, had said nothing when he had left her bed.

The problem was, it was not his uneasy conscience that was giving him most pain, despite it reminding him constantly that he should never have slept with Thea, that having done so, he should never have continued and, having continued, he should do what society would consider the only right thing: marry her. The real problem was that the thought of parting from her was agony, yet it was obvious that, as good as her word, she did not want this liaison to last. And he…he did not know what he wanted.

But he was a man, not a boy to throw a tantrum over the loss of something precious. Thea had just made it clear that she expected their liaison to end but that she still wanted his company. He owed it to her to give her what she wanted.

Rhys looked reluctant to stay. Perhaps she needed to speak to him alone and assure him she had no intention of making demands on him. Absently Thea rubbed the small of her back, where a dull ache was worsening. It would be good to retire to bed and not be travelling, just at the moment. She supposed she ought to be relieved that her courses had begun that morning, but, somehow, she felt nothing of the kind. Perhaps, deep down, she simply had not been worrying because she trusted Rhys so much.

'I am rather tired,' she said. 'Perhaps you could show me to my room and send my woman to me, Mr Edgerton. I will rest until dinner.'

Rhys came to her side as she followed the secretary out. 'You look a trifle pale. Are you unwell?'

'Goodness, no. I suppose it is journey's end—I

will be much better for a few hours with my feet up and nothing rocking, jolting or shying under me!'

'We need to talk, Thea.'

'No.' She stopped and gave them a little space as Mr Edgerton walked on ahead. 'There is nothing to talk about, not in the way I think you mean, Rhys. Nothing to warrant that serious face, at least.' She smiled up at him, loving the way he worried about her. 'And we cannot talk now, in any case. I will see you at dinner.'

Polly was waiting for her in what proved to be not just a bedchamber, but a suite of rooms. 'There's the bedroom and a dressing room and a room for me and a sitting room, my lady,' she reported. 'Lovely, it is. But you come and take your gown off, and those stays, and lie down and rest. This is no time of the month to be travelling, that's for sure.' She fussed around and then, as she helped Thea into her wrapper, remarked, 'At least it means there's nothing to worry about, if you know what I mean.'

'I never thought there was.' Rhys had been very careful, Thea knew, although she supposed nothing was foolproof. Then something in Polly's tone made her look at the maid's face as she moved about the room tidying up. 'Polly… Do *you* have something to worry about? Come and talk to me.'

'Might have.' The maid put down the gown she had been shaking out and sat on the end of the bed. 'Not sure. But John will marry me anyway. He's asked me.' She fiddled with the tassel on the edge of the bed hangings.

'Before you told him there might be a baby on the way?'

'Oh, yes, my lady. I'd have married him whether I thought he was doing it out of love or duty, but I'm glad he asked before he knew. We women don't have much choice, do we?'

'No, not unless we do not mind a scandal,' Thea said, thinking of Serena. 'Has Hodge said anything to Lord Palgrave yet, do you know? After all, he employs you both. I am delighted for you, but he might think differently.' She would have something to say to Rhys if he did.

'He'll ask him today. There's sure to be an Anglican clergyman in Venice, John says, with all the English visitors.'

'Excellent,' Thea murmured, snuggling down. 'I am sure it will all work out happily.' Which was more than could be said for her entanglement with Rhys.

* * *

Thea insisted that Mr Edgerton join them for dinner. He was a professional man, after all, not a servant. The meal was excellent, with a wide range of seafood, and, with her backache subdued to a dull twinge, she was feeling considerably more cheerful.

Rhys, she suspected, was not. Despite conversing with apparent ease on a wide range of subjects, he was drinking more wine than he normally did and was picking at a superb dish of clams in cream sauce as though it was gruel.

Men always complained that women were complicated creatures, Thea mused as she speared the last prawn on her plate. In fact, she was certain that men were far more troublesome with their infuriating reticence about their true feelings.

'If you would like to go out this evening, I will put one of our gondolas at your disposal with a reliable man who speaks some English. And I will find you masks, of course,' Mr Edgerton said.

'For both of us?' Rhys queried.

'It is usual for gentlemen who wish to be discreet. It raises no curiosity, as it might in England.'

'Then I will take you up on the offer of both boat and mask. Thea?'

'I will come, too,' Thea said, reflecting that a mask would probably suit Rhys if he was in one of his enigmatic moods. He looked as though he was about to speak, but she put her hand on his wrist. 'I am feeling quite rested now.' Under her light touch she felt him tense, then he slid his hand away. No doubt she was being a trifle indiscreet in front of the secretary, but still, the subtle rejection stung. Before they had become lovers he would have accepted that passing touch without question, as from a friend. Now she was beginning to wonder what she was to him.

'I will tell the boatman to take you for a tour of the main landmarks to start with,' Edgerton said as the footman brought in a dish of sweetmeats. Thea was itching to ask him about Godmama and the prince, but she knew perfectly well that he was far too discreet.

She popped a marchpane-stuffed date into her mouth, resisted the temptation to demolish the whole plateful and stood up. 'I will go and find my cloak and change into some more suitable shoes— I noticed the gondolas that we passed all had some water in the bottom. I'll meet you on the landing stage, Rhys.'

It would be good to have a few moments to think

about what she was going to say to him, Thea thought as she hurried along the corridor. She should reassure him that there was no chance that she was with child, which was embarrassing, although considering how intimate they had been, that seemed irrational. And then she must assure him that she expected nothing from him now other than his continuing friendship, which was going to be…tricky. It would be all too easy to protest too much, she suspected, trying out suitable phrases in her head as she went down the stairs to the entrance courtyard.

It was deserted, filled only with the sound of water lapping outside and the scent of jasmine from a tub by the ancient wellhead. The surface of the canal, lit by torchères on the landing stage, was reflected back on the vaulted roof of the internal colonnade, a shifting pattern of ripples that was almost hypnotic.

These past weeks have been very special, but it is as well we have… You know how much I… Rhys, we have always been such good friends, I hope we can continue…

There was the sound of voices from the canal, the slapping of the water became louder and a series of bumps heralded the arrival of a gondola at the landing stage. Thea drew back into the shadows under the stairs. Without a mask she felt vulnerable, and there was no telling who the visitors might be.

There was a low-voiced argument going on and she thought it was in English, but she could not make out any words. A man and a woman, by the sound of it. Through the grill she could make out figures, both cloaked. One of them tugged on the bell pull and almost immediately there was the sound of feet running down the stairs above her head. One of the footmen opened the gate.

'*Madonna* is not at home,' he said in heavily accented English before the visitors could speak.

'Damn it, she must receive us!' English, educated and strangely familiar.

There was a scuffle and the footman was forced back a pace. The visitors stepped through the grill and into the pool of light cast by one of the torchères as someone else came down the stairs.

'Now look here, Edgerton, just go upstairs and tell our godmother that we are here, will you? This nonsense about her not being at home—'

But I know that voice....

'Is the truth. Lady Hughson is not in Venice at the moment and is unlikely to return for some weeks.'

'In that case, we'll stay. Don't tell me you haven't room in this barn of a place.'

'Mr Weston, Lady Serena, I have no instructions to receive or accommodate you.'

Thea sat down on the edge of the well, heedless of moss and ferns, and held on to the iron bucket winch for support as the torch-lit scene shifted and blurred in front of her. Paul Weston, Rhys's once best friend, and Serena, his fiancée who had jilted him at the altar.

She was hardly aware of a soft tread on the stairs, of the brush of a cloak as a tall figure passed her, until another man loomed up in silhouette beside the secretary. *Rhys.* Serena gave a little scream and clutched at Paul. Thea got to her feet, knowing even as she moved it was too late.

Rhys stepped forward, flicked one edge of his cloak over his shoulder, clenched his right fist and drove it straight into the other man's jaw. Paul reeled backwards, made a futile grab for the iron grill, slipped and fell into the canal with a splash that echoed round the courtyard. Serena shrieked and fainted into Edgerton's arms, the footman stood with his mouth open, gaping, and

Rhys turned on his heel and stalked back towards the stairs.

As a boy Paul Weston had never learned to swim. Thea knew that. So did Rhys. She only hoped he had forgotten that in the heat of the moment and had not intended murder. The gondola that had delivered the couple had gone, she realised as she slid to a halt on the landing stage. In the water Paul was floundering, sinking. She yanked a boathook from the wall and held it out to him. He grabbed for it, missed and sank.

'Rhys Denham!' she shouted without turning. 'Come back here or I am going to have to go in and get him myself!'

For a moment she thought Rhys had not heard her, or did not believe her, or simply did not care. Then he was at her side, shedding coat and cloak, kicking off his shoes. He hit the dark water in a shallow dive and surfaced with his arms full of struggling man.

'Keep still, you fool, or I'll hit you again.' He hauled Paul to the edge of the landing stage as Thea pushed the footman forward to help.

'Give her to me,' she told Edgerton, who was still clutching Serena. 'It is a faint at worst, play-acting at best. Help Rhys.' She pulled the other woman into her arms. Serena gave a faint moan. 'Stop that. Go and sit on the steps or I'll drop you,' Thea warned.

Serena shot her a look of deep reproach and staggered to the steps. 'Althea? Oh, how could you be so unfeeling?'

'Very easily,' Thea snapped. Paul was out of the water, gasping in a puddle like a landed fish. Rhys levered himself out with a strength that she spared a fleeting moment to admire, and sat in his own small lake, coughing.

'Go and get blankets and brandy.' She tugged at the footman's arm. 'Tell the kitchen to heat hot water for baths. Hurry.'

When she knelt beside Rhys he shook himself like a dog and spat into the canal. 'Sorry, but that is the filthiest thing I have ever tasted. If we don't come down with dysentery, I'll be amazed.'

Servants began to run downstairs, flapping blankets, supporting the men and Serena up to the main floor. In the end they all found themselves in the main salon. Rhys and Paul dripped on the marble floor and tossed back brandy, Serena lay on a sofa, moaning, and was comprehensively ignored and Thea and Edgerton were left to organise baths, dry clothes and a room for Paul and Serena.

'I do not like to have them under this roof,' Edgerton said when they found themselves outside the salon for a moment. 'Lady Hughson has no idea they are here and they have sponged enough on her goodwill and purse, in my opinion.'

'She has been supporting them? For how long?' Thea gestured a maid with armfuls of linens into a bedchamber as far as possible from Rhys's.

'Since virtually the time they eloped. If it was not for her, they would be in debtors' prison, I have no doubt,' Edgerton said, the set of his mouth showing clearly what he thought of the matter.

'I find it hard to believe,' Thea murmured. 'They betrayed Rhys….'

'Does it seem to you that Lady Hughson added to that betrayal by helping them afterwards? She told me that if Lord Palgrave loved Lady Serena he would not want her destitute, whatever happened and, besides, she had sworn to care for all her god-children. In a way, I think she felt guilty that she had not realised what was going on and that she had not been a better influence on Lady Serena.'

'I doubt anything, short of a miracle, would have changed Serena.' She stopped a hurrying maid. 'Are the baths ready? *Il bagno?*'

'*Si, madonna.*'

Thea mentally rolled up her sleeves and went back into the salon. 'Gentlemen, your baths are ready. Rhys, I have told the footman to take some clothes from your room for Paul. Mr Edgerton's would be too small. Serena, I suggest you go and lie down.' For a moment she wondered if her cavalier disposal of Rhys's wardrobe to the other man would be the final straw, but he put down his brandy glass and stalked out with a nod of acknowledgement in her direction.

'I will order refreshments for an hour's time,' Edgerton said. 'I doubt anyone wants to go out tonight.'

Chapter Twenty-One

Thea surveyed the salon and wondered if social situations ever got much trickier. Mr Edgerton had tactfully removed himself, leaving one earl; two earls' daughters, one of whom had jilted the said earl and the other who had been his mistress; and a gentleman who had wronged the earl, created a scandal and whom the earl had just punched on the jaw. *Fortunately, this is not an English drawing room,* she thought, suppressing an hysterical giggle, or someone would start discussing the weather or worrying about the seating plan for dinner.

As it was, she had the tea urn by her side and an array of tea cups before her, and that was English and unreal enough, under the circumstances.

'A cup of tea, Serena?'

'How could you?' the other woman said with a

shudder from the corner of the sofa where she was draped like a tragic Muse.

'Very easily. I am positively parched after all that excitement.' Thea poured herself a cup. 'I could order you coffee, if you prefer?'

'You were always so prosaic.' Serena turned her gaze from a moody examination of the darkening bruise on Paul's jaw and stared at Thea through narrowed eyes. 'But you've changed. What have you done?'

'Grown up?' Thea suggested sweetly. 'I am several years younger than you, don't forget, Serena.' It was unworthy, but she could not resist the barb. Serena's hair was still as blonde, her big eyes still as blue, but there were faint lines at the corners and more pronounced ones from her nose to the corner of her lips. She must have spent too much time with an expression of dissatisfaction.

'Rhys? Paul? Tea?' Neither man had spoken to the other since Rhys had hauled Paul out of the canal.

'Thank you, no.' Rhys went to the decanters, poured two brandies and offered one silently to the other man. After a moment's hesitation, Paul took it. 'You will not stay here beyond tonight,' Rhys said, resuming his place before the empty hearth.

'In Godmama's absence Mr Edgerton controls this household, and he does not welcome you here.'

'Can you not forgive me?' Serena demanded. 'I know I broke your heart—'

'No,' Rhys said, his voice flat. 'You broke your parents' hearts, you dealt my self-esteem a severe and probably very healthy blow and you caused great embarrassment and distress to a number of people. But if you have spent these past years imagining me pining away for love of you, Serena, you are much mistaken. I was infatuated and dazzled, yes. In love, no.'

She gaped at him. Thea, in a muddle of confused emotions, knew she was probably gaping, too. Somehow she had never quite believed that he had not loved Serena, but there was no mistaking the stark truth of what he was saying now.

'Then why the hell did you damn near drown me?' Paul Weston demanded.

Rhys looked him up and down. 'For betraying my trust, for lying to a friend, for distressing all our families. How is that for a start? There was no need for any of that drama. If you had been man enough to tell me that you loved Serena—and if she had not enjoyed being courted by two men quite so much—then I would have helped you, somehow.'

'But we didn't want to hurt you,' Serena wailed.

Thea wanted to leave, to get away from Rhys's brutal frankness on one side and Serena's dramatics on the other, but this was too much. *'Hurt him?'* she demanded. 'You mean you didn't want to face up to what you had done. You had no concerns about hurting *anyone*, just as long as you were not around to bear the consequences. Paul was weak and deceitful and a bad friend, but you were selfish and heedless. Did you not realise that if Rhys had come after you he could have killed Paul? He is a better shot and better swordsman.'

'What stopped you?' Paul was white-faced, the bruise still red and stark. With his blond hair and dark eyes Thea had always thought him the more conventionally good-looking, but now, comparing the two as grown men, she saw the weakness in his face and the signs of self-indulgence around his waistline and jowls.

'Thea stopped me.' Rhys did not look at her as he spoke.

'I have had more than enough of this.' Thea got to her feet. 'It was bad enough at the time without raking over the cold ashes of it now. I do not feel well and I am going to my bed.' It was true enough. Her stomach was cramping, her back was aching and all she wanted was to lie down.

Thea looked white and drawn and as though she was in pain. Rhys wondered whether he should go after her or whether it was best to leave her to Polly. She'd probably had more than enough of his company today.

'Of course! How silly of me never to have suspected it,' Serena said, her eyes bright and full of delighted speculation. 'Thea was in love with you all along, the secretive little cat! She stopped you coming after me because she wanted you for herself. And she is in love with you still—I could see it in her face. The maid said you aren't married, but you've been travelling together. Lord, who is the one making a scandal now?'

Even as he controlled his expression Rhys knew he could not stop the blood draining from his face. He could feel the cold, tight sensation over his cheekbones.

'Don't be ridiculous, she was sixteen, Serena. Hardly a *femme fatale* plotting to ensnare a man. Thea is my friend and always has been, although I realise that friendship between a man and a woman is a difficult concept for you to grasp. I have escorted her here to Godmama because she had left home after a falling-out with her father—that is the scandal if you are so avid for one.'

'And she was as plain a child as you could come across, and a tomboy to boot, Serena,' Paul chipped in, almost earning himself another thump on the jaw.

'Well, she isn't plain now,' Serena snapped. 'She's not a beauty, but she's got style.'

'What does it matter to you whether she's an Incomparable or bracket faced?' Rhys demanded, desperate to get Serena's, and his own thoughts, off the subject. 'Now, where are you two living?'

'Oh, horrible lodgings,' Serena began. 'So damp and—'

'They aren't that bad,' Paul put in. 'Just rather simple. And the rent's due,' he added.

'What have you been living on?' *Other than Godmama?*

'My father pays my allowance on condition we don't go back to England. I play cards a bit. I've acted as courier for English tourists now and again.' Paul shrugged and glanced down at Serena. 'We get by, don't we, my love?'

Her lush, lovely mouth trembled and Rhys was

reminded, painfully, of how much he had once desired her. He expected her to make some complaint, but she looked up at Paul and held out her hand to him. 'Yes, we get by.' She shot a resentful glance at Rhys. 'It is called love.'

She really does *love him,* he thought. *They have been together for six years and it cannot have been easy and yet somehow they are still together.* Paul had acted like a dishonourable idiot, but he was not unintelligent. He would have come to his senses soon enough if he had simply been infatuated as Rhys had been. Was Thea right? Was love a real, lasting emotion that could form the basis of a happy marriage under even these circumstances?

'You'd better go to your room,' Rhys said abruptly. He followed them out and went, without a word, to his own room, unlocked his writing case and drew out a *rouleau* of guineas. He was probably an idiot, but forgiveness was supposed to be a virtue, wasn't it?

Before he could change his mind he went back to their room, knocked and when Paul opened the door thrust the money into his hand. 'Call it a wedding present.'

He felt better for doing it, he realised when he got back to his room, his fingers sore from Paul's heartfelt handshake on top of the effects of that knuckle-grazing punch. It was like drawing a line under the whole damn mess.

But Thea… Could Serena possibly be right? Could Thea have been in love with him ever since she was sixteen? Hodge stood patiently and Rhys gave himself a mental shake, pulled the pin out of his neckcloth and began to undress.

His own voice seemed to echo in his head from weeks ago, as the chaise had rattled towards Dover. *Did he break your heart?*

And Thea had smiled and said, *Not deliberately. He had no idea of my feelings, you see, and besides, he was in love with someone else.*

Surely not. His fingers slowed on his waistcoat buttons. Thea was not a good actress, but she had wanted to be his lover. Would she have given herself to him if she loved another man? But then she had appeared quite calm about the end of the *affaire*, so…

'My lord.'

'Hmm? Sorry, Hodge, I was woolgathering. You're no doubt anxious to be off to your bed.'

To his amazement the valet blushed. 'Er, my lord. I wanted to ask whether you'd have any objections to me and Polly Jones getting married. Here, if we can find a clergyman. It wouldn't stop us working, my lord.'

'I can't pretend I hadn't noticed you two were courting, but this is a bit sudden, isn't it?'

'Think it might be as well,' Hodge said obscurely. 'Polly's a decent girl.'

'And you'd not want anyone to draw conclusions from a seven-month pregnancy?'

'Quite, my lord.'

'Then you have my blessing, and when we get back to London I'll see about finding the two of you some rooms.'

Hodge beamed. 'Thank you, my lord. I wouldn't want you to think I'm only marrying her because there's a babe on the way. I love her and that's a fact.'

By the time Hodge had stopped being grateful and Rhys was in a banyan and sprawled in a deep armchair by the bed, there was no escaping the poisoned dart Serena had planted so skilfully under his skin. His confidence that such a state as love did not exist was being severely shaken today, and somehow he had never been able to dismiss the reality of the feelings Thea had so painfully confessed.

And if he was the one she loved, then what was he going to do about it? She wanted a love match and he did not think he could manage to deceive her for long; she knew him too well. He liked her, admired her and desired her, but he could not live with emotion, with opening himself up to trust a single person with the essence of himself.

When he had admitted to her that he had never loved Serena, her concern, her need to understand and to question him had felt like a surgeon probing a wound. For a moment he had wondered if that would help, wondered if he could pass through the pain and be healed. And then he had known that was just a sentimental dream.

Perhaps he was wrong. After all, a sixteen-year-old girl would never be able to hide her feelings as well as Thea would have had to do.

'Coxcomb,' he told himself aloud. But he couldn't just leave it, and besides, she was unwell.

He scratched lightly on her door, expecting either no response or for Polly to open it, but Thea called, 'Come in!'

She looked pale and pinched as she sat up in bed against a pile of pillows. There was a glass by the bedside with cloudy liquid in it.

'I came to see how you were. May I come in?' She smiled and his pulse did that odd little stutter it so often seemed to do when he saw her unexpectedly, or when she smiled.

'I am fine,' she said. 'Have they gone to their room?'

'Yes. Never mind about them.' Rhys sat on the side of the bed and took her hand in his, feeling for the pulse. It seemed steady enough and her skin was cool. 'I am concerned about you, Thea. These lagoons and marsh fever...'

The colour came up under her skin and she looked down at their joined hands. 'My courses have begun, that is all. My stomach cramps, my back aches, I feel like a wrung-out dishcloth—and you may congratulate yourself on the efficacy of your precautions.'

'Ah. Oh...excellent. Not that you are feeling unwell, I mean.' Probably all men were reduced to wittering idiots by the reality of the female system. His mistresses had always managed the matter by simply informing him when it was inconvenient to call.

How to ask that other question? He suspected the answer was not going to be as straightforward to obtain. 'Thea, who was it you have been in love with all this time?' *Well done, Denham, that was subtle and tactful.*

Thea shook off his light grip and sat more upright. 'Why on earth are you asking me that now?'

'It is just that Serena was hinting.' He shrugged. 'It doesn't matter.' *That's right, belittle it. Now is a good time to remove foot from mouth.*

'What has she been saying?' Thea demanded. 'You should know better than to listen to her. She manages to tie you in knots every time, doesn't she? You have hurt her feelings and I have witnessed it. Serena may have the intelligence of a peahen, but she has an instinct for making trouble.' Thea folded her arms tightly across her chest, as if to hold herself together. She looked thoroughly upset and he felt a complete swine.

An idea struck him. 'Is it Paul? Is that why you were so upset when she ran off with him? He was always the good-looking one in our circle.'

'Paul?' She laughed unsteadily. 'You clot! Of course it isn't him. And I was upset because of what they had done to you. How would you have felt if our positions had been reversed and a man, a friend of yours, had left me at the altar?'

'I'd have killed him,' Rhys said without having to think.

'Well, there you are. Ladies don't have the luxury of being able to rush off and create mayhem, so we just have to make do with being quietly upset for our friends. Mind you,' she added, 'if I could have got my hands on Serena just then, I think I might have pulled her hair out.'

They sat in silence for a while. Rhys relaxed, leaned back against the bedpost as Thea fidgeted with the laces at the neck of her nightgown. Then she raised her head and looked him straight in the eye. 'What was she hinting?' When he shook his head she said, 'Tell me or I'll ask her myself.'

'That it was me.' He waited, braced for tears, an armful of woman, anger…

'You must think me a very good actress,' Thea said flatly. 'Do you think I could hide that, living with you for weeks? That I could accept the end of our *affaire* so easily?' She swallowed. 'I am sorry, you must find this hideously embarrassing.'

'No, it is my fault. I should have taken no notice of Serena. You are right, she is a troublemaker and, as you say, how could someone as honest as you keep feelings like that hidden?'

'I cannot imagine.' That was more like it; the tart edge was back on her tongue. 'But I think you had better leave Venice, very soon. I will be fine here with Mr Edgerton and his respectable widow, and if you go there will be less for Serena to gossip about. I would hate it if somehow your prospects of making the match you desire are spoiled by her. She still has friends she writes to in England, no doubt.'

'Leave?' *Leave you?* he almost said.

'I am sorry, because it must be one of the most spectacular of all the cities you were planning to visit, but you can always come back once Godmama is here and I have gone.'

'You are, as ever, sensible.' He supposed Thea was right—if he was anywhere in Venice it could cause problems for both of them.

'You believe now that leaving home was sensible? That becoming your lover was prudent?'

Trick questions, Rhys thought. *There are no correct answers.* 'If those were the right things for you, then yes.'

He stood up. 'I'll leave in the morning, just as soon as I am certain those two have gone back to their lodgings.'

'Where to?'

'Rome, I thought,' Rhys said, plucking a city out of the air. He bent to drop a kiss on the end of her nose. 'Goodnight, Thea.'

When he glanced back from the door she was quite composed. She must have seen something in his face for she shook her head at him, smiled and blew him a kiss.

Chapter Twenty-Two

No one would have guessed that she had spent the night wide awake, Thea reassured herself with a quick glance in the overmantel mirror as they sat around the breakfast table. She had finally dropped off to sleep as the bells were chiming five o'clock.

Paul and Serena were subdued but civil and left, to Mr Edgerton's ill-concealed relief, after the meal. Paul and Rhys, she noticed, shook hands. To her shock, there was a boat at the landing stage for Rhys, his bags already in it.

'I got up early and Edgerton arranged everything,' he explained. 'I thought the sooner the better.'

'Yes, of course. But what about Hodge and Polly?' she asked, halfway down the steps to the courtyard. How could Rhys just leave like this, as though he could hardly bear to stay another minute? Had she failed to convince him? Was he certain she was inconveniently and tiresomely in love with him?

'I am leaving Hodge with you. They have two months' wages in hand. Edgerton will help him arrange the wedding.'

'But…'

'I'll find myself an Italian valet for a while, or do without. I'm not that much of a dandy.' He stopped at the foot of the steps and grinned up at her. 'Now, am I?'

'No, but…'

'And when Godmama returns she'll find you a maid and Hodge and Polly can catch me up, wherever I've got to.'

He looked cheerful, alert, ready to move on. Thea swallowed the words that almost escaped her and said, 'Don't forget to write and tell me all about Rome, will you?' She came down until she was standing on the first step, almost eye to eye with him.

'Of course not. Goodbye, Thea. Take care and give my love to Godmama. May I have a farewell kiss?'

All she had to do was lean a little closer. Thea put her hand on the strong, steady shoulder and tipped her face, her eyes wide open. Rhys bent, then hesitated, a breath above her mouth. 'Thea.'

Then he kissed her, a light brush of the closed lips, brotherly, friendly. She fought to stop her fingers closing, gripping through the broadcloth and linen to the man beneath.

In a heartbeat something changed. He lifted his hand from the rail and pulled her to him, off balance on the edge of the step so that she had to catch at him with both hands. The pressure of his mouth increased, the familiar, intimate demand of his tongue pushed between her lips and she opened to him, forgot prudence and disguise, sank into his embrace and the heat and the passion of the kiss.

When he released her she stumbled and he steadied her, but he did not speak. His eyes were dark and wide as though he had sustained a shock. Then he turned on his heel and strode to the boat, stepped in and sat with his broad back to her as the boatman cast off the lines and the oarsmen picked up the stroke. She ran to the edge of the landing stage and watched as they reached the Grand Canal and turned, out of sight. Rhys never looked round. Not once.

'Lady Althea, are you certain this is prudent?' Mr Edgerton was as close to agitated as she had ever seen him.

'No,' she admitted. It seemed she had done nothing that was prudent since she'd stood outside Papa's study door and heard how he and Anthony had betrayed her. Leaving home had not been prudent, going to Rhys had not been prudent. Becoming his lover had been thoroughly imprudent.

Being imprudent was dangerous, and sometimes the results hurt. But pain showed you were alive. After Rhys had left she had donned cloak and mask and gone with Polly and Hodge to the Anglican minister to arrange their wedding and then to visit shops.

'Don't you want to see the sights, my lady?' Polly had asked. 'Lovely, isn't it? But strange.' She'd still been bubbling with excitement over the wedding, which had been arranged for two days' time.

'We have shopping to do for your bride clothes,' Thea had said. 'And I want to go to a map shop. We will have time to explore later.'

Now, with Polly safely Mrs Hodge, a sailing boat chartered and crewed under Edgerton's eagle eye, Thea was ready to set out on yet another thoroughly imprudent enterprise. 'I can see Venice when I return with Lady Hughson, but I find I have grown accustomed to travel. I would like to explore the coast of Italy, and so I shall.'

Her money would hold out, for she had never managed to persuade Rhys to let her pay for more than her clothes shopping. Mr Edgerton had reluctantly admitted to knowing a completely reliable captain and crew and introduced her to Signor Vincenzo, who was a courier with an excellent reputation. 'I will come back with Godmama or, if I do not find her, I will turn around when I reach Sicily and return,' she promised the secretary.

Mr Edgerton assisted her into the boat that would take them out into the lagoon and the waiting ship. 'After working for Lady Hughson all these years I suppose I should not be surprised at what her godchildren do,' he said with a sigh. *'Bon voyage!'*

Thea did not turn her head as she was rowed towards the Grand Canal. Rhys had not and neither would she. She had no wish to see the place where he had kissed and left her without a backwards glance.

The rowers negotiated their way into the crowded Grand Canal. This was the start of the rest of her life. She had lost her virginity and gained her independence. She was mistress of her own destiny now.

Venice was beautiful; the light sparkled off the water and lit the exotic curves of windows that seemed transported from some Eastern palace. Soft pink brick and white stone, stained by water and weed, riches and decay, palaces, churches, prisons. She would come back here and explore, and then where? Constantinople? Greece?

Without thinking she pointed out an exquisite little palazzo. 'Rhys, look… I mean, Polly, do see that charming little building.'

The small cold knot inside her tightened into pain. So lonely without him. She knew she would miss him in her bed, but she had not realised how much she had talked with him, how they had shared new wonders, amusements, moments of beauty.

Perhaps he would meet Giles in Rome. She hoped so; she wanted him to have a companion, resilient and independent as he was. Someone to share with.

'Pull into the landing at St Mark's Square,' she called to the boatman. 'I want a stationer's shop.'

Signor Vincenzo was instantly alert. 'But yes, *madonna*, there is a charming one under the arcade.'

He helped her out and guided her to the shop. 'I want a journal,' she explained. 'A thick one. Several, in fact.' She would record everything, her thoughts, all her experiences as though she was telling them to Rhys.

They were beautiful, the covers made with the marbled papers that Venice's book binders were famous for, feathered with patterns made by floating oils on water, stroking it into swirls and then laying on the paper. She added pencils, coloured inks, new pens. *Live for the moment and record it all for the dark days.* Because there would be dark days when she was not feeling so strong, when the memories were too much and it was no comfort at all to know that she had chosen to preserve those recollections.

The coast was every bit as lovely as she had hoped and the towns strung along it as fascinating. Tiny fishing harbours with Venetian forts towering above them, busy little ports, cities filled with treasures that left her breathless—she felt she might never recover from Ravenna—slipped past in sunlight and under blue skies as though the weather was conspiring with her.

They anchored each night as darkness fell, and as the nights passed she became familiar with the moon and stars as she never had in cloudy England or on the voyage from Toulon when she had eyes only for Rhys. Was it a cliché that every lover stood and stared at the moon and thought of their beloved looking up at the same sky? Through Signor Vincenzo she talked to the helmsman and learned the names of the stars and wrote them in her journal. *If you were here, you would draw the constellations,* she wrote to the man who would never read her words. *Orion, the Great Bear...*

Ancona, Pescara, round the spur on the heel of Italy to Bari. Two weeks after they had left Venice, dawdling on light winds, watching dolphins and stopping to buy fish straight from the nets as they were hauled ashore, they rounded the heel and reached the lagoons of Taranto. It was hot here and Thea and Polly wore light muslins and wide-brimmed hats as they strolled through the streets to stare at the forbidding bulk of the Governor's Palace and to buy in the market: dates from Africa, melons, oranges, strange fruits she had no names for. There were palm trees amongst the crumbling grey stones and a great fortress and yet another harbourmaster who assured them that *il principe*'s yacht, the *Aquila*, had moored here.

'But yes, *madonna*, they sail a week ago after being here four days. They go to Crotone, the captain says.' He gestured out across the wide bay to the south-west. 'They do not hurry. Is romantic, no? A honeymoon on the sea.'

'Honeymoon? No, you are quite mistaken, *signor,* merely two friends on a voyage of pleasure.' Thea realised she was gossiping with a complete stranger and moderated her tone. 'Thank you, we will be sailing immediately.'

There was no hiding her surprise from Polly. 'Surely Godmama cannot have got married without Mr Edgerton knowing? He is her confidential secretary.'

'They don't have to be married, do they, my lady? But she's quite old, isn't she, Lady Hughson?'

'Old? Not above forty-five,' Thea said after a moment's thought. 'When I was a child she seemed ancient and ageless, of course, but she was widowed very young. It was a true love match and a terrible tragedy that he died.'

'A long time to mourn,' Polly said as they reached the quayside. 'Especially if she has a second chance now.'

Did it really take that long to heal? Thea leaned on the ship's rail and watched the low coastline vanish into heat haze as they struck out across the wide bay. She had thought herself cured of her love for Rhys when she had agreed to Anthony's courtship. Now she realised that she'd had a fortunate escape. Even if he had been an honestly sincere man, she would never have been happy with him because her heart would never have been free. From the corner of her eyes she could see Hodge and Polly sitting quietly together, his arm around her, her head on his shoulder. At least her actions had brought two people together.

Three more days and Thea was woken by Polly bouncing into her cabin. 'Oh, my lady! Come and see—it's a volcano, a real one with smoke and everything!'

'Mount Etna,' Thea said, rubbing her eyes as Polly bundled her into her wrapper. 'It won't go away.'

'But come and see!' Polly danced out of the cabin, more excited by the mountain than she had been by Venetian canals, dolphins or African traders.

Thea had to agree that it was a staggering sight when she joined Polly and Hodge on deck. Against the pink morning sky the plume of smoke trailed sideways in long streamers from the top of the conical mountain. At its foot lay Taormina and a string of small towns and villages. 'I would not want to live there,' she said with a shiver. 'There was a city called Pompeii that was buried when another volcano, Vesuvius, erupted in Roman times. They say Napoleon had scholars digging it up.'

'Brrr.' Polly gave an exaggerated shiver. 'We're not stopping here, are we?'

'The harbourmaster at Crotone said he thought the *Aquila* was making for Syracuse, farther along the coast, so we will go straight there.' Thea was beginning to have qualms about descending unexpectedly on Godmama. What if she really was on a romantic escape with a lover? At least with her own ship she could be independent and not intrude. She would have to play it by ear—if they ever caught up with the prince's yacht.

'Dolphins,' Signor Vincenzo called from the stern. He had learned that Thea had an inexhaustible passion for the creatures, however many they saw and, in the absence of much else to do, he had become dolphin lookout.

Thea joined him. 'We are being followed.' Well behind them another ship of a similar size was on the same tack.

'He has been there since dawn,' the Italian said. 'Heading for Syracuse, too, I hope.'

'You hope?'

'Black sails, fast lines. Perhaps he is a pirate. With the end of the fighting there are no French or British warships to keep them in check.'

'That is perhaps more excitement than I wanted.' Thea shaded her eyes to watch the sinister ship in the distance. 'Will you tell the captain that I wish to make straight for Syracuse with good speed?'

And here we are, safely in Syracuse harbour, Thea wrote in her journal that evening. The night air was cool and she had gone to her cabin after dinner, leaving Hodge and Polly the privacy of the deck to stroll, hand in hand.

We have found the Aquila *and the harbourmaster at Taranto was right: Godmama is in love. We saw the yacht at once: sleek and white with brown sails and a huge figurehead of an eagle in gold. I did not want to intrude so I borrowed the captain's telescope and there they were on deck, arm in arm, so intent, with eyes only for each other. Just talking, but I could feel the closeness even across the water.*

I will send a note over tomorrow morning to

warn her, then Godmama can make certain I see only what she wants me to see. I hope he is a good man. I pray he makes her happy, for she deserves joy for herself after all she has done for others.

The black 'pirate' ship came into harbour before we sat down to dinner, so it is a harmless voyager after all. You would laugh at me if you knew I was quaking in my shoes at the thought of pirates, Rhys. Or perhaps the fluttering in my stomach was caused by foolishly romantic ideas of a corsair: I have definitely been reading too many novels from the Minerva Press!

I am sure the reality is far more sordid. Besides, what use is a dashing pirate villain if you are not there to rescue me? I can imagine you, knife between your teeth as you swing on board to do battle....

The cabin door creaked open and Thea pulled a sheet of loose paper over the page. This journal was her private letter to Rhys.

'Polly?' She looked up to find the narrow doorway filled, not with a woman's slender figure, but the bulk of a broad-shouldered man silhouetted against the bulkhead light behind. The pen dropped from her fingers, leaving a splatter of ink across the paper. Hodge would not open her cabin door without knocking and no other man would approach her here.

Thea got to her feet, sending the chair thudding to the deck behind her as she reached for the paper knife. Were her lurid imaginings real after all?

The man ducked his head and came into the cabin and she found her wits and her courage. 'Get out or I will scream!'

Chapter Twenty-Three

'I would rather you kissed me.' Rhys closed the door and leaned back against it. The candle flames on her desk flickered and steadied as the air stilled.

He was wearing a white shirt, open at the neck, form-fitting black breeches, soft black boots and nothing else.

'I was thinking about corsairs,' Thea said and he caught her meaning and laughed as he pushed his over-long hair off his face.

'I am sorry. I should have swung on board at the head of a gang of ruthless pirates, I suppose.'

'Just you is enough.' Enough to remove the air from the cabin and the sense from her head. Enough to leave her so weak she had to grip the edge of the desk to stay on her feet. 'Is the black schooner yours?'

'Yes. Is that what put corsairs into your head?

It was the fastest thing I could find at Venice.' He studied her face, but made no move to approach her. 'Why are we discussing corsairs and ships?'

'Because I am in shock and I have no idea why you are here.' It was the truth. 'I thought you had gone to Rome.'

'Yes. Dreadful journey. I felt…wrong. Didn't know why, thought I was coming down with marsh fever perhaps. First thing I did was to go to the British Consulate to sign the book and the third person I saw there was Benton. He took one look at me and said, "You left her, then, you bloody idiot?" No greeting, just a flat statement. I hit him.' He rubbed the knuckles of his clenched right fist into the palm of his left and winced.

'Poor Giles! Was he hurt? And in the Consulate of all places.' Thea groped for the chair, set it upright and sat down before her legs gave out.

'No, he wasn't hurt and I bribed the porter not to make a fuss. Benton took me back to his lodgings—he's having a fine old time in some library or other—poured a large brandy down me and observed that I might be a fool, but at least I had a respectable right hook.'

'What…what did he say about me?' Surely Giles would not have betrayed her?

'Beyond enquiring punctiliously about your health, nothing. Nor did he explain himself. We went out to eat, got roaring drunk. I woke up the next morning rolled in a blanket on the floor of his parlour with a head like a steam hammer, but a very clear understanding of why I felt so bad. I left for Venice just as soon as we'd downed a pot of coffee.'

'Why did you go back?' It took her two attempts to get the words out of her dry mouth.

'For you.'

'We…agreed that it was not a good idea to continue our affair. We agreed there might be scandal and that would affect your chances of making the marriage that you want. We had *always* agreed that you would leave me in Venice.' It was not easy to sit there and not go to him. All that kept her in the seat was the knowledge that to be with him again and then face another parting would break what was left of her heart. 'This is not sensible, Rhys.'

'I love you.'

No. No, he does not believe in love. He does not mean it. Does not want it. 'No.' Apparently she had been wrong. All it took to break her heart was to hear Rhys say those three words.

'Yes. And I think you love me.'

'No! I told you…'

'You never denied it. I should not allow myself to forget how very good you are with words when you need to be, Thea.'

'So you believe I love you and your gentlemanly conscience has driven you back to Venice and then right along the coast of Italy in search of me to do the decent thing, has it?' She pushed herself upright and flung away to stare out of the porthole into the darkness.

'No, the realisation that I cannot live without you has done that.' From his voice, he had not moved from his position flat against the door. It was as though he would not use his touch, his body, his lips—only his words.

Somehow that was the most convincing thing that he could have done. Faint hope began to flutter deep inside her. 'You do not believe in love.'

'I was wrong. I did not understand how being with you made me feel. At first I thought it was a mixture of friendship and lust. Then we made love and I understood that I desired you, that I felt more fulfilled in your arms than I had with any other lover. But I talked myself into believing it was our friendship that made it special.'

Thea kept her gaze on the porthole. She could see Rhys reflected in it, just part of his hand and arm where he had rested his palm on the bulkhead. His hand was shaking. Tears she could not understand and did not know how to stop began to run down her face.

'It was not friendship,' Rhys said, his voice as steady as his hand was not. 'It was our love.' He must have heard her sob, despite her effort to choke it back. 'I know how much love means to you, Thea. I would never tell you I loved you if it were not the truth, even if you begged me on bended knee. I would not lie to you—'

And then his voice did crack and he moved, caught her by the shoulders, pulled her round. 'My love, say something, for God's sake. I never meant to make you cry, Thea.'

'I think it is happiness overflowing. I love you, Rhys. I have loved you since I realised why I was so jealous of Serena. That she was beautiful and I was ordinary did not matter, but she had you, and that did.' Her face was buried in his shirt front now, her wet cheeks dried by the soft, warm fabric, her senses full of the feel and scent of him. 'I thought I had managed to suppress it. After all, I cannot fly, however much I might want to—yearnings can be accepted and controlled.

'I thought it was safe to come to you, to travel with you. I thought, fool that I am, when I sensed that you desired me, that it was safe to be your lover, that you would never know.' His hands were warm and steady now, one around her waist, the other gentle on her hair. 'It was almost more than I could bear to hide my feelings and to know it must end.'

'Will you marry me?' His voice was muffled in her hair.

Thea pushed a little so she could look up into Rhys's face. He looked very serious, but there was joy and something more, deep in those blue eyes. 'I am not at all the sort of wife you wanted. I will get involved in causes and argue with you about politics. I will probably say the wrong things to important people and I will not stand for being left in the country with the children.'

'You will, will you? That sounds remarkably like a *yes*, Thea.' Rhys dropped his head so his forehead rested on hers. 'I was an idiot. I wanted to shut all the messy, difficult, painful, emotional stuff out. We will argue sometimes and it will hurt. It won't be calm and safe, Thea.'

'I can promise to be difficult and messy. And probably painful.' Thea reached up and took a handful of hair and tugged. 'Very painful if you don't kiss me.'

'Is there a lock on this door?'

'A wedge.' Thea ducked down and pushed it into place as Rhys hopped on one foot, dragging at the other boot. They fell on the bunk together, both of them laughing and jostling as they pulled at each other's clothes.

When they were naked Rhys looked down at her and shook his head. 'Why didn't I realise?'

'You had to outgrow an adolescent yearning for blue-eyed blondes of a coming disposition and I had to grow up,' Thea suggested as he bent to her breasts, her eyes drifted shut and all desire to tease and laugh fled.

He was not gentle or respectful or careful. This was a claiming and a masculine shout of triumph and Thea revelled in the strength of his body as he bent her this way and that, as mouth and hands explored her as if they had not been lovers for weeks.

She gave back with a fierceness that matched

his own, leaving the marks of her nails and her teeth on his back and shoulders as he ravaged her body. He was determined to reduce her to quivering submission; she was desperate for his possession. When he would only tease her with the pressure of his erection against her she wrapped her legs around his hips and clung, arching up to capture him.

'Witch,' he groaned in surrender, and thrust hard and deep. She was ready for him, more than ready, but she saw his set face and the hard lines of the tendons in his throat as he plunged and withdrew, mercilessly possessing her; he wanted to make this last for ever, yet he wanted to reach that peak of fulfilment. She wanted it, too. As he lodged deep inside her she gripped, held, refused to yield.

'Stay with me,' she gasped and for the first time in their lovemaking he lost control, shuddered and hung above her as the heat of his climax flooded inside her and she screamed and reached for him even as she shattered and fell, knowing only that he was with her, totally. And for ever.

The wedding, in the chapel of Prince Frederico's residence in Syracuse, took place a month later, the day after Agnes, Lady Hughson, became *la*

Principessa d'Averna. The ceremony was performed by the British consul's chaplain, ably assisted by Reverend Giles Benton in borrowed vestments. It was attended by a small but select party of guests, including the bride's father, the Earl of Wellingstone, who appeared faintly stunned that his difficult daughter had made such an excellent match and was off his hands at last, and, to the delight of the gossips, Mr Paul Weston and Lady Serena Weston.

The wedding breakfast lasted well into the evening, but finally Rhys took his wife by the hand and led her, without ceremony, out into the great square in front of the cathedral and down the slope to the ancient spring by the harbour. 'See?' He pointed at the strange plant growing in the clear water with trout weaving through its stems. 'Real Egyptian papyrus. No one knows how it comes to be here. Shall we take it as an omen and visit Egypt on our honeymoon?'

'I don't mind where we go, as long as it has a bed and you.' Thea took the corsage of flowers that was pinned to her shoulder and tossed it to a group of little girls who were staring open-mouthed at her wedding finery.

'We will set sail at dawn and head east, then

see where the winds take the *Aquila*. After all, the prince said we can use it for as long as we want.' He looked down at her as she smiled at the children, wondering why he had ever thought her ordinary or could have taken her for granted. 'Come, we have a wedding night before us.'

He swept her into his arms when they reached the yacht and carried her up the gangplank to the applause of the crew, then into the sumptuous master cabin. He was alone with his bride, at last.

'Oh, look, a proper big bed!' Thea gasped as Rhys lowered her onto it.

'I know.' He began to unbutton the gown of pale gold silk. 'We may never want to go home.'

He made love to her slowly, carefully, as though it was the first time. Her flesh softened for him as he caressed her, her body opened to him as he entered her and his strength overwhelmed her as she clung to him. More than words, the certainty of his claiming convinced her of his love.

The tension grew and spiralled and Thea opened her eyes to find Rhys watching her, his face stark with the effort to control his building climax. 'I love you,' she gasped and he smiled and kissed her so she took his shout of triumph into her and she fell free into a swirl of light and dark and, finally, peace.

She woke to find dawn light flooding through the portholes and the ship in motion. Rhys was propped up on one elbow, looking down at her.

'What is it?' Thea scrubbed at her eyes. 'Is my hair in a tangle?'

'I was just making up for years of not looking at you properly,' her husband murmured. 'Just this past hour I have found three new freckles and discovered that there is a tiny mole behind your left ear.' He bent to kiss it. 'How long is it going to take for me to discover everything about you?'

'Seventy years?' Thea hazarded as Rhys threw back the bedclothes and began, with a growl, to explore.

'At the very least, my love.'

* * * † *

MILLS & BOON®

Why shop at millsandboon.co.uk?

Each year, thousands of romance readers find their perfect read at millsandboon.co.uk. That's because we're passionate about bringing you the very best romantic fiction. Here are some of the advantages of shopping at www.millsandboon.co.uk:

* **Get new books first**—you'll be able to buy your favourite books one month before they hit the shops

* **Get exclusive discounts**—you'll also be able to buy our specially created monthly collections, with up to 50% off the RRP

* **Find your favourite authors**—latest news, interviews and new releases for all your favourite authors and series on our website, plus ideas for what to try next

* **Join in**—once you've bought your favourite books, don't forget to register with us to rate, review and join in the discussions

Visit **www.millsandboon.co.uk**
for all this and more today!